THE COLLECTIVE

Book 2, The Breeder Files

About the Author

Eliza Green tried her hand at fashion designing, massage, painting, and even ghost hunting, before finding her love of writing. She often wonders if her desire to change the ending of a particular glittery vampire story steered her in that direction (it did). After earning her degree in marketing, Eliza went on to work in everything but marketing, but swears she uses it in everyday life, or so she tells her bank manager.

Born and raised in Dublin, Ireland, she lives there with her sci-fi loving, evil genius best friend. When not working on her next amazing science fiction adventure, you can find her reading, indulging in new food at an amazing restaurant or simply singing along to something with a half decent beat.

For a list of all available books, check out:

www.elizagreenbooks.com/books

BOOK 2 IN THE BREEDER FILES

THE COLLECTIVE

ELIZA GREEN

ISBN: 9781098530082

Cover by Deranged Doctor Design
Copy Editor: Andrew Lowe
Proofreader: Rachel Small

For those like me who hate being told what you can't do.

1

ANYA

Day One

Anya woke to a gentle humming noise. She sat up too fast, kicking off a deep pounding in her head. The last time she'd had a headache this bad was... never? The pain eased for a moment and her hands sank into a too-soft mattress as she looked around the darkened room. The noise was definitely nearby.

This wasn't Brookfield, nor was it her bedroom. So where was she? Her last movements were but a distant memory. She'd been in Brookfield with her brother, Jason. Both of them had been violently ill, unable to keep anything down. Her parents...

She pressed a fist to her mouth. Both murdered. The illness had followed some kind of explosion in the land beyond Brookfield.

The skin lesions on her arms and face during that time, blotchy and red, would be etched on her mind forever. Her pallid skin had glistened with sweat.

1

Food and water had acted like poison.

Another memory hit her. Two men dressed in white protective suits waited by the door where she and Jason had collapsed. One of them had spoken in an icy tone.

'Don't worry. You're safe now.'

Had the men brought her here?

Anya shook away the last thought, too unclear for her to say if it was real or a dream.

The humming got louder, sounding more like a song with short breaks than a random occurrence. Her eyes adjusted to the dark. A deep-blue carpet covered the floor and a pair of thick red velvet drapes loosely covered a window.

A sliver of brick peeked out from behind the curtains, and Anya shivered.

She looked around at the walls, adorned with painted landscapes set in gilt-edged picture frames. Nobody in Brookfield could afford this kind of opulence. Castles or mansions didn't exist in her world. So where the hell was she?

On the other side of the room were two white doors with gold handles, set into two facing walls. One door had to be the exit.

Her hands sank further as she shifted position on the squishy bed. The brick wall, coupled with her lack of knowledge as to where she was, sharpened her senses.

She ripped back the covers and glanced down at her clothes. A soft breath escaped her lips. She wasn't naked, but the leggings and camisole weren't hers.

She placed both feet on the floor. The details in the low-lit room opened up to her some more. A large chest of drawers was against one wall, and to its right, a chaise longue. A vanity table and a backless chair with a cream-cushioned seat and ornate edges sat between the drapes and chaise longue.

The drapes reminded her of another room, a large open space split by a similar velvet covering. The sound of crying babies had dominated that space. Was it a real place? A real memory of the towns, or somewhere else?

She walked over to the window and pulled the drapes back, feeling the weight of the fabric in her hand. Her fingertips grazed the brick wall.

The only place she'd been to outside of the towns was Praesidium, to visit the library filled with books, not babies. Anya shook her head to dislodge the memories she began to doubt were even hers.

The humming drew her attention away from the drapes. A chill shot up her spine as she searched for a floor lamp and groped for the switch.

Then she saw it: a chair on the other side of the room. And a blond-haired boy sitting in it.

Anya gripped the flimsy material of the camisole, which she was sure was transparent.

'Who... the hell are you? What are you doing in my room?'

The boy got to his feet and smiled at her.

More of a smirk than a smile.

He walked towards her forcing her to step back. He was a head taller than she was, with messy hair and the greenest eyes she'd ever seen. She tried not to blush as his hot gaze ran over her body.

'I asked you what you're doing here!' She backed up when he got closer.

He held his hands up, eyes sparkling with mischief. 'Relax. I'm supposed to be here. Did you sleep well?'

'Were you here the whole night?'

The boy's smile transformed into a shit-eating grin. He was dressed in a loose pair of khaki trousers and white T-shirt—clothes that hid a lean body with a hint of muscle.

He nodded at the bed. 'You don't think that bed's just for you, do you?'

Panic swelled inside her. What exactly had happened last night?

Anya's uneasy gaze settled on the boy, stood too close for her to feel in control. 'Where are we? What is this place?' She stepped back.

The blond boy played it smart and stayed put, giving Anya the opportunity to claw back some dominance.

She placed him at around eighteen; a year older than her.

'You're different from the others,' he said. His grin dropped back to a smile.

'Different? What are you talking about?'

'They were more accepting of their fate. You, on the other hand, are feisty. I like feisty. It's a challenge.'

Anya hugged her body tighter. 'I'm not here to

challenge you. And I'm not going to do whatever it is you have planned.'

The boy just looked at her.

'Why am I here?' Anya lifted her chin. 'What's your name?'

'Alex.'

'Well, *Alex*. It seems as if there's been some kind of mistake.' Her back hit the door and she groped for the handle. It opened into a large bathroom. 'I'm not supposed to be here.' Alex didn't move as she raced over to the second door.

She tried the handle, but it wouldn't open.

'Oh, you're supposed to be here,' said Alex.

She rattled it again. Nothing. 'You don't even know me. How do you know where I'm supposed to be?'

'I know your name is Anya Macklin. You're from a town called Brookfield and you have one brother, Jason. Your parents were killed recently, by the rebels.'

Anya spun around to face Alex. He stood near the vanity table, arms folded, and with a look that needed to be slapped off his face.

'How do you know all of this?'

'I'm supposed to know everything about you.'

Anya gave a short laugh. 'Yeah? You sound like a stalker.'

'Had I known you'd fight me on this, I'd have woken you up earlier, not let you sleep in. You looked so innocent with your eyes closed. You even snored a little.' Alex cocked his head to the side. 'If I knew there was a beast hidden beneath your vanilla exterior... This will be fun.'

'Stop talking to me like I'm up to speed. What will be fun? Why am I here?'

'Over the next week, you and I will get to know each other very well.'

Anya scowled, but her heart thrummed at the innuendo. 'Whatever you think is going to happen... well, it isn't. I don't even like you.'

Alex laughed. 'That's the beauty of this place. You don't have to like me. But you're attractive, so that helps.'

His gaze made her feel naked. She glanced at the chest of drawers. 'Helps with what? What do you think I'm here for?'

Alex took a step towards her, cutting off her means of escape. She pressed her back up against the locked exit.

He lunged for her and a scream bubbled up into her throat. She prepared to hit him when he grabbed her fist and pulled her into the centre of the room. She stumbled a little as he twirled her around.

'Welcome to the Breeder programme. You and I are going to have sex, and there's nothing you can do about it.'

Anya yanked her hand from his. 'Sex? In your dreams.'

'It's not my dream. It's theirs.'

'Who?' When Alex didn't answer, she demanded, louder. 'I said, who?'

'We've been genetically matched to create the

perfect child. It will happen whether you want it to or not.'

Alex's insistence stirred a memory of a boy forcing himself on her. Strawberry-blond hair and freckles; nobody she recognised. But it felt real. She would not let Alex intimidate her in the same way.

'I'm not having sex with you, Alex. So you can forget about it.'

'You don't have a choice.'

'Says who?'

The fire in Alex's eyes died a little. 'Says Praesidium.'

Anya's gaze roamed the room. 'Is that where we are? Why is the only window boarded up?'

'We're deep underground. Nothing to look out at. There's no point.'

A short laugh escaped her. 'Breeder programme, though? You're joking, right?'

'Nope. It's why I'm here.' Alex stroked her arm. She shivered and jerked away from him. 'You and I are literally perfect for each other.'

The pain in his eyes hit her like a punch to the gut. This was real. Her shallow breaths winded her as her back touched the exit.

'I don't want to be here. I don't want to be part of a Breeder anything.' She locked eyes with Alex. The thought of kissing him, of having sex with a complete stranger, made her feel sick.

Alex followed her to the exit and leaned against it. His mood turned sombre. 'Like I said, you don't have a choice.'

Anya hugged her middle. 'So you're going to force yourself on me? Is that how you get girls to like you?'

'Not force.' Alex's cockiness wavered for a moment. 'The programme, it's designed to make us fall in love. At the end of the week, you won't have a choice.'

'I always have a choice and so do you.'

His jaw clenched.

Alex's vague answers irritated her. 'So what's this *Breeder* programme for, exactly?'

'To create a genetically perfect child. I told you.'

'I am not having a baby. And I won't to be part of some stupid Breeder programme that forces me to.'

Alex's tone softened. 'I wish it were that simple. It's not about what you want. It's about what the city needs.'

She couldn't believe she was having this conversation. 'There are other ways to do that. Artificial insemination, test tubes. These days, you don't have to be present for the task.'

'All fine examples. But the Collective is addicted to learning, and it has already learned everything it can from test tubes, from laboratory conditions. Now it's after results. It wants to see what happens when two genetically compatible people fall in love and conceive. It wants to learn how a baby created from love differs from one created in a lab. But what it really needs is the babies. So it can create something new. That's why you're here. You're not the first to be in this room and you won't be the last. The results vary from subject to subject.'

The Collective. She'd never heard of them, yet the name sounded familiar.

'So you're saying the Collective's watching now?' Alex's gaze lingered on her covered chest. Anya folded her arms higher. 'I'm not here to be part of some pervert's experiment. And falling in love takes longer than a week, you know.'

Alex laughed. 'I'm not a pervert, but thanks.'

'Maybe you are. I haven't decided yet.' She stepped around him and went to the chest of drawers, looking around. 'Are there cameras in the room?'

'Just one.' He followed her and leaned in close to her ear. 'But I've worked out where the blind spots are.'

She tore her ear away from his hot breath. 'You're disgusting. Don't think I'm sneaking off with you so you can do what you like. I told you, I'm nobody's experiment.'

A vague memory of an atrium and a camera blind spot surfaced in her mind. She was standing beside a different boy, one with dark hair.

Alex's eyes darkened. 'Soon you won't have a choice.'

'Yeah? You keep saying that. And I keep telling you it's not going to happen. There will be no conception. I've no interest in touching you. And you won't touch me without my permission.' She opened one of the drawers and let out a breath when she saw a grey hoodie with a zipped front. She put it on and yanked the zip up fully before turning back to Alex.

His smile, sad not cocky, both surprised and disarmed her. 'I like your optimism and I've tried to fight them but when they inject us with Rapture, we won't be able to keep our hands off each other.'

2

CARISSA

Carissa shielded her eyes from the sun's glare using the book in her hand. *The Peculiar Child with the Curious Eyes* didn't make much sense. It was just a series of black marks on paper. She knew how to read but not how to put words into context.

What was Vanessa thinking, giving her the book, knowing her limitations as a Copy?

She tossed the book away; it hit a tree with a soft thud. Had Carissa known reading would be so hard, she'd have downloaded a summary instead.

The paperback with a fresh mark on the cover lay on the ground, an innocent victim of her frustration. There wasn't even that much to the story. A girl had encountered a peculiar child with curious eyes in the woods behind her house. But what she couldn't understand was why the girl had met the child daily and lied to her mother about it.

She pressed her back against the gable of an

apartment block in Zone D, where the Originals lived. She liked the quiet of the zone during the day. With so few people around, she could sort through her memories and erase the ones that didn't fit with the Collective's impression of her. Memories like the one of the book. Her orb zipped playfully around her head then circled the tree. Carissa didn't have time for games.

Why had the girl in the story lied to her mother? The tale mirrored her own because Carissa had also lied to her own creator: the Collective.

Being connected to the Collective had its advantages. Carissa had known about the arrival of the five participants from Arcis just over two hours ago. She also knew that Quintus had ordered decommission of Essention and the other urbanos in the region. He'd said the programme in Arcis, designed to identify the most suitable females for the Breeder programme, had served its purpose. But a far more likely reason was because the rebellion had rattled the Collective. Rebels had bypassed Arcis' impenetrable defence system to attack the facility. Now the ten masters were accelerating their plans for the Breeder programme.

The real reason Carissa hid certain memories was to mask evidence of her growing empathy. She'd ordered the Inventor to delay decommission to give the people in Arcis and Essention time to escape. Quintus, the Collective's spokesperson, could never find out. The Inventor, her friend, would never betray her secret.

Her Original's sister had been one of the five brought to Praesidium. She'd watched their time in Arcis, feeling a connection to more than just June.

'Miss, I've been so misled by this place, I never even noticed. You don't know how long I've waited for one of you to finally develop a conscience.'

It was what the Inventor had said to her, after she'd ordered him to delay decommission. Carissa didn't know what a conscience felt like, or why the Inventor thought she had one now. But seeing how Anya and June, her only link to her dead Original, had been mistreated had kicked her into action.

Connection to the Collective's network had its disadvantages, too. The daily uploads shared her thoughts, experiences and feelings with the ten masters. Copies had been created to experience life, but how could Carissa live a full life spent under the microscope?

The Inventor regularly called the Ten an oxymoron.

'The Collective insists its Copies experience humanity first-hand, yet it monitors their activities to make sure they don't stray outside their original design parameters. Ridiculous.'

Carissa couldn't agree more.

She looked at the book with a mark on the cover that contained a story close to her own. Why had the girl risked her safety to meet a girl she knew nothing about?

Because that's what humans do.

Carissa wanted to be more human. As a Copy,

she could process information, but a deeper understanding of life was always out of reach.

That's what the newborns were for; newborns like the one copied from Anya Macklin's DNA and under Vanessa's guidance at the library. Carissa's neuromorphic chip allowed her to detect other Copies in Praesidium. But newborns without a chip were unconnected and undetectable.

The newborns were made of biogel, which covered a supporting skeletal frame and a functioning synthetic brain. During maturation, the biogel created hearts, lungs and entire systems, from cardiovascular to endocrine. The final stage created a connection point to receive a neuromorphic chip. To ensure a newborn reached maturation, they received regular infusions of biogel.

Carissa no longer had her original biogel heart. Hers was made of titanium, replaced because of a flaw in the copy process. Maybe her imperfect body meant an imperfect brain, and explained why she hid so much from the Collective.

She stood up and collected the damaged book. She tucked it into the waistband of her leggings, hidden under her long white dress, then snapped her fingers for her orb to follow. It hovered by her side while she called up old footage of her playing with it. She used this footage to overwrite her thoughts of the book and anything else incriminating.

The Collective had yet to notice the similarity of her uploads. She thanked the distraction of the new arrivals for that.

Ω

It was nearly closing time at the library when she approached the glass and wood exterior. With her hands cupped against the glass, she watched Vanessa pick up books off the floor. Several Copies were connected to the download terminal by the door. Carissa considered grabbing a synopsis of *The Curious Child with the Peculiar Eyes* from the archives, but that's not how the humans did it. The Inventor had told her she was developing a conscience. It intrigued her to learn what that meant.

Carissa entered the library, keeping an eye out for Anya's newborn. There was no sign of her. Vanessa had moved away from the download terminal just inside the main door to collect more books from the floor.

'Damn disrespectful Copies,' she said with a sigh.

The Copies didn't respect books. The Inventor had said that respect should always be given to the items most likely to disappear.

When Vanessa didn't acknowledge her, an impatient Carissa strode up to her.

'I need to speak to you, now.' Vanessa didn't look up. 'Explain the book you gave me. Tell me what the story's about.'

'Not now, Carissa. I'm busy. Come back tomorrow.'

'I need to know now.'

Vanessa carried a stack of books to a trolley and set them down. Then she wheeled the trolley along one row, slotting the books back into their rightful places. Everything in the library was categorised alphabetically, regardless of genre.

'You know full well the participants arrived today, Carissa. The Collective assigned one of the newborns to me for the week. She's here right now.'

The Inventor had said it was unusual for a newborn to be assigned to an Original during maturation. Carissa didn't remember her own beginning, but the Inventor had told her he'd raised her after finding her in his workshop, hiding from the Copy put in charge of her.

Vanessa moved on forcing Carissa to follow. 'Yes, I know. But this is more important.'

'Aren't you impatient today? Does the Collective know you're here?'

'No. And I'd appreciate it if you didn't tell them.'

Vanessa stopped and turned to Carissa. 'Is that so? How long have you been hiding things from them?'

Ever since the most recent recruits entered Arcis.

'I'm not hiding things. I require knowledge so I might learn and add to the Collective's database of experience.'

Vanessa perched a fist on her hip. 'But you just said it doesn't know you're here. So how will the Ten learn from your experiences?'

Carissa froze at being caught out in her own lie.

She lifted her chin to assert control, a gesture she'd seen other Copies use with humans. 'Stop asking questions, Librarian. I demand you tell me what I need to know.'

Vanessa narrowed her gaze. 'I've got a frightened, disorientated girl in the room downstairs. She's unconscious for the time being, but when she comes round she'll need my full attention. So forgive me, 173-C, but it's closing time. I need to get down there, so she doesn't wake up alone. I'm sure the Collective wouldn't appreciate you demanding my time during a newborn's maturation week.'

Newborns were wilful, bratty and dramatic. The Collective had no desire to absorb those experiences. While the newborns matured, the Collective gave them free rein. Then right before connection, the Collective wiped the newborns' memories of that first week.

According to the Inventor, Carissa had been a handful that first week, and she'd clashed with his wife, Mags, on more than one occasion. Mags was dead now, and the Inventor didn't like to talk about her or that time.

'So can I come back tomorrow?'

Vanessa nodded. 'In the morning. I'd like you here when the newborn wakes up. It would be good for her to meet a Copy, so she can understand what she will become. The first week is usually a little erratic. They're like toddlers, figuring out the world.'

'I'll help, Librarian, on one condition. That you explain this book to me.' She pulled up her dress and showed it to her.

'I promise. And, please, call me Vanessa, not Librarian.'

Carissa nodded to the stairwell at the back of the library that led down to a single room. Vanessa had shown her the room once, when Carissa had insisted. 'What's her designation?'

'She's called 228-C.' Vanessa closed her eyes briefly. 'Lord, I can't keep straight all the damn numerals for each of you.'

'Should we call her Anya then?' said Carissa.

'No, her Original is in the city. The name clashes.'

'Copy Anya?'

'Still pretty formal.' Vanessa paused. 'What about Canya?'

Carissa nodded. 'That will be an acceptable compromise. I'll see you tomorrow.'

She left Vanessa to lock up and climbed the stairs to the train platform; the train tracks were set one level above the concentric city. A white building in the distance dazzled her: the Learning Centre, located at the heart of the city. The Collective lived there. It was also the location of the main terminals, where Carissa carried out her daily morning upload. But tomorrow she wanted to be at the library first thing.

She boarded the only train in Praesidium and rode it to Zone A. She got off and crossed a circular courtyard to the front of the Learning Centre. The setting sun bathed the steel lobby in a faded-orange wash. Her human-eye implants leaked only a quarter of what she knew they could. She followed the left corridor that housed the main terminal room and the Great Hall, where the Collective minds lived.

She stopped just short of the Great Hall. Inside another room, a dozen receptacles were nested into both walls. A single wire hung down from the top of each receptacle. Other Copies were there, mostly medical staff or guards assigned to protect Praesidium's perimeter with orders to upload more frequently than Carissa. She watched them for a moment as they stood inside the receptacles facing out, the single wire connected to their disc on one temple. Their closed eyes flickered rapidly, as if they were in deep sleep. But Carissa knew it was the process of upload or download that made their eyes do that. She waited until they were finished, disconnected and left the room before she connected.

She stepped inside one of the receptacles and linked the magnetic disc on the single wire to her own for her neuromorphic chip. The NMC, implanted after maturity, gave her synthetic brain most of the abilities of a real one.

Carissa pulled up footage of her orb play from two days ago. She'd committed every detail of the play to memory, making it easy to turn it into a real memory that the Collective would mistake for a girl's obsession with her toy.

Reworking. Reordering. This was her life now.

The Collective could never learn of her evolution.

3

ANYA

Alex leaned against the wall beside Anya, grinning. 'So where do you want to do it?'

She relocated to the bed, to get away from him.

'Well, that's as good a place as any,' he said, following her.

She moved over to the chaise longue.

'Or there. I've done it in both places.'

'Could you stop being gross?'

He laughed. Anya noticed his perfectly straight teeth.

'I can't help it. I've been programmed to seduce you.'

She scoffed. 'You think *that's* seducing me?'

'I haven't even brought my A game yet.' He pushed his messy blond hair out of his eyes and stepped in closer. Anya's pulse raced at his proximity. 'Or would you prefer to dance first?'

'I don't want to do anything with you.' She

20

turned but Alex grabbed her wrist.

His other hand found her face. 'You're prettier than the others. Don't get me wrong. They were attractive. They always are. But you have the most alabaster skin I've ever seen.' He leaned back. 'And those eyes. Wow! A guy could fall under your spell in an instant.'

His thumb stroked her jaw line—a move that felt too intimate. 'Get your hands off me.'

Alex let go and stepped back. His green eyes sparkled in the overhead light. 'Am I stepping on someone's toes? Who's the lucky guy?'

'None of your business.' Her cheeks flushed. There had only been a couple of boys at school who showed a fleeting interest in her. Awkward kisses. Hands trying to go places they shouldn't. Whispers to their friends that they'd made it to third base.

All lies, because they'd never even made it to second. And the kisses weren't even that memorable.

Alex gave her a guarded look. 'There's someone, I can tell. But it doesn't matter. There's no point in resisting. It would be easier to just do it. Then we won't need to keep up this charade.'

'If we do it, will they let us go?'

Alex flinched. 'Sure. Why not?'

'Why did you just flinch like that?'

'I didn't.' He turned away.

'Yes, you did.' Anya bridged the gap between them. 'Why did you flinch, Alex? *Are* they going to let us go after we have sex? Will it be that easy?'

'What things in life are ever easy?'

She tugged on his arm, forcing him to face her. A smile replaced the pained expression on his face.

'Don't worry, Anya. It's not that bad. You're hot, and I can tell from that look you keep giving me that you're curious about me.'

She ignored his attempts to distract her. 'How long have you been here?'

'What does it matter?'

'It matters. How long?'

He moved over to the bed, taking her with him. He sat down and pulled her between his legs. 'Now, isn't this more interesting? We know practically nothing about each other, but I can tell things are going to be easy between us.'

Anya tried to escape, but Alex was too strong. 'We're not doing this,' she said softly. She'd already seen too much in her short life; her parents' murder. Rebels destroying their town. Pity, not fear, consumed her.

'I like that you fight me. It's a turn on, if you must know.'

She stepped out of his space. 'How long have you been here, Alex?'

His gaze clouded over. 'Long enough to know how this works.'

'A month? Two?'

Alex met her gaze. 'Try eight months.'

'Are you serious?'

'I never kid.'

'What about your life outside Praesidium? What town did you come from?'

'What does that matter?' Alex stood up, hooking his thumbs into his pockets. 'This is my life. I've come to accept that.'

'So the city keeps you in this cage, expects you to perform? Is that what's expected of me?'

He shrugged. 'I never see the girls again after they come through here.'

Anya sat down in the spot Alex had vacated. For some reason she didn't fear this boy. If he really wanted her virginity, he wouldn't have asked. 'What happens to them? Why am I here?'

'I'm not told anything about what happens outside of my room.'

Anya looked around. 'I'm in *your* room?'

He flashed a grin at her. 'Yeah. You like?'

She took in the chaise longue and vanity table. 'It's not very manly.'

'I get frequent enough visitors. It's dressed up to make the newbies feel at home. Nobody cares about what the Breeder wants.'

'Breeder?'

'That's what the Collective calls me.'

Anya wanted to keep him talking, to learn what she could. 'Are there more Breeders?'

Alex shrugged again and folded his arms. 'I told you. I don't know what goes on outside of this room.'

She studied the space—a mix of masculine and feminine. 'So if you could decorate this place how you wanted, what would you go for?'

'I don't know.'

'What if the Collective said you could do what

you like?'

'I don't really rate in the Collective's opinion. The group doesn't get that humans like different things. And space?' He tugged on his hair and laughed. 'Not too pushed on giving me much of that.'

'Who is the Collective?'

'A group of ten masters that run Praesidium. Quintus is the spokesperson for the group.' He frowned. 'You said you visited the library here. They would have given you a rundown of how the city works.'

Quintus. She'd heard that name before. But not then. More recently.

'That was over five years ago. I don't remember. Have you ever met the masters, or Quintus?'

'No. The Ten have no corporeal form. This is a machine city.'

Anya knew about the machines, but not the masters. 'So how can you be sure the ten masters exist, or the Collective? Or Quintus?'

'Because the Copies live to serve the masters, providing them with the corporeal form they lack. The Copies are connected to the Collective ten's network.'

Anya focused on the details of Alex's wild story. She had heard the term 'Copies' before from her memories, or dreams—whatever. If these Copies were linked to the Collective, maybe they were also her way out of this room.

'What is the Collective's purpose, Alex?'

'To explain would take longer than I have.' Alex

unfolded his arms. 'Look, I don't like to think about them while I'm working.'

But Anya persisted. 'Okay. Explain exactly what the Collective wants to happen here.' To reason with the group, she first needed to understand its motives.

Alex relocated to the wall. He leaned against it and buried his hands in the front pockets of his khakis. 'Okay, if helps speed things up. First, the Ten lets you get acquainted, like we're doing now. In the beginning, the group had expected the magic to happen naturally.'

'But attraction doesn't work that way.'

Alex nodded. 'But the Collective doesn't understand that. Everything it knows about us it learns from the copies of humans. The group assumes that because we look the same—upright, breathing, walking bags of skin—we're all similar.'

'Copies? Of humans?' This was getting too weird.

Alex looked confused. 'Yeah. There's another you walking around Praesidium right now.'

The thought made her shiver. She rubbed her arms. 'I don't even know how I got here.'

'Oh, shit, I forgot. Your memory is wiped before you get here.' He walked over to Anya and sat down. 'You were in a place called Arcis. The Collective used a machine on the ninth floor to download your experiences. Then the machine made a copy that's biologically identical to you in every way, right before it wiped your memories.'

Arcis? The name, like the term "Copies", was

familiar. But her last memory was of being sick in her town. 'Why would it do that?'

'The Collective wanted your experiences in Arcis. It uses them to teach its Copies and hybrids to become the perfect specimen.' Hybrids? Anya shivered again. 'Think of the group as puppet masters. It controls the Copies and experience life through their eyes.'

'But if the Collective is only after experience, why does it need to perfect its Copies or... hybrids?'

Alex shrugged. 'I've heard rumours it's part of a greater plan to escape.'

'I thought *we* were the prisoners.'

'Like I said, I don't know. I'm only told the essentials.'

Anya stood up and crossed the room for a little space. Turned back. 'The last clear memory was of my hometown. My parents were killed. I was sick. Jason, my brother...' She locked her gaze on Alex. 'Is my brother here? Jason Macklin. Is he okay?'

Alex shrugged. 'The machine brought just five of you here; four females and one male, dark haired. If Jason went through Arcis, he's probably here.'

She bent over at the waist, her breaths coming fast and uneven. Jason had light brown hair. It wasn't him.

Alex's hand on her back surprised her. She straightened up and he pulled his hand away. 'It will get easier, I promise. You won't remember everything, but some stuff will come back to you in time.'

26

'Tell me about these Copies. If humans aren't considered unique to the Collective, then why am I here, or you? Are you a Copy?' Alex was too perfect looking not to be.

'Copies are different from their human Originals. For the first week, they're closer to newborns in behaviour. Not actual babies, but everything is brand new to them. They are sexually aware, have heightened emotions. They're also incapable of reproducing. When the Collective first brought pairs of humans together to mate, it assumed their sexual appetites would be similar to that of the newborn Copies. But humans process things differently, and most need a connection before they can have sex with someone. The Collective is impatient. It wants results quickly.'

Alex hadn't answered her question. 'I said, are you a Copy?'

He flashed a smile that would have turned all the popular girls' heads at school.

'I'm all human. Where it counts, if you know what I mean.'

She tried not to think about it.

'Okay. So say the "magic" doesn't happen. What then? Will the masters let me go?'

Alex shook his head. 'Rapture will speed up the attraction. The injections, low doses at first, are built up over time. After each injection we're left alone with everything we need to... you know. We have music, alcohol, a bath and shower through there.' Alex pointed at the bathroom. 'Everything to put us in the mood.'

'So, the Collective wants me to get pregnant? Why?' The idea of a forced pregnancy made her sick to her stomach.

'To create a genetically perfect child. I told you already.'

'But you said something else, about helping the masters to escape. Escape what? Why?'

Alex sighed. 'I told you I don't know much beyond the essentials.'

Tears pooled in her eyes. Her odds of escape were narrowing by the second. 'I'm too young. I don't want this.' She groped for the handle to the exit. When the door wouldn't budge, she slid down to the floor and buried her face in her knees. 'I don't want to get pregnant and I don't want to be stuck here for nine months.'

Alex hunkered down to her level. 'It's not for that long. Only three months.'

She stared up at him through wet eyes. 'Three?'

'Remember I said the Collective was impatient? Your body will act as an incubator for the foetus for the first three months. Then the baby is taken out and its growth accelerated in specially adapted machine incubators. And in a couple of weeks, a new baby. They grow the babies pretty fast after that. '

Three months and two weeks? That wasn't possible. 'What are the babies *used* for?'

'Test subjects, mostly. They're prepped from birth to be integrated into the neural network. The Collective needs control over their minds.'

Alex knew a lot, but not why the Collective was doing this. 'And the ones who can't be controlled?'

'They're sent to the harvesting centre where their living organs are replaced with Praesidium tech. It's another form of control—through the body, not the mind.'

Anya hugged her legs to stem the nausea. She looked up at Alex. 'What if I don't go through with it?'

Alex gave her a sad smile. 'That's never happened. Rapture will see to that.'

4

CANYA

The room didn't feel right, filled with dusty books that...

She sneezed.

I hate this place. Wherever I am.

She'd woken up an hour ago in a bed that was barely big enough for a child, let alone an almost adult. At five foot six she wasn't tall, but single beds were for losers.

Or kids.

Alongside the bed and wall shelves filled with books that smelled of old leather, there was a writing desk and a locked door. She chose to sit on the bed, where she had the best view of the exit.

Where was Dom? She'd just left him inside a holding room. A woman with dark skin and a long green dress had taken her from the room and brought her here. The rest was hazy. Whatever Vanessa had given her must have knocked her out.

Ever since she'd woken up, Vanessa had shown up every ten minutes to sit with her and ask her a bunch of questions about Arcis. Vanessa didn't like it much when she said nothing. Half an hour ago, her memories of Arcis had returned to her. She assumed that's what Vanessa was after.

Vanessa kept calling her 'Canya'. She preferred Anya, but Vanessa had said it wasn't possible to keep the name, not while her Original lived in the city.

Canya remembered the giant machine on the ninth floor; the soldiers arriving with Anya's brother to attempt a rescue; the Copy supervisors murdering some of the soldiers. She had a vague recollection of her Original's past, but Vanessa's intervention had turned those recollections into real memories.

Nothing had hit her quite as hard as the memory of Dom Pavesi.

'How can I have Anya's memories if I'm not her?' she'd asked Vanessa.

'A duplicate of her memories was imprinted during the copy phase. I activated that imprint.'

And Canya was glad she had; the memory of Dom gave her hope.

After each visit, Vanessa would lock the door on the way out.

She sat up straight when she heard the door unlock once more. Vanessa entered the room, but this time Canya saw a second person behind her, a girl aged around thirteen, dressed in white. She glanced down at her own pale skin, which matched her white dress; some sort of uniform, apparently. She studied

Vanessa's bright green dress, feeling envious at how the colour complemented her dark skin.

The quiet child with strange, restless eyes unsettled her. She looked around the room, more interested in it than Canya.

Vanessa stayed by the open door, as if she was eager to leave.

'She needs to leave this room, Carissa,' Vanessa said to the child.

Carissa sat down beside Canya on the bed, prompting her to shift away.

'I agree.' Carissa narrowed her gaze at her. Canya matched her stare, refusing to let this child intimidate her. 'It will take some time to get used to how things work around here. First, you're not connected. Second, your biogel body needs a full week to reach maturation, and you'll need regular injections to top up the biogel required to create your synthetic organs. You have the basics now. Bone structure and a functioning brain. The biogel will give you a heart, lungs—anything necessary to survive long term. Being unconnected can feel scary, but I can help you to adjust.'

But Canya didn't *feel* scared. She remembered her old life as if it were yesterday. Who was she supposed to be 'connected' to?

She just needed to see Dom. Then everything would be okay.

Carissa continued in a business-like tone. 'The last thing the biogel does is build a connection point to accept your new neuromorphic chip. The NMC will connect you to the Collective's network. You're a newborn now. But post-connection, you'll be a Copy.'

Vanessa nodded and said, 'Lucky for us, the Collective doesn't take an interest in your maturation week. The biogel in your system acts like an overdose of hormones. The Collective prefers logical and rational behaviour, which means you're a free agent until your biogel balances out and your body matures.'

Canya might be a biogel newborn, but inside she felt human. She would succeed with Dom where the pathetic, virgin Anya had failed.

Vanessa continued. 'You will feel on edge while you're a newborn. Your emotions will run high. You will have extreme appetites for things you've never experienced before, like sex. I can help you control your urges until maturation is complete and you're reset.'

Canya's mouth fell open. 'Reset?'

'Yes.'

'Why would the Collective reset me? I'm more human than Anya.'

Carissa touched her hand; it felt cold. Canya yanked it away from the creepy child.

'All newborns are reset,' said Carissa. 'You're an exact replica copied limb for limb. But you are not human.'

'I was born in Brookfield and I have a brother, Jason.' She almost mentioned her boyfriend, Dom.

Almost.

Carissa glared at Vanessa. 'You gave her back her memories? Why would you do that?'

Vanessa shushed her. 'Because I need her to remember something.'

'I must report this anomaly to the Collective.' Carissa stood up and touched a disc embedded just above her ear.

Canya mirrored her stance. No way in hell was this child taking away her memories.

But Vanessa surprised her by grabbing the child's hands. 'You can't connect to the Collective down here. This room is off the network.'

'Why?'

'I brought you here to help, not to tell the Collective about the existence of Canya's memories. I know you hide stuff from the Collective. What would Quintus do if he found out you were overwriting your memories?'

The girl stared at their joined hands. 'How did you know?'

Vanessa frowned at Carissa. 'Why else would you ask me about the book? You possess a natural curiosity that the others don't have.'

That news seemed to rattle the child. 'I don't want them to find out. Please, Librarian, I've been so careful.'

'So you'll help me with Canya? Overwrite our discussion about me returning Anya's memories to her?'

Canya's memories.

If the girl refused, Canya would find another way

to stop her. She examined the two discs the child carried: one embedded in her temple, the other just above her ear, partially hidden by shoulder-length blonde hair. Canya felt around for her own discs but found none. Would she receive similar discs upon connection? She noticed Vanessa had only a single disc, above her ear.

To her relief, and Vanessa's, Carissa nodded.

Vanessa turned to Canya. 'This is a really difficult time for all the newborns. You come out of the machine with a vague tie to your Original's memories. The tie creates a bond. But you must understand that you are not *her*. The real Anya is alive and well. You're only borrowing her memories, until reset.'

But Canya didn't agree. 'They're my memories. It's my life I'm remembering.'

'It's not your life,' said Vanessa. 'The memories belong to your Original. You have them now because I need you to recall a place. Anya's parents might have mentioned it.'

'I won't help you!' Canya rushed for the open door that Vanessa no longer guarded. 'I want to get out of here.'

Dom would make everything better.

Vanessa blocked her exit, managing to close the door with a soft click. When she pulled a syringe out of her pocket, Canya backed off.

Vanessa waved the syringe at her. 'Just because you're not connected doesn't mean I can't control you with this.'

'You can't keep me here. I want to go home.'

'You *are* home, Canya. You belong here, in Praesidium.' Vanessa put the syringe back in her pocket. 'The Collective created you. The sooner you accept that, the sooner we can get on with your orientation.'

Canya charged at the door again, but discovered it was locked. She rattled the handle, fighting the rage inside her. 'Let me out of here. These are my memories. It's my life now.'

'This is a problem,' Vanessa said to Carissa.

Carissa agreed. 'If the Collective discovers she's more than a blank Copy, she will be terminated. The Ten don't like variables they can't control. She must not mention her memories around the other Copies. She must stay off Quintus' radar.'

'*Terminate* me?' That sounded worse than being reset. Her hot temper cooled.

'Yes,' said Carissa. 'If you don't accept what you are, your life will be over before it's begun.'

Canya slumped to the floor. 'But I *feel* like her.' She looked up at Vanessa through wet eyes. 'Why can't I just *be* her?'

'Your emotions are running high. Your bond with your Original is strong. You feel everything that she felt.'

Canya wanted to say it was more than just a possession of memories. She felt a disconnect with the old Anya. It felt like she was shedding her skin.

Shedding her past.

'So I won't remember her in a week?'

36

'All memories, including your own, will be stripped from you at reset,' said Carissa. 'You will get her memories back, but only when you're mature enough to handle them. What you will lose is the connection you feel now to Anya's past.'

And her connection to Dom.

'Newborns with Original memories are too influenced by past traits and decisions. Quintus demands all newborns be created as blanks so the final Copy is pure and untainted.'

'Why bother?' said Canya.

Vanessa shrugged. 'The Collective obviously sees value in doing so.'

'Because,' said a miffed Carissa, 'it is a more efficient way of creating and managing Copies.'

Vanessa couldn't hide her shiver.

Canya got to her feet. If escape was no longer an option, maybe negotiating would work.

'I want to see Dom. Where is he?'

'You can't see him,' said Vanessa.

'Why not?'

'He's not *your* Dom. We talked about this. They're not your memories. They're Anya's. Whatever you think you know, it didn't happen to you. It happened to Anya.'

Canya folded her arms. 'Okay, let me see his Copy.'

'Dom Pavesi didn't copy correctly,' said Carissa. 'Only one of him exists.'

Canya fixed Vanessa with her best intimidating stare. 'I still want to see him.'

'No, Canya.'

'What part of the city is he in?' Her heart beat too fast thinking about never seeing him again. 'You can't keep me locked up forever. Or would you rather I tell the Collective about my memories?'

A bluff, but she took the risk that Vanessa needed her alive.

The Librarian closed her eyes. 'He's being held in the medical facility. But you must stay away, pretend you're a blank. *She* shares a connection with him, not you.'

Canya wanted to scream, to punch the wall. Dom was hers, not Anya's.

She pushed down her hate for this woman.

Vanessa forced a smile. 'Why don't I give you a tour of the city? When you're up to it, let me know.'

Canya took a deep breath and returned the fake smile. 'I'm ready now.'

5

CANYA

Outside the library, Canya's eyes pricked with the worst pain imaginable.

'It's your human-eye implants,' said Carissa. 'They can't handle the sun's glare that bounces off the white buildings.'

The pain settled behind her wet eyes. She absorbed the blurry view of the city around her.

Someone—Vanessa, she presumed—pushed a pair of glasses into her palm. She put them on and her discomfort eased. She wiped away new tears to see everything clearer.

'It takes a while to get used to the implants,' said Carissa. 'I've had mine for six months now. I'm still not used to them.'

'Will you be joining us, Carissa?' said Vanessa.

The girl shook her head. 'I must attend my lessons.'

'Lessons?' said Canya, as the girl walked away.

'When you're connected, you'll be doing lessons, too.'

'I don't think so.' She was too old for school.

Canya followed Vanessa up a flight of stairs to a train platform set above street level. The set-up reminded her of the Monorail in Essention.

Zone D – Library.

From her new height, she saw much more of the city—large, bright and white. With the glare safely muted behind her tinted glasses, she tracked a solo train moving past a cluster of white buildings in the distance.

Vanessa handed her a tissue. 'It will help.'

Canya dabbed at her eyes and continued her examination of Praesidium. The city was split between two levels: the upper, where the train ran, and the lower, set out in a concentric-ring design. The rings decreased in size the closer to the heart they got. Two roads cut through the centre like a cross and finished at the edge of the city. Smaller roads cut through the rings at forty-five-degree angles to the centre.

'There are tag stations where two zones intersect. You enter and exit the different zones from there.' Canya followed Vanessa's finger to a silver station below them no taller than head height. The area swarmed with people dressed like her.

'How does the tag station detect them?'

Vanessa held up her wrist and Canya made out the tiniest of incisions on her skin.

'Our locator chips talk to the tag station.

Proximity sets them off. Same process when you enter buildings.'

Canya ran a finger over her own scar.

'Copies wear white, Originals colours. In case you were wondering.'

Open-sided cars travelled the roads beneath the platform. Copies streamed in crowds towards the building at the heart of the city. Those dressed in bright colours appeared to walk stiffly among them.

The train came to a stop in front of her. It was bigger, sleeker and quieter than the Monorail in Essention. Both Originals and Copies boarded. Her white dress marked her as something she wasn't. She would rectify that soon.

The whites boarded the first carriage while the colours boarded the second. The division appeared to repeat all the way to the last carriage, but Vanessa broke the pattern and boarded a white-only carriage with Canya.

Canya pulled off her glasses and dabbed at her eyes using Vanessa's tissue. Dozens of receptacles dominated both sides of the space. A solitary wire hung down over each receptacle. These wires connected to the whites' discs. Their closed eyes flickered, and she wondered why.

'They're uploading their experiences while on the move,' said Vanessa. 'Normally the Copies upload in the Learning Centre. The mobile receptacles are a new way to upload, so the Collective doesn't miss a thing. Right now, it's not mandatory. The receptacles can also be used to download new information from the Collective.'

'Like what?'

'News of the participants' arrival from Arcis, for example. Or the existence of four new Copies in the city.'

Canya nodded to the second carriage, where the colours had gathered. 'Why are they separated?'

'The Collective doesn't like Originals to mix with Copies. It wants Copies to experience a pure life without outside contamination.'

'The Originals. They don't upload or download?'

Vanessa tapped her only disc. 'Just a communication disc, I'm pleased to say. We don't have NMCs. We're not connected. We do things the old way—read books, talk and learn from each other. The Copies learn human behaviour through observation, not interaction.' Vanessa pointed to the receptacles. 'There are hundreds of these dotted around the city, but the main upload rooms are in the Learning Centre, in the heart of the city. The wires connect to their NMCs. The neuromorphic chip gives them the ability to process sensory data like sound and images, so they can become more responsive beyond their programming.'

Canya's fingers fluttered over her smooth skin. 'If I'm supposed to be like them, shouldn't I have a disc?'

'Soon, right before you're reset.'

Three unconnected Copies stood near one of the carriage doors. They ignored her. 'Why don't they interact with me?'

'They can't sense you because you don't have your NMC. Copies learn from life through downloads, and the chip helps them to process the info. It's my job as your carer to help you navigate your first week. To make you more human, so to speak.'

Canya already felt human, and she had the memories to prove it. But if she wanted to avoid termination, she had to keep her mouth shut.

'So I'm more like them.' She thumbed at the second carriage, where Originals talked to each other. Vanessa nodded.

She preferred that carriage to the one she was in. She and Vanessa were the only ones engaged in conversation, and it felt too much like the Copies were eavesdropping.

The train moved off in the direction of the outer ring. Vanessa and Canya stayed by the window.

'See that there?' Vanessa pointed to a road on the outer edge of Praesidium. Dozens of giant wolves roamed the area.

'That's Zone E, and the furthest point out. An energy barrier with a high electrical current surrounds the city. If you want to leave the city, you need permission first.'

The barrier separated the neat manicured lawn of the city from the stony, vast plains of the world beyond Praesidium.

'What are they?' She pointed at the wolves.

'Officially? Guardians. They patrol the three sections of Zone E. See there?' Vanessa pointed at a long grey single-storey building with several doors to the front. 'That's where you arrived from Arcis. There's a portal inside. The rooms serve as holding areas. The rest of the zone is divided between accommodation for the Copies and the Business District, where we *Originals* are given a little freedom. You'll find a large plaza with a fashion, food, art and music area. While it's mostly for us, some Copies have been known to visit. I say "a little" freedom because the Collective uses camera orbs to monitor our activity there. It's all part of its learning experience, to understand us better.'

Canya pointed at the three-tiered accommodation. 'Is that where I'll live?'

'Eventually,' said Vanessa. 'For now, you'll stay at the library.'

'Have you ever left Praesidium?'

'No.' Vanessa's voice hitched slightly. 'The only safe way inside the city is through the portal that brought you here.'

'What about the main gates?' She saw them shimmer in the distance.

'Protected by an energy barrier.'

'How far does the energy barrier extend?'

'Twelve generators equal twelve segments that encase the city in an invisible bubble.'

'Does it ever rain?'

'Out there it does. Not inside the city, because of the barrier. That's why the city is so damn bright. It's not just the Copies who struggle with the unnatural glare.'

The train glided over the lower street, above the heads of the wolves that patrolled Zone E. One of the creatures looked up just as the carriage moved overhead. Canya jerked her head back from the window.

The train tracks above the city were laid out like a spiral, loosely matching the concentric design below. The track circles shortened the closer the train got to the heart of Praesidium.

'That's Zone D. The Originals' accommodation.' Vanessa pointed at a group of four-tiered buildings in the distance. 'I live in Section C, apartment twenty-eight.'

The space allocated to the accommodation blocks was a quarter of the size of the area given to the Copies. 'You don't live in the same zone as the Copies?'

'I told you, we don't interact with the Copies.' She pointed to another building made of glass and wood. 'And that's the library.'

The train spiralled from Zone D towards Zone A —the heart of the flat city. 'Zone C houses the medical facility. It's where...' Vanessa sighed. 'It's where the Collective studies Originals.'

That's where Dom was. Vanessa had said as much. Canya's heart beat so fast she had to hold on to a vertical bar for support.

The facility, a long grey structure that occupied half of Zone C, looked innocent enough. That innocence disappeared when she saw patrolling guards outside.

'What happens in there?'

'The Breeder programme. A study of how boys and girls—teenagers—interact.'

'And what else?'

Vanessa paused. 'There's a Harvest programme. Originals are tested to see if Praesidium's tech is compatible with their anatomy.'

Dom's scars. He had to be in the Harvest programme.

The train moved on. 'This is Zone B. There used to be a school for the Original children here to keep them separate from their Copies. The children are all gone now. The Collective reallocated the space to more receptacles.'

'Why the separation if the Collective wants to learn about you?'

Vanessa shook her head. 'If I knew what went on in the ten heads of the Collective, I wouldn't be here.'

'And you've never tried to leave the city?'

Vanessa didn't answer as the train moved on to the last zone. It slid to a final platform above a large white building with a circular courtyard to the front.

'Zone A and the Learning Centre. This is also where the Collective exists. When you receive your NMC, you'll spend most of your time here.'

Most of the Copies alighted at Zone A. Vanessa and Canya stayed on board and rode the train back to Zone D.

The orientation wasn't as boring as Canya had expected it to be. At least now she knew where to go next.

'I want to see Dom in the medical facility.'

Vanessa glanced at the emptying platform and lowered her voice. 'We already talked about that. You need to stick to the other zones. It's safer if the Collective knows nothing about you having Anya's memories.'

'But I can go where I like?'

'Well, technically, yes. You're not hooked up, so you don't have access to the Collective's knowledge. You're not a threat. Quintus doesn't care where you go.'

'So I can go to the medical facility?'

Vanessa sighed as she headed for the library. 'I advise against it.'

'What do you need from my memories?'

Vanessa stopped and placed a hand on Canya's shoulder. 'Can I trust you to help me?' She nodded. 'I need you to remember Anya's time in Brookfield. There's a place in the mountains, a place Anya's parents might have mentioned.'

'What's in it for me?'

'What do you want most, Canya?'

To see Dom.

'To be human.'

Vanessa's fingers curled into her flesh. 'If you could live outside Praesidium as a human, would you?'

Canya's heart fluttered. 'Yes.'

'Then do what I say and I'll make that happen.'

She was about to ask 'What about Dom?' when her chest tightened, forcing her to stop. She bent over while her heart pounded in her chest.

'What's wrong, Canya?'

'I feel weak. My heart... It's beating too fast.'

'They warned me of this. Your biogel reserves are too low. Take a deep breath. You're putting too much strain on your underdeveloped heart. I'll need to top up your biogel to continue the maturation cycle.'

Canya nodded, too weak to argue.

'Jacob gave me everything I need. It's at the library.' She pushed her on. 'You'll feel much better soon.'

6

DOM

Dom Pavesi's white-walled cell matched his tunic and trouser set. He looked down at his bare feet. Where were his shoes?

Except for the male medic who'd brought him to the room and checked on him once, he'd had no visitors. That suited him just fine. The medic gave off a weird vibe.

His only other interaction had been with the food guy. Not exactly a chatty sort, and Dom had only seen his hand. Ten minutes ago, he'd slid a food tray through the slot at the bottom of his door; the third one in over three hours. It contained runny stew—too salty for his taste—a dinner roll and a bottle of water.

Dom kicked it over to the other two trays, one tested, the other untouched, probably laced with some drug other than Compliance. Compliance sweetened food.

The machine on the ninth floor of Arcis,

designed to erase his memories, had done little more than give him temporary amnesia. The details of what had happened in Arcis had mostly returned to him.

His stomach growled, and he pressed his fingers into his middle. The tray taunted him from across the room.

Screw it.

He dragged the tray over and spooned the stew into his waiting mouth. The bread went down just as easy. His stomach finally quietened. He waited for the drugged dizziness. Nothing came.

He cracked open the water and drank as his last few moments in Arcis came back to him. He swallowed past the lump in his throat when he thought back to Preston, a boy who'd facilitated communication between Dom in Arcis and Max and Charlie. Two boy soldiers were also dead. Sheila and June had been with Dom. Anya too, and her brother, Jason. Dom had gone last through the machine. He hadn't seen what happened to him.

The holding room came next. All of them together. Then a woman in a green dress came for Anya. Others dressed in white came for Sheila and June, and Yasmin, whom he didn't know all that well. But he hadn't been alone for long.

Male medics had joined him, said something about him not copying and that the memory wipe had failed. Something about tech he'd carried from age seven.

Dom drained the bottle. In his heart, he knew that Sheila and June—his rebel friends—were okay. He had no worries about Yasmin either. She had been tough in Arcis.

Only one person occupied his thoughts: the girl with the brown hair and deep blue eyes who'd shocked, surprised and angered him. And tamed his inner lone wolf. They had been forced together in Arcis. Were their feelings for each other even real? He wanted to find out. Wherever she was in this place, he'd find her.

And his mother. The reason for him enduring all this crazy shit.

A noise alerted him. His gaze flashed to the opening door. The male medic was back, locking Dom in a hateful stare, as if he were some diseased lab rat. A female medic stood behind him.

'Collect the trays, 148-C,' she said.

'Yes, 118-C.' The male picked up the two spare trays off the floor, shooting Dom another look of disgust as he snatched up the one in front of him. Dom watched the food go, wishing now he'd kept the spare rolls.

'On your feet,' ordered the female medic.

Dom complied, noting her more authoritative tone.

'Walk outside.'

Dom looked down. 'I need shoes.'

'They are unnecessary.'

He disagreed as the cold concrete floor chilled his feet. With the door open, he could overpower the medic, make a run for it.

But two additional male medics waiting outside

put paid to that idea. They pulled him forward by his arms while the female followed. The cold cement of the corridor floor shot fresh chill pains through his feet.

They entered a large space with two doors on one side. One of the males pulled Dom through the left door and into a large, bright room with a gurney in the centre. An overhead light attached to a moveable arm illuminated the gurney. The smooth and glossy walls showed the faint outline of a hidden set of panels. The ceiling above him contained similar hidden panels. He feared the worst.

One of the males dragged him towards the gurney. His feet slipped on the white-tiled floor as he tried to resist.

'Lie down, Dom Pavesi,' said the female.

'Why?'

'Because I told you to. This will go easier if you comply.'

Dom continued to put up a fight. 'I asked you why. I'm not getting on that thing without a good reason.'

He glanced up at the closed ceiling panels.

'I can order the medics to break your arms and legs and lift you up, if you'd prefer.'

Dom called her bluff. 'Well, I guess we have a problem then.'

He caught her nod too late. The male who hated him grabbed his arm and twisted. Dom heard something crack. A blaze of heat set his arm on fire.

He gritted his teeth and hissed out a cry. 'What

are you doing?' He fought against the blaze and tried to reclaim his arm, but the strong medic held on.

Dom sucked in a breath as the medic twisted again. He heard another snap, felt a deeper blaze of agony. A deep, guttural scream passed his lips. His head swam and he groped for the gurney.

The two medics lifted him up the rest of the way and strapped both arms and legs down. Heat licked at his broken bones.

He gasped, dry heaved, turned his head to one side, just in case. A panel in the ceiling opened and a metal arm descended to the hand on his unbroken arm. Dom recoiled from the needle but his restraints kept him in place. The needle slipped into a vein in his hand and stayed there. The pain lessened.

Morphine?

'What are you giving me?' His words came out thick and heavy.

'A sedative. Not enough to knock you out. Just to keep you calm.'

Another arm with a second needle shot down and disappeared under the table. He felt a pinch at his spine.

'Keep still, Dom Pavesi. It's just a spinal anaesthetic.'

Distracted by the numbing sensation in his torso, he almost missed another two metal arms extending down, both with sets of pincers attached to the ends. The pincers clamped above and below the break in his arm and twisted it the opposite way. The pain silenced Dom's screams. He gasped for air as a fifth arm slipped down and bathed the area with the break in a blue light. The pain lessened instantly, and Dom had just enough energy left to flex the fingers of his bound hand. He felt no pain.

'What the hell was that? What did it just do?'

The female moved to his side. 'We fixed the break in your arm. Then healed the tears, cartilage, bone damage.'

That kind of break would have taken six weeks to heal in a cast.

'How? It was so fast.'

'Our medical equipment is advanced, Dom Pavesi. I expect you to cooperate, unless you'd like to see how well you heal without our assistance, or without a cast.'

Dom nodded. His eyes grew heavy. The needle with the anaesthetic was still attached to his hand.

'If you plan to experiment on me, sorry to say you're several years too late.'

The males stepped back, allowing the female full access to the gurney. She was in charge. Maybe he could try reasoning with her.

'We are aware of the technology you carry, Dom Pavesi. The machine was unable to copy you in Arcis. The Collective wishes to understand why. The Collective also wishes to know how you evaded us for so long.'

His stomach rolled at the mention of Mariella. 'Where is my mother?'

'Cooperate and you will have your answers. First, I need you to relax. If you don't, this part will hurt more than the broken arm.'

'What part? What are you going to do?'

'We're just taking a look inside you today.'

Three new arms raced down from three separate ceiling panels, silencing his next question. The light repositioned itself over his torso. The first arm had a laser cutting tool attached to the end; something he'd seen Charlie Roberts use to cut steel in Essention. It sliced his skin at the exact point with the scar on his torso: an upside-down *T* that cut across his stomach and travelled up to his breastbone.

A second arm peeled back the skin to reveal his innards. Dom released a silent scream.

'Try to relax, Dom Pavesi,' said the female medic. 'Your heart rate is too high. It will help if you take a few deep breaths.'

'Stop! Please... I need to get out of here.'

He glanced down at the open wound in the middle of his chest. A third arm scanned his full liver transplant—the metal alternative he'd been given at age seven. He looked away from the butchery.

'The Collective's records show that you've had this for twelve years. But this is Second Generation tech. That makes you part of the Generation Two programme. The Collective presumed all the test subjects from that batch had expired. With no viable way of tracking you, you were lost to us. Your mother said you'd died, but by that time we'd already begun experimenting on Generation Three subjects.'

The medication kept him in a sleepy haze that allowed him to feel sensations but not pain. The arm with the laser sealed up his scar, leaving a puffy red mark. The table flipped him over, and the restraints stopped him from falling to the floor. He felt his other two scars being opened: the *C* scar running from below his right armpit to the small of his back, and his horizontal scar running at hip level along one side of his back. He closed his eyes as he felt his skin being pinned back, followed by a small tingle as the scanner checked his lung and kidney replacement. Then a final tingle as they closed him up.

The bed flipped him right side up. All but one of the metal arms retracted into the ceiling. A new arm with another syringe stabbed his other arm.

'What did you just give me?'

'It's to accelerate your healing.'

His skin tightened where the laser had made the new cuts and reopened old scars.

'We're done for now, Dom Pavesi,' said the female medic. 'You can return to your room.'

The anaesthetic needle slipped out of his vein and the medics undid the restraints on the gurney. Dom placed one shaky foot on the floor. His legs gave out and he collapsed. The male medics lifted him upright and walked him back to his cell.

A drugged and disorientated Dom committed what he could of the route to memory.

7

ANYA

'Why haven't you tried to leave?' said Anya.

Alex lay on the bed—his bed, she'd recently discovered—with his arm draped over his eyes. Anya, too wired to sit, leaned against the dresser.

'And go where?'

'I don't know. Anywhere has to be better than this place. I can't believe you've been here for eight months.'

'So what? Look, I don't want to force you into anything, but believe me, having sex now before they inject us is a far better option.'

From the second Anya had made her feelings clear, Alex's charm and brazen attitude had vanished.

'Why?'

Alex sat up. 'It just is. Okay?'

'No. Tell me why it's better to get it over with now rather than wait.'

Alex sighed. 'Because Rapture slowly eats away

at your self-control. It feels like someone else is directing you. Everything is heightened. Every feeling you have for me will surface.'

'I don't have feelings for you, Alex. I don't even know you.'

He groaned as if she were an idiot. 'But you will. Have feelings for me, I mean. I told you already. It's what happens. It's the whole point of the injections.'

Anya paced with nervous energy. 'Why are you so against waiting? What's so bad about a couple of injections? It can't be worse than us having sex like this'—she waved her hand around the room—'in a place where you say we're being watched. You're a total stranger.'

'So you'd rather wait until you've been injected and can't help yourself? Wouldn't you rather be in full control of your mind?'

His argument meant little to her. 'I'm not going to have sex with you. With or without the injections. I have great self-control.'

Alex scoffed. 'That's what they all say. Then they give in. Believe me. I've tried to fight it. It doesn't work.'

'I won't give in. You want to know why?' Alex shrugged as if he didn't care. 'Because I'm going to *resist*.'

That earned her a laugh. 'You can't. That's what the injections are for. They undo all your hard work and mental power. They tap into your primal instinct. Man. Woman. Sex. Procreation is the most basic of our urges. I'd rather do it while I'm still in control, in the driving seat. The other way makes me feel cheap, like I'm part of some experiment.'

Anya lifted her brows. 'From what you've told me, you are.'

'But at least if I'm in control, I'm doing it because I want to, not because of some hormones. *Jesus.*' He grabbed a clump of his hair. 'Why are you fighting this? The others understood. Some didn't at first, but most I could convince.'

Anger pooled inside of her and she stopped pacing. 'I'm sorry if won't let you have sex with me. But that's my decision, so live with it.'

For the second time, a particular image popped into her head: a time when she had struggled against someone stronger than her. She was in a bathroom, her back pressed up against a cold wall. Someone was hurting her.

The memory caused her to stumble. She fought against the weakness in her legs and stomach. It wasn't her memory. It couldn't be.

'Are you okay?' Alex was perched on the edge of the bed, coiled like a spring.

'I'm fine. Just felt a little dizzy. I think I need to eat something, that's all.'

'Food comes *after* the injections. Nothing before.' He tilted his head. 'Are you sure you won't reconsider? I'll be gentle.'

She gave him a look. 'No.'

Alex got up. Punched the wall.

'Fine! Don't say I didn't warn you.'

Ω

An hour later, the exit swung open to reveal a woman and a man, both wearing white uniforms with bright-red collars and cuffs. The pair stayed outside.

The woman called her name and Anya jumped up from the seat, ready for a change of scenery. Alex was getting on her nerves. The man called for Alex in the same way.

'Yeah, yeah. I know the drill.' Alex was slower to his feet. He passed Anya at the door and flashed her a quick smile. Her insides curled tight when she caught the flicker of fear in his eyes.

The woman—a medic, Anya assumed, based on the white of her uniform—led her down a long corridor. With hair as black as coal and eyes as grey as the sky, she had a familiar face—a face she'd seen in one of her dreams.

The concrete floor sent chills through her shoes. A sharp right at the end then a left turn brought them to a trio of doors and a stairwell. The medic ushered Anya inside one of the rooms.

Anya shielded her eyes against the harsh hospital light reflecting off the all-white, sterile room. A partially reclined dentist's chair was in the middle with a mobile trolley to its left. She counted six vials on a tray and one large hypodermic needle.

She wasn't afraid of needles, but this one freaked her out.

The medic instructed her to sit. Anya eased into

the chair and focused on the plain white ceiling. Another hazy memory hit her, this time of a similar chair with a screen attached. It was a game of some sort; she'd been answering questions. No needles, though. Her pulse raced.

'Just relax,' said the medic, with a coldness to match the room's sterility. 'The procedure will go more smoothly if you do.' She tied both of Anya's arms down with leather straps. Her breathing hitched.

Resist.

'What's going to happen? What are you going to do? Where am I?'

The medic's short black hair clarified Anya's hazy thoughts about a different woman: a supervisor of some kind, but with differently styled hair and not as skinny.

'This is the preparation room.' The medic's eyes lacked warmth. 'You'll be injected with a low dose of Rapture to begin with, to wake up your libido.'

'What's Rapture?'

'A precise cocktail of drugs to increase dopamine and stimulate blood flow, to help you maintain a constant sexual high.'

A constant *what*? Anya struggled against her restraints. 'Why am I being forced to have sex? You know there are ways to bypass the act itself? You've heard of artificial insemination, right?'

'The Collective wishes to understand the act of love, so its creations can learn. The Breeder programme is about more than just the beginning of life. It is the study of the emotions that precede that act.'

'Act of love? Isn't your Collective missing the point by forcing these injections on us? If it's non-consensual, it's not real.' Anya twisted her bound wrists; the leather bit into her skin. 'Your Collective is sick, do you know that? Alex says the medics watch us. Is that true?'

'Yes.'

'Do you watch, too?'

'All the medics have access to the footage, if that's what you mean. We have access to everything that the Collective deems important for us to know. Because of my work in the medical facility, I am aware of everything that goes on during the Breeder programme.'

Anya balled her fists. 'I don't want this. Let me go.'

'That's not an option. Please stay calm. It will be much easier on your body if you relax. The procedure will take just thirty-six seconds.'

There were six vials on the tray. The medic drew a precise amount from each vial into the syringe. She swabbed Anya's arm with what smelled like rubbing alcohol. Anya turned her head away when the medic jabbed her upper arm.

She didn't feel any different.

Resist their treatment, Anya. You can do it.

About half a minute later, the medic untied Anya's hands and feet and led her back to Alex's room. Alex was already there, sat on the edge of the bed, his head in his hands.

At the exact moment the door closed, he looked up at her. 'So how's that resistance working out for you?'

Anya felt a stirring in her belly. She tried not to notice the shape of his body beneath his tight T-shirt. 'Fine. If I can do it, so will you.'

It surprised her to see Alex close to tears. 'I wish I had the same strength as you. When Rapture kicks in, it will be impossible to ignore.'

'I feel fine. It will all be okay, Alex. Trust me.'

Alex huffed out a breath and stood up. 'You don't get it. This is only the beginning. A test amount to see how much it takes to turn you into a sexual deviant. The more you resist, the more you get.'

She followed the movement of Alex's muscles and swallowed. The overhead light enhanced the shape of his jaw, which was covered in light stubble.

She closed her eyes. 'I don't plan on giving in to my feelings.'

'Ha! So you admit you have feelings.'

Anya opened her eyes and folded her arms. The movement attracted Alex's hooded gaze, and she uncrossed them. 'I don't have feelings for you.'

'But you will, soon enough.'

'We'll see.'

Her nerves jangled when Alex walked towards her. Such an innocent act, yet her body was tight with anticipation. 'So how much did she give you?'

Anya tried to remember, biting her lip. 'I don't know. The total was definitely less than a quarter of the syringe size.'

Alex nodded. 'A low dosage. They're being cautious.' He stopped a foot away. 'Do you remember a floor in Arcis where they put girls and boys together, and they had to rely on each other to rotate?'

Anya shook her head, but the memory of the bathroom taunted her. Someone had pinned her against a wall. 'What happened there?'

'Girls and boys were separated, made to compete against each other. But there was one task that guaranteed rotation: sex.'

Anya's stomach did a sudden flip. While she had never been to Arcis, Alex's description of the floor sounded familiar.

'That place is a lot like this one.' Alex inched forward, forcing Anya to hide her gasp. 'Eventually, you give in, because your instincts take over. The treatment will kick any higher brain function to the kerb and force those instincts to take the lead.'

His fingers grazed the outside of her arm. She jerked away from his touch, but not too far. 'I never talked this much with any of the other girls before we had sex.' He held her wrist gently and ran a finger over the skin on her forearm. 'There used to be a mark here. They've repaired it, but I can still see the faint and slightly rough edges.'

Anya's mind raced back to the bathroom incident. There had been pain, lots of it—someone had dug their fingers into her, right where Alex had just touched.

Just a couple of inches of space separated them. Alex's hot and intense gaze was on her. His neck bent forward. 'Have you ever been kissed in places you can't see?'

She felt her cheeks redden. 'Stop it, Alex.'

'I can't. I'm not strong like you. I usually get a stronger cocktail than the girls to make me more alluring. My looks usually persuade the girls to go the rest of the way.'

Her pulse raced; her whole body felt hot. She stepped out of his space. 'I think we should go to sleep.'

'Okay.'

'I mean, you sleep on the floor and I'll take the bed.'

Alex shook his head and smiled. 'You're serious about this resisting thing, huh?'

'Deadly serious.'

She squeaked when he grabbed her wrist, pulling her into the bathroom. He shut the door and turned on both sink taps.

His eyes were wide. 'They can't hear us over the water. While I don't think resisting will work, I'd like to try something different this time. Let's do things your way.' He offered his hand and she shook it. 'So what's this plan of yours, besides resisting?'

His thumb working circles on her skin distracted her. She snatched her hand back. Maybe it would be better if they didn't touch. 'If we don't do what the Collective wants, we won't be of use to it.'

'Won't work.'

'So you've said. But have you tried?'

'No.'

Alex's blistering gaze melted some of her resolve. She shook her head to dislodge her fake feelings. 'Then until you come up with something better, that's the plan.'

'Yeah, okay.'

Her resistance was the only thing Anya had control over. Escape wasn't an option. Not yet. Neither was sleeping with Alex: a total stranger.

Anya turned off the water, and they returned to the bedroom with their new agreement in place.

8

CARISSA

The Collective built Praesidium and controlled every part of the city, including its Copies. In turn, the Copies shared their experiences with the Collective. The Collective could not leave its neural network prison, while the Copies sacrificed their freedom for loyalty to its creators. A symbiotic relationship, where both had limited freedom.

Carissa hadn't thought too much about the Copies' other reason for existing. The Collective's plan was for Copies to live outside of the city. But the city was all Carissa knew. It was hard to imagine living anywhere else.

She had told the Inventor about the Collective's plan. He had dismissed the idea, said the Copies wouldn't pass as humans; the Collective still controlled their behaviour too much. Spending time with the Inventor and Vanessa, and watching the five in Arcis, had taught Carissa one thing.

In their attempts to understand humans, the Collective still thought too much like a machine.

Carissa sensed she had evolved beyond her original design—a design that The Collective preferred. The book hidden under her mattress was proof of that. But while she could process information faster than humans, her machine mind made it difficult to understand empathy and love. Only one thing set her apart from the other Copies: her curiosity. Her latest interest? The newborn.

She found the Inventor in his workshop assembling a Guardian from parts that came from hooks in the rafters. She gave him a hurried explanation of Canya's behaviour.

'You overanalyse every little thing. It's what all you Copies do.' He applied flux to the ends of two wires and fused them together with a piece of solder and a soldering iron. Carissa hovered at his shoulder while he worked on the inside of an inactive wolf, supine on his table. She didn't mind being this close to them when they were offline.

'But how are the newborns different from Copies?'

'Well, for a start, the newborns are not mature enough to survive on their own. Their bodies are still developing and they need regular biogel top ups to complete the cycle. During that week and until they receive their NMC, they maintain a strong link to their Original.'

Carissa wasn't convinced. 'I remember my Original, Inventor, yet my behaviour and Canya's are not the same.'

The Inventor paused with the iron and rocked with laughter. 'Is that what you're calling her?'

'It was Vanessa's idea.'

He smiled and shook his head then resumed his soldering. 'Of course. That woman puts a positive spin on every situation.'

'Why am I different from the Originals, Inventor?'

'You don't go with your gut feeling.'

'What's that?'

The Inventor looked up and tapped his chest. 'More of this.' Then his head. 'Less of this. Humans rule with both heart and mind. Sometimes the best decision is the one made with the heart.'

'Will I ever be able to make decisions like a human?'

'Not while you're connected to the Collective and living in the city. Free thinking doesn't exist here, miss.'

The idea of a life beyond Praesidium terrified her. 'Can I even exist beyond this city?'

The Inventor shrugged. 'I know of only one Copy that exists outside of Praesidium. No name, no photo. He escaped about four years ago. It was before your time and mine. Never heard what happened to him.'

Carissa had been created six months ago. The Collective's records said the Inventor and Mags had arrived in Praesidium a year ago.

'Did the Collective look for him?'

'You have access to the records, not me. But I don't believe so. He was a newborn, never connected to the network. I don't think he was seen as a threat. To be honest, Copies don't have the best survival instincts. The Collective probably expected him to perish out there, with a half-formed biogel body and just the basic towns to survive in.'

Carissa checked the time and gasped. 'I've got to go, Inventor. It's time for my morning upload.'

'Make sure to present me in the best light.' The Inventor knew all about Carissa's memory alterations.

She left the workshop and climbed the stairs to the outside. The daylight blinded her, making her eyes instantly water. She hated everything about the inconvenient sun. The Inventor said the sun gave life, and provided warmth. Carissa had no way to prove it; the invisible energy barrier around the city kept everything inside the same.

She erased that thought as she crossed the courtyard.

A group of white-clad Copies streamed out of the nearby train and raced towards the Learning Centre. Carissa sped up to beat the group to the upload rooms. Sessions could get busy at this early hour. Several Copies shoved past her to get inside the building first; Copies rarely liked to change up their routines. Carissa was no different, but she didn't like crowds.

A voice echoed in her head as she slowed her walk: a connection made possible by her NMC.

'173-C, please proceed to the Great Hall. You

will carry out this morning's upload in the presence of the Collective.'

She replied 'yes' and reorganised her thoughts of that morning's conversation with the Inventor. She had already switched up vital information from the day before, including her questions to Vanessa about the book and her conversation with Canya. She replayed old footage of her downloading information from the terminal in the library and playing with her orb. Since she first started caring about the participants in Arcis, she had presented a steady mix of new and old footage to the Collective.

The Great Hall was where the Collective lived, housed on a network independent from the rest of the city. It was also the place where rogue Copies were terminated. Carissa feared the hall, even though the Collective could sever a Copy's link at any terminal if it wished. An electrical blast during upload or download would see to that. Fry the NMC, stop the mechanical heart. The Collective liked control. That's why Quintus had chosen electroshock as punishment on the first floor in Arcis.

She steadied her racing heart as she entered the hall. Dozens of monitors covered one wall, black and idle. Members of the Collective used the screens to give themselves human representation. The face of Quintus, the spokesperson for the group, appeared to her most often.

Carissa approached a white podium in front of the idle screens. She placed her hand down on its flat top, which was level with her chest, and closed her eyes. Her palm tingled as the surface connected to her interface and the upload began.

'Welcome, 173-C.' A dark-skinned man in his early thirties appeared on one of the many screens: a human representation of Quintus. 'It has been a while since you've been to see us. The Collective wishes to know what you've been doing to occupy your time.'

'Nothing unusual, Quintus. I attend my lessons every morning. Then I play with my orb in the afternoon until it's time to eat. In the afternoon, I also attend art lessons. My Original was interested in art.'

'Yes, your routine is becoming just that. Routine. We noticed you've been spending quite some time in the library.'

'Yes. I like to learn.'

'But you haven't been downloading anything. Your log times are short. Not long enough to use the terminal in any meaningful way. Why have you been going there if not to use the terminal?'

Carissa froze. She'd been too distracted by the book Vanessa had given her to check her memories for consistency. 'I prefer to read their books.'

Quintus' almond-shaped eyes narrowed at her. 'Explain.'

She shifted from one foot to the other. 'It helps me to understand them better, Quintus.'

'And the Librarian. Has she been helping you?'

'A little. Other than to point out books for my age, she doesn't really speak to me.'

'Expected behaviour,' said Septimus, one of the usual voices of disagreement. 'The Originals we brought to the city a year ago have distanced themselves.'

Vanessa, the Inventor and Mags had been in that group.

'Interacting with them gives us nothing that cannot be achieved through observation of their behaviours,' said Octavius. 'They are disruptive and will only undo the learning our Copies have amassed.'

'And yet we have one Copy that is interested in the Originals,' said Quintus. He turned his distorted gaze to her. 'Carissa, we've been studying your memories of the time you watched the participants go through Arcis. Please tell us why you showed such an interest in them?'

Carissa had been careful to erase the stronger emotions but had left in the parts where her curiosity didn't venture beyond the parameters of normal Copy behaviour.

'I was curious to see how they dealt with the floors and the obstacles in Arcis. I had permission to observe them.'

'We are not upset with you,' said Quintus. 'We just need to understand why you spent more time watching one particular group, the group that recently came to Arcis, over other groups.'

Easy: June. For Quintus' benefit she pretended to think about it. 'Their complex behaviours exceeded those of the previous participants. I was curious to know why they fought against the tests more than the others. I imagined myself there, doing the same tests, and wondered how I would have fared.'

Carissa also left out the part about her fascination with Anya. At least the Collective couldn't detect new memories during upload.

'173-C's understanding of humanity is developing at a more accelerated rate than the other Copies,' said Septimus, ignoring Carissa. 'But I fear her interaction with the Librarian will limit her ability to unlock the secrets of the human mind.'

'How so, Septimus?' said Unos. Carissa watched new faces flash up on screen as other members of the Collective joined the discussion.

'The Librarian does not speak to her much, or any other Copy for that matter. From what we have observed, the Originals are usually much more conversational. If this is not typical human behaviour, how can we learn from it?'

'Why do we challenge our Copies to think for themselves then forbid them to talk to the Originals?' said Unos.

'Because they need direction,' said Quintus. 'If we are to succeed in breaking free from our confines, we still need control over them.'

'We caught rebels in the recent group from Arcis,' said Unos. 'And one of the subjects didn't copy.'

'Dom Pavesi,' said Septimus. His face disappeared from screen. Quintus was alone again, but Carissa still felt the others through her connection. 'He is in the Harvest programme in the medical facility. We must determine how he has lived with Praesidium tech for twelve years. And early Second Gen technology, at that. All the prior subjects were lost to us.'

Dom was who Canya was risking everything to see.

'How did we lose track of him?'

'His father told us he was dead.'

'And we didn't check?'

'He found a way to disable the boy's tracking device when we stopped paying him.'

'There are Originals in the current Breeder programme who are uncooperative,' said Unos. 'What is to be done with them?'

'They will succumb to their fate. Rapture is powerful,' replied Quintus. 'We should learn from them, add their human behaviour to our catalogue of knowledge, so we may blend in when the time comes.'

'And create a child that can be grown quickly and can be controlled,' said Unos.

Carissa heard the others, the silent members of the Collective, murmur in her head.

'Our tests are taking too long,' said Septimus.

'We need to be patient, Septimus,' said Quintus. 'The Breeder programme is yielding results.'

'The medics have reported that 230-O has bitten her suitor, even with the injections,' said Septimus.

Sheila.

'What about the blonde girl?' said Octavius.

Carissa's artificial heart skipped a beat. *June.*

'We have different plans for her. She will not be

paired up with a suitor like the others,' said Quintus.

What had they planned?

'173-C, I detect an elevation in your heart rate,' said Unos.

Carissa calmed her breathing. 'It must be a fault.'

'Go see the Inventor for a check-up after you are dismissed.'

Carissa nodded as the Collective ten resumed their discussions.

'We should give all the Copies access to the new arrivals,' said Quintus. 'We might learn faster from their interactions. The recent group from Arcis is less compliant than we had anticipated.'

'I think it's a mistake,' said Octavius.

'And I agree with Quintus,' said Unos. Quatrius echoed Unos' opinion.

'173-C, would you benefit from having access to the Originals?' said Quintus.

Carissa looked up, surprised; she hadn't expected Quintus to include her in the discussion.

'Yes.' The word rushed out of her. She had to see June. She also wanted to know what Anya remembered of her time in Arcis.

While her palm was pressed to the plate, new thoughts would remain private.

'Your heart rate has spiked again,' said Quintus. 'Complete your upload and go see the Inventor for a diagnosis. It is too late to visit the medical facility now. You may go there tomorrow morning after you carry out your upload here. The Ten would like to keep your experiences off the Copy network for now.'

'Of course,' said Carissa.

Any uploads carried out in the Great Hall would be added to the Collective's independent network. Carissa had no idea how much the group shared with the main network.

She disconnected and walked away from the screens. Her shoes made the same sound on the white-tiled floor as her thumping mechanical heart made in her chest. She left the Great Hall behind and thought about the Collective's desire to make its Copies human, yet retain their machine-like, controllable minds. Carissa's own mind confused her. The Collective controlled her through fear, but she risked her life by altering her memories.

She thought about the Breeder programme, just eight months in existence. The purpose of the children? According to Quintus, they would live outside of Praesidium and have the ability to cross over to a place the Collective referred to as the Beyond.

A place that the Collective and existing Copies could not currently access.

Carissa pondered life outside of Praesidium as she crossed the courtyard. What was her Original like? What was June's town like? What was the Beyond?

Why did it matter? Her purpose was to serve the Collective.

She arrived at the Inventor's workshop out of breath.

'Quintus detected an elevation in my heart rhythm. He sent me for a check-up.'

The Inventor nodded and ran a set of fake diagnostics on her for the purposes of Carissa's upload the next morning. As he worked, Carissa planned out her visit to the medical facility. A strange, tickling sensation filled her stomach when she thought about seeing June the next day.

9

CANYA

Day Two

The morning sun bounced off the almost-invisible barrier, giving Canya a rare glimpse of the bright halo that encased the city. She shielded her eyes from its usual glare as she left the library behind.

Biogel shots were amazing. Before Vanessa had given her one, she'd felt weak and light-headed. After, she'd been filled with a new desire to explore. Vanessa had warned her to take it slow; the more she expended herself, the faster her biogel would be used up.

Just Vanessa fussing over nothing. Canya skipped, jumped and twirled all the way to the train platform, just to prove her wrong.

Her eyes landed on the medical facility in the distance, a place she wanted to visit.

Not yet. She needed something first.

The Business District in Zone E, run by and for

Originals, sported fewer whites than other areas. She stood in the middle of a large semicircular plaza surrounded by an arc of single-storey units with stores selling clothes, baked goods, old curiosities, art supplies and shoes. Camera orbs buzzed overhead while a few perched on roofs. Some Originals cast uneasy glances her way. Others continued to set up outdoor displays and check crates of supplies as they opened for business. A customer picked up a bar of soap from one crate, but dropped it when an orb swept in for a closer look.

I'm human, just like them.

Yet, out in the open and dressed in white, Canya didn't feel it.

She plucked at her stupid white dress. If Dom was to accept her as the real Anya, she needed to look the part. This colour wouldn't work. By the time she'd finished with him, Dom would be asking, 'Anya, who?'

Her biogel heart fluttered in a way that made it feel real. But it was not. And neither was Carissa's, according to Vanessa. Apparently the Collective believed that metal hearts made its Copies more durable.

If Canya ever met this Quintus person, she would ask for a human heart, not a mechanical one like Carissa's.

A warm, yeasty aroma wafted from one of the open-front units, reminding her of a time in Essention. Her brother had brought home a loaf of bread from the factory.

Except it wasn't her brother and it wasn't her memory.

She shook the thought away and perused two spaces, one selling pottery and the other an array of art supplies.

The Originals' gazes switched from her face to her white dress. They didn't want her here? Too bad. She owned this district. Well, she would when she became a Copy. She moved on from their rude stares to stop outside a clothes store. A bright-yellow floor-length dress with half sleeves in the window caught her eye.

She entered the store and a bell rattled overhead. A woman tending to a messy rail of clothes looked up and smiled at Canya. But the half-second smile fell away when she saw the white dress. Canya lifted her chin high and flicked through a bunch of clothes on a different rail.

Her chip contained credit that could buy her anything in Praesidium. When she finished in the store, she would look for a gift for Dom. Vanessa's warning rang loud in her head: 'Don't visit him. You're a blank.'

Okay, maybe she hadn't said that exactly, but it was Vanessa's fault she knew Dom. With the real Anya out of the way, Dom would *have* to accept her.

She stopped at a rail of dresses that matched the yellow display model.

The assistant's eyes tracked her. Canya kept her anger in check.

Colours had an attitude problem. She had every

right to be here. Maybe if she reported this colour to Vanessa or Carissa, they might pass it on to the Collective and have her terminated.

Canya picked out her size. She was about to ask where she could try it on when two more customers entered the premises.

'Would you look at that?' said one. 'A Copy in your store.'

Canya gripped the yellow dress in her hand. She couldn't wait to look less like a Copy.

'See the way her eyes water like that? It's the human implants. Their eyes are supersensitive to light. They never really get used to it. And they shouldn't. I mean, who had to die to give her sight?'

'Why did you let her in here, Nora?' said the second customer to the assistant.

'I can't stop them from coming in, Louise. This district may be for our use, but they can come and go as they like.'

Louise peered into Canya's eyes. 'Do you think she's a newborn? She seems very brazen to be in here with a bunch of humans.'

'Very likely,' said Nora. 'She probably hasn't been told the way of the city yet. Vanessa should have done her job and warned her off this place. We don't need the Collective or its creations here.'

'If she's new, she's not connected or recording, so it doesn't matter,' said the first customer. She gave her a nasty look that made Canya want to scratch the woman's eyes out. 'The Collective probably isn't interested in her. Newborn emotions run too high and too hard. And the temper tantrums? The Collective thinks it knows humans, but it hasn't a clue.'

'Still, I don't like one being in here,' said Louise. 'This place is ours, where we get to be ourselves for a while.'

'If you can call a place crawling with orbs "private",' said Nora.

Colours appeared to be much more talkative and brazen in the Business District than in other areas.

The women continued their discussion. They had no business talking about her, but they did it anyway. Canya squeezed the hanger; the metal bit into her skin. She was more real than they were. And she would prove it. But not today.

Her eyes leaked fresh tears as she dropped the dress on the floor and ran out. She heard one of the women shout, 'Good riddance!'

Without a backwards glance, she ran from Zone E. Her location chip tingled as she passed a tag station. Her heart pounded too fast during her jog-walk to the nearest train platform. She needed another biogel shot. Canya ignored her spinning world and boarded the silent machine. When her stop came up, she got off.

She should have gone back to the library; her heart may have slowed, but she still felt weak. Instead, she approached the facility, the one she wasn't supposed to visit. The three women and Vanessa had made their point. Now she would make hers.

With Dom.

The grey structure spread out lengthways, one-storey high with a grassy area to the front. Three guards wearing white uniforms with gold trim on their collars and cuffs patrolled outside the entrance.

One of the guards stopped her. 'State your designation.'

'I don't have a designation. I'm a newborn. I've been told I can go where I like.'

The guard pulled out a scanner and waved it over her. 'Ninety percent biogel, ten percent human. Your biogel reserves are depleting fast, newborn. Make sure to report to your carer soon for your next injection.' Canya nodded. 'You must not interfere with the work at this facility. If you do, we will report you to the Collective.'

'Understood.' Canya swayed as she entered the facility, unsure if her shaky legs were due to her depleting supply of biogel or because she was close to seeing Dom.

How would he react when he saw her? The last time she'd seen him was in the holding room with the others. He'd called her Anya then.

The glass roof in the foyer allowed a steady stream of natural light in. To her right was a corridor and before that an elevator; to her left a booth with a guard inside. She approached the booth and asked for a map.

The guard pointed to a screen near the elevator. 'For the Originals and newborns. Your chip already gives you access to any room in this city.'

The screen map showed four levels. Three were

underground, with the Nurturing Centre on the lowest level. Two levels below her was the Breeder programme, and the Harvest programme was just one floor beneath her.

Dom.

Her nerves—depleting biogel, whatever—jangled as she rode the elevator one floor down and exited into a soft-lit corridor that was easier on her eyes.

The space widened further on, branching off into three new right-angled corridors. She entered the first corridor and checked all the rooms she came across using the spy holes.

She drew in a breath when she spotted him.

He looked so vulnerable on the single bed, dressed in white separates. He almost blended in with the walls. One arm was draped over his eyes. His slightly curly dark hair peeked out over the top.

She steadied herself as she used her chip to unlock the door.

Her preformed heart shuddered in her chest as she closed it behind her.

He didn't look up.

Maybe she should do something, make the first move? He must have heard her enter. Surely their bond ran deep enough that he could just *sense* her presence? She resisted the childish urge to demand his attention.

Dom stirred from what she realised was sleep. He opened his eyes and blinked at her.

She grinned.

He sat up slowly in the bed. 'Is this a dream?'

'No dream, Dom. I'm really here.'

Then his eyes widened. 'Anya, you're okay! You know who I am?' He glanced at the door. Frowned. 'How did you get in here?'

She loved that he called her by Anya's name. She ran to him without answering his questions. The force of her hug caused him to wince. 'Easy! I'm a little sore.'

She slammed her lips against his. Biting him, tasting him.

He laughed. 'Anya. I'm a little fragile. Ease up.'

'Sorry.' She touched his hair. She was sure it had grown since she'd last seen him, just two days ago. It was definitely longer, with a soft curl.

Dom smiled at her interest. 'It's a side effect of the drugs they give me. They're designed to accelerate healing, but they also make my hair grow fast. It's become a nuisance in a very short space of time.' He sat up, clearly in some pain. 'Tell me what happened. When did your memories start to return? Was it after the holding room?'

Canya wanted to tell him she never forgot, but she had to pretend. So she shrugged. 'Soon after the holding room, I guess.'

'But they said the memories were gone.'

'What about your own?'

Dom shook his head. 'Mine never left. The procedure didn't take. It was just an effect of stepping through the portal. Temporary amnesia. Have you seen the others? June, Sheila? Are they okay?'

Canya remembered them from the holding room.

'Not yet. I'll find them. But first I wanted to see you.'
A heady rush of desire caught her unawares. She
kissed Dom's neck, his face. Went to unbutton his
shirt.

He put his hands on hers. 'If you got in, can you
get me out? Is anyone helping you? What about that
woman in the green dress who took you from the
holding room?'

Canya didn't want to talk about Vanessa. She
pushed Dom back onto the bed and laid her head on
his stomach.

He squirmed. 'Anya, what are you doing? Please.
We don't have much time. You need to get me out of
here.'

If she did, the Collective would revoke her
visiting privileges. She liked having Dom here, far
away from the real Anya, and where she could access
him any time she wanted.

'I'm sorry, I can't do that.' She smiled up at him.
'You don't know how happy I am to see you, Dom.'

'Anya, please.' He pushed her away until they
were both sitting up. 'Talk to me. What's going on?
Are you in trouble?'

Canya shook her head.

'Then why can't you get me out of here?'

'Because I'll lose my access to you. I just wanted
to see you.'

She tugged his top up before he could protest.
'Anya...' Her hands roamed over his chest, across his
fresh scars, causing him to gasp. 'Anya, I can't.
Please get me out. You've no idea what's going on

here.'

Canya kissed his stomach, around his weeping scars. The sound of his breath hitching fuelled her. He twisted his hands in her hair and pulled her on top of him. He ran his hands under her white dress, along her bare thighs. Canya shivered when Dom tasted her skin.

She tugged at his waistband, and he gasped when she pulled his trousers halfway down. It wasn't her fault. An entity inside her pushed her on.

Control. Seduce. Take.

But Dom straightened up too soon and pulled his loose-leg trousers back up.

'What's wrong?' She reached out for him, but he held her hands down at her lap.

'Why are you doing this?' said Dom.

'What do you mean?' She leaned forward against his restraints and stole kisses along his collarbone.

He pushed her away, much to her annoyance.

'This doesn't feel right.' Dom studied her face. 'Why are your eyes different?'

'I'm the same.' She averted her gaze.

'No, you're not. You refuse to get me out of here. You're not the Anya I know.'

'It's not possible. I wasn't lying about that.'

He held on to her hands. 'Why?'

'Because it just isn't!' She failed to keep the irritation out of her voice. Why was Dom being difficult?

She caught a flicker of change in his expression. Then he released her.

She tried to get closer, but his hand on her shoulder kept them apart.

'Who *are* you?'

'I'm Anya.' Partly true; she felt like Anya.

'It doesn't feel like you. You've changed.'

His words cut her deep; Canya folded her arms to stem the bleeding. 'How do you know? You've been drugged.'

'Because the Anya I know thought of others. She would have understood I need help, not kisses.'

'I *am* her.' She uncrossed her arms and reached out for his face. 'I'm your Anya.'

Dom's soft, pleading gaze almost broke her. 'Then get me out of here.'

Canya snatched her hands away. 'I can't.'

'Then I don't want to see you. Please leave me alone.' He turned away.

'I don't want to leave.'

Dom growled as he pushed her away. 'You have no choice. This is my room and I don't want you here. Get out.'

10

CARISSA

June and the others had arrived from Arcis two days ago, and Carissa finally had permission from Quintus to visit the medical facility. She pushed down her nerves as she completed her morning upload in the presence of the Collective ten. She was about to see her Original's sister. After visiting June, she would see Anya, and ask her about her time in Arcis. Quintus would be expecting her report.

Carissa paused. She'd forgotten the machine had wiped the real Anya's memories. That left Canya, the wilful newborn, who had refused to tell Vanessa what she wanted to know. And Canya seemed to hate Carissa for no reason she could find.

She had tried to see the good in the newborn; it wasn't her fault she was overrun with emotions. But Carissa couldn't shake the feeling that Canya was up to something.

In five days, Canya would be connected to the

Collective's network. Though June was her priority, Carissa would ask Canya all she could about Anya's time in Arcis. Those experiences mattered to Carissa; they had woken up her humanity.

Her NMC vibrated as the upload completed. She disconnected from the podium and left the Great Hall behind, relieved that Quintus hadn't commented on her altered memories. Nor had he remarked on her memories of Canya, who, in her newborn state, was acting far more human than the Copies the Collective attempted to humanise. That oversight could cost the Collective big because in five days, when Canya was reset, all her knowledge would be lost.

She glanced at the grey building across the courtyard that led to the Inventor's workshop. The other access point was a retractable roof a short distance from the single-storey structure. She recalled nothing of her first week as a newborn, but the Inventor had assured her she'd been as wilful and difficult as Canya.

Her first memory had come to her just after she received her NMC and was connected for the first time. It had belonged to her Original. She was frightened, crying, and pleading for someone to let her go. After connection, Carissa had felt no strong connection to her Original. But after listening to the Inventor's stories, she began to miss her. It had been easier for her to betray her Original back then.

Carissa left the Learning Centre and made her way to Zone C and the medical facility.

C, D, E. It didn't matter as long as she was far

91

away from the Collective.

It was just after her connection that she'd learned about the Inventor's plans to escape from the city. *Her* plan to warn Quintus was meant to protect the Inventor. She'd delayed him long enough for the others to carry out the attempted escape without him. His wife Mags, Carissa's Original and others had died that day. While Quintus had been responsible for their deaths, Carissa sensed the Inventor hadn't forgiven her for the part she'd played that day.

But all that was in the past. Carissa wanted to do right by her Original and earn back the Inventor's trust. It started with June.

Her pace, quick and light, slowed in the presence of other Copies. Her mind, preoccupied during upload, played back snippets of Quintus' conversation with the Ten.

They had discussed Dom Pavesi. The Breeders. The girls with the Breeders.

They had argued about ways to create a perfect, controllable human. And they had settled on a scattergun approach for now: try everything until something produces the best results. They would merge the best of their tech with selected humans.

The Collective's arguments often continued long after Carissa lost interest. But something Quintus had said forced her to replay the conversation in her mind.

He'd mentioned 229-O.

June.

What about her?

'She will not be paired with a suitor,' he'd said.

Why?

But Quintus hadn't explained. Her upload had finished and she'd already disconnected before hearing the rest.

Carissa's mechanical heart thrummed in her chest. What had the Collective planned for June?

She cut through a few back streets to reach the medical facility faster. The location chip in her wrist tingled as she left Zone B behind. Zone C swarmed with white-clad Copies. The Originals didn't visit the area much.

She approached a trio of guards at the entrance to the facility.

One of the guards stepped forward. 'Designation?'

'173-C.'

The guard's eyes flickered as he checked her clearance. 'The Collective has approved your access to this facility. Keep your visit brief and do not interfere in the work.'

Carissa nodded and entered the building. Her chip connected remotely with the proximity chip in the tag station beside the guards' desk.

Quintus had given her a map of Praesidium; it provided a layout of the building and others. The map appeared as a file in her peripheral vision. While her ocular implants were human, her NMC enhanced them so she could see the files. But her eyes weren't as efficient as synthetic ones for processing detail.

'Eyes are the windows to the soul,' said the Inventor. 'Humans can always tell the difference.'

She had been given human eyes to make her look more human.

Another flaw in the Collective's methods: the sacrifice of efficiency for authenticity.

She rode the elevator down two floors and exited into a plain white corridor. According to the map, it ran in both directions to two sets of treatment rooms. Ahead of her was another corridor leading to the Breeders' rooms. The hybrid children—from a Breeder and a human girl—could accept the tech faster than human children but didn't yet possess the 'human' look.

Three female medics approached. They wore white tunics with bright-red collars and cuffs, unlike the guards who wore white with gold trim. Two of the medics dragged a girl each. Carissa pulled in a sharp breath when she recognised them: Sheila and Yasmin.

One of the medics stopped while the other two continued dragging the girls towards the treatment rooms.

'Designation?' said the medic to Carissa.

'173-C.'

'You're here to experience and interact with the Originals?'

'Yes, the ones who arrived in the most recent transfer from Arcis.'

Carissa kept her tone businesslike, careful not to mention June by name, and nodded at the guards who had Sheila and Yasmin. Familiarities caused alarms, and alarms got back to Quintus.

'Follow me.'

Carissa followed the medic to the trio of treatment rooms and up a set of stairs nestled between two of the doors. In some kind of viewing room, Carissa saw three spaces, each containing a single reclining chair. Yasmin and Sheila took up two; the third was empty. Carissa wondered where June was.

'What's happening with these two?' She watched the medics below her attach restraints to Sheila's and Yasmin's wrists.

'Originals 230 and 231 are not cooperating with the programme.' She knew that 230 was Sheila and 231 was Yasmin. 'They both fight their suitors. They both leave them battered and bruised. Especially the one on the left.'

Sheila.

Carissa hid a smile as she thought back to Sheila in Arcis. The boys admired her from afar while the girls hated her. Carissa had grown fond of the feisty girl.

'And the injections?'

The medic stood with her hands behind her back. 'Rapture isn't working with these two. They resist it better than the others.'

It hadn't escaped her attention that Sheila and Yasmin had become close in Arcis. She knew from library downloads what it meant to be gay. The Collective believed everyone could be changed, given the right motivation. And Rapture was that motivation.

Sheila struggled against her restraints. 'You can inject me as often as you like. But you overlooked one detail. I don't fancy boys. So unless you put me with a girl, and I don't know how that's going to work for your weird child project, nothing's gonna happen. You hear me? No amount of treatment is going to change me into something I'm not.'

The medic nodded at Yasmin. 'This one is less vocal but more vicious.'

Yasmin grunted and twisted. She kicked the tray away and bit the medic's arm. The medic shook off the pain and picked up the scattered instruments as if nothing had happened. She grabbed Yasmin's arm and jabbed her with the needle.

'Bitch!' said Yasmin.

Carissa checked what little information Quintus had allowed her to access. There was nothing specific about June. 'The third female. 229-O. Where is she?'

'229-O is not part of the Breeder programme.'

Carissa feigned surprise. 'I understood all the females would be part of the programme. How will that Original be used?'

'Studies show a child born naturally has a higher survival rate. She is being prepped to place a three-month-old foetus into her womb. She will be used as an incubator for the foetuses produced by the Breeder programme.'

'Will she give birth?'

'Yes. We will use the growth accelerator on the foetus to speed up birth.'

'Has she been prepped yet?'

'No, she is still in her room. You may interact with her while she waits.'

'Number?'
'Seventeen.'

Ω

Carissa's heart bashed against her ribs, making a sound similar to when the Inventor hit steel against steel. It had beaten pretty fast when she'd watched Lilly shoot Ash before she jumped to her death. But now, as she got closer to room seventeen, it almost leapt out of her chest.

She worried for her health; she was a long way from the Inventor's workshop.

The chip in her wrist unlocked the door to June's room. She slipped inside, just under the camera's gaze.

June sat on her bed. She was dressed in white separates with her blonde hair tied up in a ponytail. Either she hadn't seen Carissa come in, or she didn't care.

Carissa opened her mouth then shut it. What did she want to say? She had no idea if Quintus was even aware of the family connection: she was designation 173-C to the Collective, not a name. Quintus had said it wasn't important for the Copies to know where they came from.

June's gaze drifted from the bed to her. Her eyes widened.

Carissa touched a finger to her lips and dragged over the only chair in the room. She stood on it and disabled the camera.

The second Carissa returned to solid ground, June jumped off the bed and pulled her into a tight hug that brought tears to Carissa's eyes. She smelled of lemons: a familiar scent for her Original. June pulled away, keeping hold of Carissa's arms.

'How? I thought you were dead.'

She pulled Carissa back into a hug before she answered, feeling her nervousness melt away. She wished she were the *real* Carissa, the one June had grown up with. She'd taken her Original's name after the real Carissa had been killed by the Collective.

'I'm not her. I'm not your sister.'

June laughed. 'Of course you are. You look exactly like her.' June froze, studied Carissa more closely. 'You're a Copy?'

Carissa nodded.

'Where's my sister?' June's voice tightened. 'Where is she?'

'She died several months ago, trying to escape. She was killed.'

She left out her involvement.

June stared at Carissa. 'Did she suffer?'

'No. She wouldn't have felt any pain.'

They had planned the escape during a temporary power-down of the grid. The real Carissa would have made it through the energy barrier, had the Collective not sent a surge of power to the specific area Carissa was passing through, killing her instantly.

June pressed her face into her hands and wept. Carissa just sat on the bed, unsure of what to do.

June dried her eyes and looked at her. 'Were you

two friends? Did she know about you?'

Carissa shook her head. 'We never met, but we were connected through her memories. I recognised you instantly when I watched you go through Arcis.'

'Arcis?'

Carissa forgot that June's memories had been erased.

'Was she frightened here?' said June, her voice lifting. 'Oh, God. Did she know I was looking for her?'

'She never gave up hope that you would come for her. She died trying to get back to you. She loved you.'

June wept some more. Carissa waited some more.

'You look just like her.' June sniffed and wiped the last of the tears away.

'I am her, in every way, except... I'm not human.'

'Why did you disable the camera?'

'Because they don't know about our shared family connection.'

June paused. 'So are you here to help or harm me?'

'*Help*. Do you know why you're here?'

June glanced at the camera. 'Some damn Breeder programme. I guessed when I saw the beautiful boys walking around. I've heard them talk about how some of the patients are resisting their genetic matches. You said you were watching the footage from Arcis. Are Sheila and Dom here?'

'Dom is on a different floor. I just saw Sheila receive her injections.' She didn't mention Yasmin or Anya. June would have known only Dom and Sheila, fellow rebels, before Arcis.

June huffed. 'I guess it's only a matter of time before I get my own genetic match.'

'I don't think they plan to pair you up in the same way as the others.'

'What do you mean?'

'You're to be an incubator. You'll grow the foetuses inside you.'

'No!' June got up and paced the tiny room that held just a bed and chair. 'I can't stay here. You have to get me out of this place. I can't even go to the bathroom without a Copy accompanying me.'

Carissa touched June's arm and she stopped pacing. 'I will. That's why I'm here. But first I need to reconnect the camera, and we need to pretend we don't know each other. Okay?'

'Okay... Why?'

'Because to help you escape, I have to pretend I don't care. Can you get back into the same position you were in when I entered the room?'

June scooted along the bed until her back was against the wall. 'I'm ready.'

Carissa reconnected the camera feed, and this time June played her part. Carissa sat down and asked her about her experience in Arcis. June replied in a cool manner.

Carissa spent just ten minutes on camera with June. The five minutes prior to that, spent off-camera, guaranteed her termination. With the recordings of the camera feed stored in the Learning Centre, she had until tomorrow morning to delete the incriminating footage before the Collective used it to verify her time spent there.

She left the medical facility and went to the only place she felt safe. She had no idea how to help June. Maybe the Inventor would know.

She arrived at his workshop to find him out. She sat in a chair and overwrote details of the early five minutes with June with static moments on replay.

But overwriting wouldn't be enough. She had to delete the actual footage of her visit.

She left the workshop and arrived at the viewing room in the Learning Centre, the place where Copies could watch the live camera feeds around the city.

To her relief, she found the room empty. She sucked in a breath as she connected to the system. There was no other way to access the raw files.

If the Collective found out, detected her illegal connection, she would be terminated.

11

DOM

Dom knew she'd come. It gave him hope that not all the medics were cold-hearted, or capable of worse acts than breaking his arm. A nervous Anya had shown up in a white dress that accentuated her already pale skin. Had the female medic brought her?

Her visit should have thrilled him but instead something bothered him. How had she opened a locked door? Why had she left him here? The medics, usually noisy outside his room, hadn't made their presence known. If she'd come alone, why hadn't she helped him to escape?

His scars, puckered and red just after surgery, continued to heal, thanks to the healing accelerator in his body. The anaesthetic, no longer in his system, had left him with a slow burn across his new scars. He lay on his bed trying to forget the feeling when they'd opened him up to study his 'Second Gen' tech.

He switched his thoughts back to Anya. *His*

Anya, yet somehow different. Less courageous. Her skin, usually so warm, had felt cold to the touch.

The air was cooler underground. That's all it was. It could lower anyone's body temperature.

But her eyes were different, too. Not as bright or as dark blue as he'd remembered them.

Maybe it wasn't the brightness or colour of her eyes that bothered him but the lack of something behind them. The visiting Anya had the temperament of a younger girl—emotions running wild. *His* Anya, the one he'd gotten to know in Arcis, kept a guard around her emotions.

Dom draped his recently healed arm over his eyes.

Maybe it wasn't Anya who'd changed. Maybe he had.

The hatch at the bottom of the door slid back and Dom jumped off the bed as a new tray of food was pushed through. He eyed the steel spoon on the tray, then slid down onto his stomach and slipped a hand in the hatch before it closed.

'Move your hand, human. Unless you want to lose it.' It was 148-C, the male medic who had broken his arm.

'Please. I just want to talk. Can you come inside the room?'

A full day had passed since his arm had been broken and reset, and three food trays later, Dom was still trying to coax 148-C inside his room. Now was the time to escape, not when he was too weak to try.

'Remove your hand. I won't tell you again.'

The hatch started to close. 'Wait... I have something to tell you that I think you'll find very interesting.'

He held his breath as the hatch touched his hand. 'What?'

Dom pulled his hand out. 'Come inside and I'll tell you. I feel stupid talking to you through a food slot.'

He'd seen evidence of the Copies' curiosity first-hand. It was his only leverage.

The medic was quiet for a moment. 'Step back from the door.'

Dom grabbed the spoon off the tray and jumped to his feet. He stood by his bed, hoping the medic would come all the way inside. He slipped the spoon up his sleeve.

The medic did, but not far enough. He kept a hand on the door.

'What is it?'

'Come closer. It's a secret.' It was such a childish thing to say. Dom's heart thundered in his chest. The spoon handle bit into his skin.

The medic walked further inside and, to Dom's relief, he left the door ajar. Just one swift move could stun him before he escaped and locked him in. He had no idea of the floor layout—only the route to the testing room. Never mind, he'd figure it out as he went along. He would locate Sheila and June first; they both had combat training. Then, Anya.

'What do you have to tell me, human?' The medic kept his distance. The Copies weren't friendly, but this one actually despised him. Was it germophobia? Max had once said the organic bodies of the Copies left them vulnerable to human diseases. It was one of the reasons they kept their distance from humans.

'I wanted to tell you I had a visitor just now.'

The medic looked surprised. 'Who?'

'A girl. I don't know where she came from. But she said I should ask you about my mother.'

The medic barked out a laugh. 'I don't know anything about your mother, human. And I don't care. But you must tell me the girl's name.'

'Okay, but I need to whisper it to you.' Dom made a show of looking around. 'I don't want to get her into trouble.'

The medic inched closer, but he was still too far away. If Dom lunged too early with the spoon, the medic might have enough time to react. So he waited, trying to keep calm. The handle of the spoon slipped a little.

'Okay, but make it quick.'

The medic leaned his head in, keeping his body back.

Dom slipped the spoon down his arm with the handle pointing out. Then he lunged at the medic's exposed neck. The medic grunted when the handle lodged a quarter of an inch into his flesh.

Dom yanked the spoon out and was about to strike again when it slipped out of his hand. He lunged for it, but the medic caught him around his neck and forced him backwards. Dom's head rattled when it hit the wall with force.

'You dirty liar! There was no girl. All you humans are filthy liars.' The medic's hand squeezed tighter causing Dom's windpipe to constrict. He spluttered as the medic said, 'The Collective thinks you filthy humans have a purpose, but I don't agree. I knew from the moment I saw you that you were beneath me.'

Dom croaked out his reply. 'The Collective won't like that you killed me.' The medic kept his grip tight and Dom inched closer to passing out.

'The Collective doesn't control me. Some of us have our own minds. I don't take orders from anyone. I am an individual.'

The medic's hand tightened even more. Dom's vision blurred from the pressure.

'Stop what you're doing!' said a female voice.

The male loosened his grip. Dom coughed and protected his neck. The female medic, 148-C's supervisor, stood there looking furious.

'148-C. The Collective commands that you step away from the subject. Unless you wish to be terminated?'

The threat propelled the male away. He flashed Dom a venomous look.

'Please leave this room, 148-C, and report to the Great Hall. Quintus wishes to speak with you.'

'It was self-defence, 118-C. He attacked me.' He showed her his injury.

The female kept her expression neutral. 'Quintus would like a report on what happened here. Hurry. He

106

won't wait for long.'

The male grunted and stomped out of the room. Dom sat down on the bed nursing his aching throat.

'Stand up, Dom Pavesi.' The female was still by the door.

Dom did, keeping his eyes on her.

'Were you planning to escape?'

'Yes,' he croaked. 'You're holding me against my will.'

The female closed the door. 'The Collective needs you alive, so you are lucky. Your life is of no concern to me, but try to escape again and I will order your destruction myself. Are we clear?'

Dom nodded.

The female opened the door. Dom panicked; he had to know something before she left. 'Please, what about my mother? Mariella Pavesi. Is she here?'

She stopped and turned. 'What does it matter?'

'It matters to me. It matters to humans.'

She closed her eyes and her eyelids jerked and twitched.

She opened her eyes. 'Dead.'

'When? How?'

'The Collective terminated her when she attempted to escape Praesidium.'

Dom wanted to throw up. 'When?'

'Six months ago. She was helping others to escape.'

A lump rose in his bruised throat. It was just like his mother to think of others. His father Carlo used to beat the crap out of her, and she'd taken every hit to protect Dom.

Anger kept his sorrow in check. 'What the hell's wrong with you people? Why am I here? Why did my mother have to die? Why are you putting your tech in me? Why are you copying us?'

'We wish to understand you and learn from you.'

'If you want to understand us, start by showing us compassion. Start by treating us like equals. That will get you much further than torture.'

'I understand all I need to, Dom Pavesi. Your outburst over your mother's death makes you weak. Copies can separate thoughts from actions. We can function without emotions; do what needs to be done.'

'That makes you cold.'

'But functional.' Her hateful stare chilled him. 'Remember where you are, human. I have control in this city. You do not.'

'You mean Praesidium?'

The female lifted her chin. 'Yes. It's all I've ever known.'

'But there's a whole world out there beyond machines, Copies and rules.'

The female shuddered. 'The towns are unclean. Disorganised. Rural. Not worthy of a Copy's time.'

'And who made them rural? The towns survived on the technology Praesidium gave them. If you wanted them to thrive, then you should have given the people better tech. You kept the towns in a poor state.'

The medic's demeanour softened a fraction. 'The

Collective did not deem the towns worthy of that kind of investment. Humans cannot understand the dynamics of the Copies or the Collective. We serve the Collective's purpose, not the other way around.'

Dom coughed. Massaged his throat. 'And what is my purpose?'

'To help us evolve.'

12

ANYA

Day Three

One visit on her first day. Two visits to the treatment rooms yesterday. Two quarter syringes of Rapture: one in the morning and another in the evening. 'The second one's a top-up,' Alex had said, 'to keep the sexual high going.'

He'd only been for treatment twice, but according to him, his dosage was much higher than the girls'. Alex's ability to resist concerned Anya.

'Don't worry,' he said. 'I'm stronger than I look.'

If Alex was willing to try, she would keep going. The weak cocktail made her head and thoughts feel light, but she could resist. The longer she held out though, the sooner they would up her dosage.

There was nothing to do in Alex's room; nothing lasting to distract them. Anya slouched on the backless chair, thinking back to the card game they'd played last night—gin rummy, the only card game her father had taught her. An hour in and right in the middle of a game, they both fell asleep. When Anya woke, she was in the bed. Alex slept on the chaise longue covered by a blanket.

That morning they sat on different chairs as they waited for the medics to show. Her stomach rumbled. She hadn't eaten anything since her last treatment over fourteen hours ago. Rapture first, then food. That was the rule. In her weakened state she willed the medics to hurry up, to get it over with so she could eat.

Anya jumped to her feet when she heard the familiar sound of a door unlocking. Both medics entered wearing matching outfits and scowls. Anya didn't bother arguing with her medic. Alex wasn't as cooperative when the male grabbed at him.

'No need to be rough, Dennis.' Alex tried to pull his arm from him.

'My name is not Dennis.' The male dragged him outside and past Anya, who walked politely alongside her medic.

Alex dragged his fingers along the wall, as though he was trying to slow *Dennis* down. 'In all the time I've been here, you've never once told me your name. I could call you "medic" if you'd prefer? Nice and cold. Like your personality.'

'My name is of no relevance to you.'

'Dennis it is. Like it or don't. Not my issue.'

'My name is 148-C, not Dennis.'

'Like I said, cold. *Brr.*' Alex pretended to shiver.

They entered an open space with two adjoining corridors, one running left, the other right. Both corridors led to different treatment rooms. This was the point where Anya and Alex were separated.

The male yanked on Alex's arm, a little too roughly. Anya's heart leapt into her throat when she saw him stumble.

'See you in a while, honey!'

She hoped so.

Anya allowed her less-aggressive medic to steer her in the opposite direction. While Alex had been antagonistic with his medic, she tried a more friendly approach with hers.

'Do you have a name?'

'118-C,' said the female.

'Your number is lower than the other medic's. Does that mean you're his superior?' Or he was hers. But from what she'd seen so far, she doubted it.

'It means I was created before him. I am in a position of power over anyone with a number higher than mine. Stop talking.'

'So who's number one?'

'The Collective ten hold numbers from one to ten. You talk too much, Anya Macklin.' She gritted her teeth. 'Stop or I will gag you.'

Other medics passed, offering 118-C a brief nod. A memory of a gaunt woman wearing a black uniform flashed in Anya's mind. She said, 'Welcome to Arcis.'

Arcis? Not a place she remembered.

Inside the treatment room, the medic pulled her

over to the reclining chair. Anya flinched at the sight of the six vials waiting on the trolley. Before she had a chance to protest, her wrists were strapped down.

She twisted beneath the leather. 'This is too tight...'

118-C glared at her then opened a hidden panel on one of the glossy white walls and removed a syringe. She brought it over to the trolley and used it to draw liquid from all six vials. She jabbed Anya's arm, causing her to flinch.

'Ow!'

She could find no reason for the medic's anger, frustration—whatever this was. Unless she'd heard her talking to Alex about how she planned to resist.

The camera! How could she have been so stupid? They had talked about many things on camera.

The medic prepared a new dose designed to fast-track her attraction to a boy she'd barely known two days. The combined liquid filled just a quarter of the syringe. Not much more than she'd received the first couple of days. She was confident she could resist Alex, even though her attraction to him was growing. Not that she'd ever admit it.

Alex wasn't bad looking. In fact, he was cute. Most girls who came through here probably fell at his feet. But Anya wasn't most girls.

Besides, she had a thing for guys with darker hair.

The medic jabbed Anya's arm. 'Hey! Watch it.'

118-C ignored her and drew another round into the syringe. Anya squirmed in her seat. She was doubling the dosage. The medic injected her with the same roughness as before.

She yelped when the needle broke the skin. 'What did I ever do to you?'

The medic's gaze bore into her. 'You are a substandard. You shouldn't exist.'

'A substandard?'

'Less than perfect.'

'You mean human?'

118-C placed her mouth by Anya's ear. 'I know all about your plans to resist.'

Anya suppressed a shiver. 'What does it matter to you what I do?'

'The Collective ten is in a hurry and you're creating problems. You are not cooperating.'

'I'm here, aren't I? Letting you inject me?'

The medic pulled back, her tone icy. 'The injections are only the beginning, to help you consummate faster.'

'Yeah? Well having a baby is a big deal for someone my age. And I'm not ready.'

'It doesn't matter what you want. The Collective needs this to happen. You are delaying their evolution.'

Anya sat up as far as the restraints would allow. 'It's my body and I'll do what I want with it.' Why was she even having this discussion? The choice was hers.

The medic ignored Anya's words. 'You will not resist the treatment. You will comply, as others before you have done.'

'I'm too young to have a baby.'

'I don't care, ingrate.'

'How exactly am I ungrateful?'

'*Because you don't comply.*'

The shift in her medic's voice was subtle, but Anya caught it. Was that jealousy she heard? 'Does it annoy you that I have free will and you have none?'

118-C glared at her. 'You have no idea what you're talking about.'

'You work for the Collective, which you say runs this place. You do what you're told, when you're told. Your life seems pretty boring to me.'

The medic busied herself with the tray, but from the noise she was making it was clear Anya had hit a nerve. 118-C carried the tray to the open panel. 'The logical thing would be for you to accept the sequence of events.' She slid the tray inside and clicked the panel closed.

'Even if that means doing something I don't want to do?'

The medic turned round. 'We all have to do what's necessary for the order of things.'

Anya leaned forward. 'Well, the difference between you and me is I maintain my right to choose.'

A voice interrupted the medic's reply. '118-C, please refrain from engaging with the subject or I will report you.'

Anya looked up to see another medic—a female —in a viewing room set on the floor above. How had she missed it the other times she was here?

Her medic looked contrite under the second female's glare. 'Apologies, 28-C. I will not make that mistake again.'

She undid Anya's straps and led her back to her room. The silence between them lingered. Anya had upset 118-C—maybe she could use that to her advantage.

One of these damn Copies had to see sense.

There was no sign of Alex when the medic returned her to the room. A grateful Anya used the alone time to get to grips with her new feelings.

Twenty minutes later, the food she'd been so desperate for arrived: a container of soup, some bread and a bowl of chicken and pasta. Anya snatched the tray from the Copy and placed it on the bed. The door closed, and she climbed on the bed and tore wedges off the bread, stuffing them her mouth. It tasted of nothing, as usual—a side effect of her Rapture treatment—but she chewed and swallowed to quiet her stomach pangs.

Her eyes flickered to the door as she ate. If Alex didn't hurry up, she might eat everything. Where was he, anyway? He was usually back before her.

Ten minutes later, the unfriendly medic shoved Alex through the door. Anya dropped her fork into the pasta when she saw a fresh bruise under Alex's eye. The medic didn't stick around. The door slammed shut and Alex slid down to the floor.

Anya clambered over to him. 'What happened?'

He coughed and winced. 'It appears that I have an attitude problem.' He crossed his arms over his stomach.

She couldn't see any injuries other than to his face, but when she touched his folded arms, he flinched. 'Don't... I got punched in the stomach. Those damn Copies are strong.'

She tilted his chin gently so she could examine the bruise. Alex hissed as her fingers grazed the puffy area.

'What did you say to your medic, exactly?' She went to the sink and soaked the edge of a towel with water. She returned and knelt down beside him.

'I told them I didn't find you the least bit attractive and you should be allowed to leave.' Alex laughed a little, then grunted.

'Why did you say that?' She pressed the towel's wet edge to his eye.

Alex winced. 'Because I don't want you to go through what the others have. It breaks your mind, your spirit.'

'You've been here eight months, Alex. You suddenly care?'

'Yeah, I guess I do. So shoot me.'

'If you're not careful, they might do that first.' She pulled him to his feet. 'I need to see your eye. The light in the bathroom is better.'

She closed the door and ran both taps in the sink before turning to him.

'What's changed your mind?'

'You.' Alex tilted his head, looking down at her. 'The girls who came through here were always too weak, too willing to give me what I wanted,

117

especially after the injections. Some of them became more demanding after the treatment, took their anger out on me, hit me if I didn't tell them how pretty they were. The treatment turned the already uptight ones into demanding divas. I couldn't keep up with their changing moods. The medics were pleased because the Collective was pleased. The Collective doesn't punish the Copies if things go the group's way.'

Anya knew what he was going to say. 'But then I started talking about resisting,' she said. 'And now you have a black eye.' She looked away. 'The medic was rough with me today, said I was delaying evolution. She heard me telling you I was going to resist.' She looked back. 'She confirmed that the medics watch us on camera.'

Alex nodded and leaned against the counter. 'The Copies are curious about human behaviour but not enough to interact with us. To them, we are dirty vermin, riddled with disease. They view themselves as a perfect version of us. A happy Collective equals happy Copies.'

'Remind me what the Collective is again?' While Alex had explained it to her earlier, she still didn't understand the dynamic.

'A group of artificial minds that exists in the network.'

'A network? Like a computer?'

'The Collective cannot perform tasks in the real world. It relies on the Copies to do its bidding, and the Copies rely on the Collective to keep them alive. It's a symbiotic relationship. But the Collective doesn't directly control the minds of its synthetic Copies. Most likely the Collective conveyed its irritation to the medics about the delay, and your medic took out her frustration on you.'

'How do you know all of this?'

'Eight months is long enough to pick up on how things work.' He turned and examined his face in the mirror.

Anya twisted the wet towel in her hand. 'Why would anyone think I'd want to have a baby this way?'

'Because you're different from the other girls. The Collective is used to things happening a certain way. It doesn't like resistance. It doesn't like change. I've heard the medics talk about a group from Arcis that is causing trouble for the Collective. When you were all in Arcis, the Collective viewed your antics as a challenge and a valuable learning experience. But I guess you became a nuisance as time went on.'

That place again.

'How am I connected to Arcis?'

'That's where you were before here.'

'Was it a prison?'

'Of sorts.' Alex turned round. One eye was open, the other puffy and almost shut. 'Your memories were wiped, but it doesn't mean they're completely gone. Are you experiencing flashes of events?'

Anya nodded. 'Bits and pieces. I thought I was taken from Brookfield and brought straight here.'

'That's partly true. Essention and Arcis is the bit the machine wiped. You were sick in Brookfield. Do you remember?'

She nodded again. She didn't know why she remembered that.

'Then the Collective allowed you to keep that memory. What is your last one?'

She and Jason had collapsed on the floor in her home. 'Men from Praesidium came to rescue me and my brother.'

Alex nodded. 'The memories might come back. Just take it one day at a time, okay?'

But Anya didn't want to wait. She wanted to know what memories had been stolen from her.

When Alex said nothing more about Arcis, she changed the subject.

'Tell me about the other girls who came through here. Were they pretty?'

Alex rested his hands on the edge of the counter. 'It sounds like every guy's dream. Attractive girls throwing themselves at you. But it wasn't.' He sighed. 'I told you about the girls who became demanding after treatment. Well, others used to sit in a corner of my bedroom and cry. I hated my time with them. It felt wrong. Even though the physical attraction was mutual, it always felt as if the sex wasn't consensual.'

Anya wet the towel again and pressed it gently to Alex's eye bruise. 'So why now? Why change things up? Why haven't you convinced me more to have sex with you? It's not like resisting is going to change anything and the Ten are going to just let us go.'

'Because you cared enough to fight me on it.'

Alex's green eyes, marred by sadness, shone under the light. 'And you weren't angry with me because you were frightened or because the treatment turned you into a sex-crazed maniac. You fought because you saw the injustice of the situation. Not just for you, but for me.'

His words stirred something low in Anya's belly. She felt the heat from his skin, even though only the towel touched him. She continued to dab at his eye. Then his hands found her hips. She gasped and jerked the towel away, feeling his hot gaze on her.

The sound of the running water cut through her thoughts. She shook her head. 'We've been in here too long. We need to get out there, to pretend for the camera.'

Alex took the towel from her. 'I hate to say it, but Rapture is working.'

Anya focused on his mouth. 'I hate to say it, too.'

'So what do we do?'

'Anything we can to resist. I'm serious about that. No matter how I feel right now, I don't want to give in.'

'Yeah, neither do I.' Alex cleared his throat and tossed the towel on the counter. 'You go back out there first. I want to look at my new shiner a bit longer.'

'Try not to piss them off again, okay?'

That earned her a smile.

'But what if I were covered in bruises?' he said teasingly. 'Would I be less attractive to you?'

Anya grinned. 'Possibly. Do you mean the face?

A nasty bruise on your other eye?'

Alex touched her hips again. 'Or one on my cheek.'

Anya tilted her head. 'Or maybe one on your chin.'

'Or on my lip.'

Anya's gaze lingered on Alex's full lips. Her own parted as she imagined tasting him. His good eye had widened, and she could hear his shallow breaths.

'Anya, I'm struggling here.'

'Me too. But we have to try.'

She relocated to the bed not believing her words. Through the open door Alex watched her with a hunger that made her want to throw the rules out.

'It will only get better or worse from here on in, depending on how you look at it,' he said, then turned to the mirror.

Anya pinched the skin on her arm—anything to distract her from the deep ache inside.

13

CANYA

Canya slouched in a chair by her bed while Jacob and Vanessa talked about her. The old man had turned up that morning. No announcement. Neither of them had bothered to ask what *she* wanted.

'The newborn needs freedom,' he said.

'Well, I disagree. I need to monitor her stores of biogel daily. She's too new. She won't top up when they run low. She needs constant care.'

'But locking her up isn't the answer. Look at her.' Canya straightened up when they both turned in her direction.

Vanessa's brown gaze held little sympathy. 'Here, I know where she is at night. I can keep her safe. She's already acting like a stroppy teen. I don't want that in my home. Not yet.'

They went back to ignoring Canya. 'Taking care of a newborn is a Copy's job,' said Jacob.

Vanessa smiled. 'And yet, you took care of Carissa. You don't think I can do it, old man?'

123

'That was different. That was before...' Jacob drew in a tight breath. 'Before the escape attempt.'

What escape? Canya leaned forward just as Vanessa touched Jacob on the arm. To silence him?

'Of course I think you can handle it,' he said, patting her hand. 'I just don't like variables, not here where machines follow order and logic. Anything out of character makes me nervous.'

What escape? If only she could find out. Maybe Carissa could tell her. But the girl barely acknowledged her. *Bitch.*

'The Collective doesn't like problems, and the Copies can rarely handle the newborns' behaviour,' said Vanessa. 'I guess they're more like us at this stage in their lives. So when I volunteered, they accepted.' She glanced at Canya. 'Plus, she has all of Anya's memories. She has information we both need.'

Canya knew exactly what the woman wanted: the name of a rebel camp in the mountains. It was a memory that Anya had buried deep and took some digging to release it. If Vanessa wanted it, she'd have to bargain big to get it.

Jacob frowned. 'Are you still looking for that place—the Beyond? What's the point if we can never leave the city? Besides, it's only hearsay. We have no proof it actually exists.'

Canya folded her hands on her lap just as Vanessa locked her gaze on her.

'It does exist, Jacob. The camp set up close to where they think it is. Evan and Grace Macklin told me they saw physical evidence of it once, before the border vanished. If we find the camp, we find the Beyond.'

Canya flinched at the mention of Anya's parents. Through her borrowed memories, Canya felt Anya's love for her father and hate for her mother.

He waved his hand. 'A fictional place. A place Mags was obsessed with. A place she died for.'

Vanessa switched her focus back to Jacob. 'Yet the Collective believes it exists.'

'Only because the rebels say it does. You know what exists?' Jacob pointed at the ceiling. 'A machine city with defective programming and a bunch of towns. That's all. My wife died for nothing.'

Canya smiled at the volleying conversation. This was more entertaining than sitting alone.

Vanessa sighed. 'The Beyond is no fantasy, Jacob. It's real and Anya's parents saw it. But Canya won't say.'

Why should she? Vanessa didn't care about her. She kept her around for a secret. What would happen as soon as she gave up that secret?

She'd even told her not to visit Dom.

Rookie move, Vanessa.

'Did you know Carissa has been helping me with *her*?' said Vanessa.

That hurt Canya. She couldn't even say her name.

Jacob nodded. 'Carissa's a good kid. She listens to the Collective but she follows her heart. I worry for her. She's been altering her memories prior to upload.

If the Collective finds out, Quintus will terminate her.'

'I had my suspicions when I gave her a book last week. She returned to ask me to explain the contents.' Vanessa folded her arms. 'Had to play it cool, you know, in case she was recording the interaction. Took me by surprise, if I'm being honest. I didn't expect one of them to break away from the pack. We've been here a year—I'd given up hope that any of them were even capable of it.'

Jacob nodded at Canya. Canya hadn't made up her mind about the old man yet. 'And this one? What kind of life will she lead when she's connected to the network?'

'I have no idea, Jacob.'

She was done listening to the pair of them. 'I want to go out.'

Vanessa blinked as if she'd forgotten Canya was in the room. 'Fine, but stay away from the medical facility.'

'Okay.'

She would keep no such promise. Dom needed her. The last time she'd seen him, he'd acted so cold towards her, ordered her from his room. She had to fix things.

She blamed it on the pain. Or the drugs. Whatever. Dom would come around, see her for what she was: a person worthy of his love.

But she still needed a new look. Her white dress with a dirty hem would no longer cut it.

Ω

Canya strolled through the bustling Business-District plaza with its arc of units on both sides. Chatter gave way to silence and whispers from the colours as she passed. She couldn't wait to blend in, to ditch her 'Copy' label. She returned to the store with the yellow display dress. Snide insults from passersby began. 'Non-human' and 'Imposter' were the worst. Her preformed heart thumped too fast in her chest.

If she was an imposter, then why did she care so much about Dom Pavesi? She held her head high and entered the store. Canya flashed a sweet smile at Nora, the sales assistant, in an effort to cancel out her look of disgust.

'I'm surprised you have the nerve to show your face in here, newborn. Didn't you get the hint yesterday?'

Canya ignored her and went straight to the only rail of clothes that interested her. What if she threw a tantrum? She giggled as she pictured Nora standing over her with a shocked look on her face, and no freaking idea what to do. But to do so would be an immature move, and Dom didn't like immature girls. Dom wanted a quiet, well-behaved girl. She would learn to be just that.

She considered meeting the real Anya. Maybe she could copy some of her traits and transform into the girl Dom had fallen for in Arcis.

She selected a yellow dress in her size.

Nora rolled her eyes. 'If you insist on being in

my store, then I guess I should offer you some advice. Yellow is all wrong for your pale skin colouring and brown hair. A nice moss green or purple would work better.'

Canya gripped the dress tighter. 'I want to try it on.'

Nora shook her head and showed her to a room at the back. She snapped the curtain closed after Canya entered.

Canya slipped off her white dress and stood in front of the mirror in her camisole and underwear. Except for the eyes, which were a lighter blue, she saw no variations between her and the real Anya. Dom would soon accept that. She grinned when she pictured his reaction to seeing her in the yellow dress.

She slipped it over her head and bit back her disappointment when she realised Nora had been right about the colour.

What colour did Dom prefer? Maybe he *liked* yellow.

Good enough for her. She rolled up her white dress and left the changing room.

Nora looked her over and then walked to the sales counter. 'Taking the yellow one, huh? Okay, but don't say I didn't warn you. No returns. I assume you've got credit?'

Canya held up her wrist just as Nora pulled out a flat plate from beneath the counter. She pressed her wrist to the plate.

'A Copy's credit is only worth half of what I can get if I barter with humans. You want to be like humans so much, hun, then learn to do business like one.' She fired the flat plate back under the counter and left to tend to a customer who had just walked in.

Canya left the store with her old dress tucked under her arm. Despite the colour and Nora's rudeness, the new dress gave her confidence. Plus, it didn't attract negative attention like her white one did.

She caught a glimpse of herself in a store window and smiled. A dozen display boxes sat outside, crammed with crappy handmade items. She stuffed her old dress into one of the boxes and skipped away.

Ω

Dom was exactly where she'd left him the day before: in his room, on his bed. She closed the door and twirled to show off her new dress.

Dom sat up, alert. Her skin buzzed when his eyes swept the length of her. He wanted her. She could tell.

Maybe she'd make him work for it a little first.

But then his gaze lingered on her face, on her eyes. The eyes she could do nothing about. With a heavy sigh, he looked away.

She tried to keep the mood casual, like the real Anya might. 'You don't like the colour?' She stepped closer to his bed.

'I told you to go.'

'You were sad, so I did. But now I'm back.'

'I wasn't sad. I asked you to help me escape, and you wouldn't.' Dom pinned her with a hard gaze, and she shivered. 'Your eyes are all wrong.'

'Light sensitivity, that's all. The sunlight is too strong on the surface.'

Dom's eyes widened. 'You've been to the surface? When? How?'

Canya realised her mistake; the real Anya would also be prisoner here. 'They let me out for an hour.'

Dom shook his head, his interest waning. 'That doesn't make sense. And now you're in here? How?'

'I guess they felt sorry for me. I needed to see you. One of the medics let me in.'

Dom shifted his feet from the bed to the floor. He grimaced. 'Which one?'

'What?'

'Which medic let you in here?'

'I don't remember.'

Dom stood up—with great difficulty, she noticed —and walked towards her. 'Come on, Anya. We're prisoners down here. We can't have too many medics visiting us. Which one let you in here? Male or female?'

Canya backed up, not liking the look he gave her. 'Why are you asking? Okay. Male.'

Dom's gaze, cold and clinical, raked over her. 'Anya would never wear that colour.' He returned to the bed and eased himself onto it.

'*I'm* Anya. What are you talking about?'

'I wasn't sure the last time, but I'm sure now. You're not her. You're the Copy. I remember you from the machine in Arcis. Except you were a blank then.'

She rolled her eyes. '*Okay*, so I'm a Copy. But I look exactly like her and I'm definitely not a blank. I have her memories, her personality. Why are you being like this?'

Dom snorted. 'You *do not* have her personality.' He winced as he readjusted his seated position. 'There's more to attraction than what someone looks like. It runs deeper. It comes from here.' Dom pressed his hand to his heart.

She sat at the foot of his bed, inching closer when he allowed it. Her hand grazed his and he flinched. Pulled away. 'What does she have that I don't?'

Dom laughed. It was the most magical sound in the world. 'For one, she thinks of others.'

'I think of others. I'm thinking of you right now. You're all I think about.'

'No. You want something from me. You're not trying to help me. You think only of yourself. '

Canya picked at the fabric of her sleeve.

Dom said, 'You would have asked how my injuries are.'

She could do that. 'How are your injuries?'

'It's too late.' Dom moved up the bed, away from her. 'And there's something off about you. Something childish that doesn't fit the Anya I know.'

Why would he say such things? Why did his words ignite her anger? She breathed in and out, slowly. What would the real Anya do? She had her memories. It couldn't be that difficult to mirror her.

'I know you're hurting, Dom. You don't have to be alone. I can be your friend.'

Dom gave her a sad smile. 'You sound like her, and it's certainly something she might say, but I still don't feel it.'

Her anger pressed against her weak biogel heart. She stood over him, forcing his eyes up to her.

'You're selfish, Dom Pavesi. Do you know how long I've waited to see you? Do you know what humiliation I had to endure to buy this stupid yellow dress? I wore it to cheer you up.'

Dom blinked. 'I'll guess you waited a couple of days to see me because that's how old you are. And you probably stole the dress because they wouldn't give it to you.'

A high-pitched sound escaped from her throat. 'I bought it, with credit!' She showed him her wrist. 'So why can't you pretend I'm her? I need to be with you. I want to sleep with you.'

The smile Dom wore didn't make her feel better. 'We still come back to one thing. You're not Anya.'

'But I can *be* her. Teach me how.'

'It doesn't work like that.' She detected a trace of anger in his voice. 'You can't teach someone to be like another person. Humans aren't carbon copies of each other. When two people look identical, it's their personalities that set them apart.'

Despite his rudeness, Canya moved closer and positioned her body between his legs. She took his frozen stature to be a good sign. He studied her. She detected a tiny fissure developing in his defensive wall.

Men were all the same. When it came down to it, they wanted sex. And if the opportunity presented itself... Anya's encounter with Warren on the fourth floor of Arcis had proved that.

Dom's eyes softened under her gaze. He protected his stomach with his hand. She avoided touching or pressing against his scars.

Instead, her fingers grazed his cheek. He shuddered and closed his eyes.

'I can be her if you want,' she whispered. 'All you have to do is pretend.'

'I really want you to be her. More than anything.' He opened his eyes.

Canya brushed her lips against Dom's, the way Anya had done in the infirmary on the fourth floor in Arcis. Just after Frank had died. Anya had sliced her arm open trying to help him.

Dom groaned and pulled her onto his lap.

A fire burned inside her, low and strong. She moved until she straddled him. His heated gaze followed her movements as she pulled off her dress, leaving her covered with only the flimsy camisole and underwear. She took advantage of his submission. Kissed him again. Pressed her body against his.

But he turned his face away, and one of her kisses landed on his cheek. She touched his face, hoping to stoke the fire in his eyes that barely smouldered. She pushed her half-naked body into him, eager for a response.

Nothing.

Canya jumped off. 'I hate you, Dom! I love you, but I hate you too. Do you know what this is doing to me? How it's tearing me up inside?'

'I have an idea.' He picked her dress up off the bed and tossed it to her. 'You'd better leave before you say something you'll regret.'

'I already regret this.'

She stormed out, pulling on her dress as she went. It satisfied her to hear the click of the lock as she walked away. She smacked her chip against the control panel and rode the elevator down one floor, to the Breeder programme. Anya was probably doing it with some other guy and not even thinking about Dom. If Anya didn't remember Arcis, she wouldn't even know who the hell Dom was.

Dom's holier-than-thou attitude was bullshit. And boring.

She stormed out of the elevator and smacked straight into two female medics. Her breaths came fast as she said, 'I want to see Anya Macklin.'

'No visitors,' said one of the medics. 'Please leave this floor or we will report you.' They both walked on.

'Fine. I'll come back later.'

The medic spoke over her shoulder. 'No visitors. Ever. The Collective's orders.'

Canya gritted her teeth and climbed back into the elevator. She needed out of this facility before she lost it with a medic, and lost her visiting rights.

Dom would come round. Until then, she'd find some way to tell Anya exactly where Dom had touched her. And how he'd liked it.

14

CARISSA

Two visits to the Great Hall in two days. Some kind of record.

She took her time crossing the white-tiled floor, grateful that Quintus could only sense her, not see how she pressed her fingers below her ribs—a soft spot teeming with nervous activity. As soon as she let go, her nerves bounced back.

The black screens provided the only contrast to the all-white room. To the Collective, white signified purity. Quintus once said that Originals used colour not to express their individuality, but to show their genetic impurities. But Vanessa had told Carissa that colour engaged the senses, and the imagination—something the Copies lacked in spades.

Carissa glanced down at her white dress and wondered how developed her own senses and imagination were. For a time she'd even managed to fool June.

The deletion of footage of that conversation gave

her some comfort as she touched the podium. Her NMC pinged in its search for a connection before changing to a steady hum. The hum—a strange, invasive thing—connected her to a group of beings that understood her.

She never wanted to be alone.

Her upload ended just as Quintus appeared on screen. '173-C, we have analysed your experiences from yesterday and noticed some anomalies that we wish to discuss with you.'

Carissa held her breath. *Don't panic.*

'You spent thirty minutes in the medical facility. You spoke to 28-C, the head medic, and asked about the humans from Arcis. Then you visited with one Original who goes by the name of June. Your recollections of the latter event and the footage don't match up. There are delays that cannot be accounted for. Please explain.'

Carissa swallowed her breath. 'Perhaps it was an error in the camera feed.'

'There are long instances in both your recollection and the footage where you and the human stare at each other.'

Carissa had added innocuous scenes to make it seem like a natural delay. Her memories matched, but she must have overlooked an inconsistency somewhere.

Quintus waited for her reply.

'I was curious about the Arcis participants, both before and when they arrived here. I was just thinking of the best questions to ask 229-O.'

'This anomaly has prompted a closer look into your Original's background.' Quintus continued. 'It appears she had a sister. And that sister is 229-O, the human you went to visit. Did you know who she was before you entered the room?'

She thought about lying. But if Quintus caught her out...

'Yes, I knew who she was. I'm sorry for lying, Quintus.'

She looked at her hand, pressed flat to the podium, and prepared herself for the shock Quintus was bound to order, at the others' command.

'We should terminate you for your insubordination. In fact, Octavius and Septimus voted for it, but Unos and Quatrius were intrigued by your behaviour.' Carissa looked up at Quintus, hopeful. 'We are interested to learn if your behaviour matches that of your Original.'

Stunned into silence, Carissa waited for the verdict.

'Your Original was a curious one. And you seem to have inherited this from her. We have reviewed your most recent uploads. You spent more time in the viewing room than other Copies watching the footage from Arcis. You also spend time at the library, although there are gaps in your time there that cannot be explained. You also spend a lot of time with the Inventor. Please explain the latter?'

Quintus' penetrating stare unsettled Carissa. 'My Original was curious. I cannot explain my own curiosity, only that I spend time in the places where I feel comfortable. The Inventor has been good to me. I understand he took charge of me when I was a newborn, though I have no memories of that time. He helps me to understand where my curiosity comes from and how to temper it. The Copies are unable to provide such assistance.'

'And the Librarian?'

'I thought I had permission to speak with her.' The words rushed out of her.

'You do have permission, 173-C,' said Quintus. 'We wish to know what you spoke to the Librarian about.'

She gazed up at Quintus' skewed on-screen image. He watched her with his catlike eyes. 'I wanted to know about the books. Van... I mean, the Librarian, loaned me a book and had promised to explain it to me. '

'And the newborn in the Librarian's care. Have you seen her?'

'Yes. The Librarian asked me to help her understand what she is and to explain how things work around here. She's not yet connected, so she doesn't understand.'

Quintus' image frowned. 'And why has none of that footage been recorded?'

Carissa decided to opt for the truth. 'The room where the Librarian keeps the newborn is below ground. There is no signal there.'

Angry faces—Unos, Septimus, Quatrius—flashed on screen. Carissa controlled her shaking hands.

'Your connection may not have been live,' said Unos. 'But a cache of your experiences there should be stored in your NMC. Yet, we see no evidence of that in your upload.'

Carissa blinked too fast. 'The location of the room must interfere with the NMC. Perhaps it also interferes with my ability to form memories.'

Septimus nodded, as if that answer was acceptable. 'The Inventor speaks highly of you. Says you like to learn.'

'Yes, I do.' She hoped that by telling the truth the Collective would choose to save her.

'173-C, we are interested in you,' said Quintus. 'Interested in your experiences thus far. We want to know if the deletion of your Original has led you to develop a greater understanding of your humanity. If that is true, there may be no need for the Originals beyond their immediate usefulness.'

'What do you mean, Quintus?'

'If a bond exists between the Original and Copy that is preventing the Copy from reaching its full potential, then we must consider breaking it.'

'Termination?' Carissa huffed out.

'Yes. Deletion of the Originals.'

'All of them?' Her heart hurt. She had just found June.

Quintus nodded. 'Including your Original's sister. Her Copy is a more than adequate replacement.' Carissa steadied her rapidly beating heart. 'There is no need for you to come here tomorrow for your scheduled upload. You may use

140

the main terminal room as normal.'

'As you wish, Quintus.'

'Stay close, 173-C. The Collective wishes to study you in greater detail.'

Carissa disconnected and forced herself to walk —not run—from the room. Outside, her body remained stiff and on high alert. She bent over at the waist, drawing stares from other Copies.

She had been altering her memories for a while, so why was Quintus only looking into her uploads now?

She might be alive, but for how much longer?

15

ANYA

118-C came for her again that evening. Anya didn't feel like cooperating. The medic gripped her arm so tight, Anya felt it tingle.

'You are delaying on purpose, Anya Macklin. Do not think your games will be tolerated here. You will be forced to comply.'

'I don't *want* to comply. You know why?' The medic glared at her, pulling her along. 'Because I think you enjoy my games. In a place where everything is planned, I'm not what you expected. Did you choose to work as part of the Breeder programme, or did the Collective place you here?'

'I was assigned this role.'

Anya's feet slipped on the floor in her futile attempts to slow the medic down. 'Still, I'm sure you had some say in that decision.'

'If I had a say, I would be working in the Learning Centre serving the Collective directly.'

The grip on Anya's arm intensified, causing her

to yelp. She stopped fighting, to save her arm. 'But now, you're forced to interact with me. A *lowly* human.'

'Humans are unpredictable, violent.'

'Humans are also compassionate and caring. And you're intrigued. I can tell. Why else would you talk to me?'

The medic flashed her a bitter look and yanked her along. 'You will comply. Rapture will make sure of that.'

Anya would never tell the medic how close she'd come to giving in. Alex had been right there, sitting on the bed, leaning back on his hands, his legs crossed at the ankles.

She had been sitting on the chaise longue trying not to look at him. They had agreed to keep things professional, but the bouts of prolonged silence were the worst.

When she thought he wasn't looking, Anya stole glances at Alex, memorising the way his messy blond hair fell into his eyes when he dipped his head. Or how the light reflected off his golden lashes. Then he'd caught her looking. His hooded gaze took her breath away. She returned the look, gripped the edges of the chaise longue and pressed her knees together.

She clawed back control, but he was like a drug, drawing her back in. One thought about Alex's green eyes undid all her good work.

The medic's rough handling snapped Anya back to the present. She was already strapped into the chair. Another round of painful injections followed.

Could she resist Alex for much longer?

Alex was already back from his treatment when she returned. No fresh bruises or black eyes to show for his time away. Good.

'I see you're intact.' The door closed behind her.

Alex ruffled his hair. 'Yeah. I decided it wasn't a good idea to piss them off while they were stabbing me with a needle.' He touched the bruise under his eye. 'Besides, I think this proves just how much of a man I already am.'

Anya laughed softly. 'Yeah, that's what my brother used to say. I think he was fifteen when he said the same thing, after trying to impress a girl in school. He was too busy watching her while walking and trying to make his friends laugh, then he smacked straight into a tree. You boys are all the same.'

Alex lifted a brow. 'Not all the same. Doesn't seem like he deserved that war wound. I bet the girl wasn't impressed.'

'No. She left with her friends. Didn't talk to him again.'

'So he learned the sharp lesson that girls are fickle.'

'How so?' Anya relocated to the chaise longue.

'When we make fools of ourselves, girls are quick to tell us we're acting like kids. When we try to act grown up, they say they wish we were more fun. We can't win.'

Anya pulled her legs up under her. 'It's not about what you do—it's about how you execute it.'

Alex leaned forward, watching her movements.

'So you think if he'd played up to the girl's idea of a perfect man, he would have had a better chance?'

His gaze caused her to blush. 'Maybe not. Girls are too fickle at fifteen. But then, so are boys. I was there that day, watching. Jason was trying to impress his friends more than he was her. He was showing off. When you're a girl and you get that kind of attention, you're not sure what's genuine and what's for show. You have to go with your gut.'

'And that's why I'm single.' Alex barked out a laugh.

'And I thought it was because you were trapped in this place.' She had meant it as a joke, but Alex dropped his gaze. 'Shit, I'm sorry for being insensitive. I was just trying to lighten the mood.'

'It's okay.' He looked at her. 'It's good that we're talking like this. It helps with, you know, ignoring the other stuff.'

Anya agreed, even though Rapture heightened her awareness of everything Alex did.

'You said you came from Brookfield,' he said. Anya nodded. 'Do you think your brother is here too?'

'Not with my group.' One dark-haired boy. That's what Alex had said.

'Another group then?'

'I don't know.' She didn't want to talk about it. 'What about you?'

He shifted on the bed. 'Parents are both dead. I didn't have a home for a while. You could say I drifted from town to town, like a nomad.'

She'd been too busy trying to figure this place out to ask Alex about his past. All she knew was he'd been kept prisoner in Praesidium for eight months. No mention of any rescue attempts. 'Did you go to school? Did you ever visit this city before you were captured? Where were you when the Copies came for you?'

Alex touched the bruise under his eye. 'Like I said, I'm a nomad. Nowhere to call home. I was in between towns when they found me.'

His long fingers distracted her—fingers she wanted touching her face and hair. She swallowed and pushed away her raging hormones. Thoughts of Jason worked as an instant mood killer. She hoped her brother was okay.

Her parents. Dead.

Jason was all she had left. Jason and her link to Arcis manifested as flashbacks. Maybe her memories would return. Maybe what happened to Jason was buried somewhere in her head.

Anya studied the self-confessed nomad sitting a few feet away. How had he survived? There was nothing but open land between the towns. No animals. No food other than what the townspeople produced. Maybe he had stolen food, taken shelter wherever he could.

She stole another glance at him, the stranger who'd been here for eight months and seemed too accepting of his fate.

Alex groaned and stood up. Every muscle in his body moved, and Anya wished. *Wanted.*

'Sometimes I really hate this place. Before you, there were pockets of time between the girls' arriving and leaving. It was a regular whorehouse, except I was the whore. In between, I'd have time to myself to think about how demeaning and dirty I felt. But with you, it's like I'm walking on eggshells. I hate this tension between us. Let's do something to break it.'

Anya's heart jackhammered. 'Like what?'

Alex strode over to one of the walls and pressed a hidden panel. It revealed a control unit. He turned a few knobs and music began to play. She didn't recognise the up-tempo song. Alex turned round and held his hand out to her.

'We're sitting here with nothing to do and I'm bored. Humour me with a little dancing.'

Anya blushed. 'No. I don't dance.' She was skilled in all kinds of sport. Ask her to run in a race, she knew what to do. But dancing? Two left feet. Word had got round about her clumsiness, and the boys had stopped asking her to dance.

Alex grabbed her hand and pulled her up.

Embarrassed, she tried to pull away, but he held on.

'Don't blame me if I step on your toes, okay?'

He gave her a slow smile that heated her insides. 'Don't worry. I'll lead.'

The music changed to a slower song. The stirrings began. It didn't help that Alex was pressed up against her. 'Uh, can we pick something a little less...'

'Romantic?' Alex grinned. 'Yeah, I was thinking

the same thing.'

He walked away and flicked the music to a more upbeat song, then returned. 'Just follow my lead.'

He twirled and turned her round. She laughed so much that she forgot her aching attraction.

'I've never had a friend in here,' said Alex. 'I kind of like it.'

'Yeah. Me too. It feels like I haven't laughed in a really long time. But it also feels as if I have. Does that make sense?'

Alex twirled her again. 'Your memories are still in there somewhere. Like an imprint. There were probably people you knew in Arcis, and some you got close to. The Collective doesn't want you remembering anything. You're more compliant that way.'

'Can the medics hear us over the music?' Anya searched for the camera she'd been unable to find.

'Probably. But they know I can't keep my mouth shut. I've already been starved, half beaten to death, put on suicide watch. The Collective finally realised their Copies couldn't break me. So the masters let me do and say what I want. I get results, and that's all anyone cares about.'

'Will the masters ever let you leave?'

'No.' He sounded bitter.

Anya moved her lips to his ear. 'I'll find a way to get us both out of here.'

He sucked in a breath and whispered back. 'I'm sick of being used in this way. I want control of my life. What if I could choose someone to be with?

Wouldn't that be something?'

Anya nodded. 'It can happen, Alex. That's why we're fighting this. This is us taking back control.'

'I wish it wasn't so damn hard to resist the treatments. All I can think about is...' He groaned in her ear, sending shock waves straight to her core.

She jerked away. Control. She needed more of it. 'Me too. But it doesn't feel right.'

'I know.'

Anya pointed to the bed. 'You. Sit. Let me tell you more about my brother's antics when we were younger.' She sat cross-legged on the floor. 'That should kill off any attraction you have to me. And mentioning my brother is a sure-fire way to kill mine.'

Alex grinned as he sat. 'That's the second-best idea I've heard today.'

'And the first?'

He locked her in his feral gaze. Her cheeks heated up as she pushed those same thoughts from her mind.

'I'd like to learn more about you, Alex. How you ended up in this place.'

'It's really dull. Nothing to get excited about.'

The fleeting look that passed across Alex's face happened so fast, Anya almost missed it.

He was nervous.

Who was this boy? What secret he was hiding?

16

DOM

Dom sat on his prison bed and examined the almost-invisible scars. A day ago they'd been red and puffy along the seam post-surgery. All that remained was a silvery trail to remind him of his new role as Praesidium's guinea pig.

For how long?

He smirked. *Since you were seven, Dom, and they put their tech in you.*

He tore his gaze away from his scars. The wounds had healed within a few hours as a result of a special healing accelerator. He'd felt the injection work almost instantly; it tightened the skin around the wounds. He could have done with that tech in Arcis when Anya had almost died trying to save Frank. Frank had died unnecessarily from a severed artery.

Yet Praesidium's minds, which built Arcis, had kept the tech to themselves. Arcis had been one giant test to record the participants' responses to danger. Sometimes it had felt as if the Praesidium-run facility preferred to watch them bleed than to learn.

Anya. The girl who'd helped him and Sheila complete Arcis' crazy test. How could he have mixed her up with that *thing* in the yellow dress? He didn't deserve Anya. While she was trapped somewhere in this facility, he'd been getting handsy with her Copy.

A ticking noise drew his attention. Soft, repetitive. He turned his head towards the source. Was it coming from outside the room? Or the room next to his? He got up and pressed his ear to the exit. The sound vanished. He listened at the wall between his room and the next. There it was again, louder than before.

The ticking noise was replaced with a new sound, like someone tapping a fingernail on the wall.

Dom pressed his forehead against the wall and smiled—it was the first sign of life he'd encountered since he'd been locked up in here.

The Copies didn't count.

Using his fist, he banged on the wall three times. Three bangs on the other side of the wall answered him. He tried again: this time one bang, a beat, then two bangs. The reply copied his pattern exactly.

'Hello?' Dom cupped his hands to his mouth.

There was no answer.

'Hello? Are you trapped like me?'

He heard a faint but indistinct reply.

'Speak louder. I can't hear you.'

'Yes!' answered a high voice. 'I'm here. Where are you?'

'In the next room, I think. How long have you

been here?'

'I don't know. A while? Where did you come from?' The thick stone between the rooms muffled the reply.

'Arcis. You?'

'Some facility.'

Max had always believed that more than one Arcis existed. His cell neighbour must have come from a similar facility.

'Do you know Morse code?' Charlie had taught it to him.

'Yes.' The voice sounded female. 'But I'm a little rusty.'

Dom looked around for something better than his fist to bang out a message with. He picked up an empty food tray and tapped out a series of dots and dashes against the wall.

Can you understand me?

After a long pause, the reply came. *Y... E... S.*

Have you been brought in for testing?

Another long pause. He waited with one hand and an ear against the cold white brick. *Y... E... S.*

Dom considered his next question. Then he thought of something Max might ask. He turned the edge of the tray to the wall.

Are you clean?

If she'd received the antidote to Compliance, if she was a rebel, she'd understand.

The reply came. *Y... E... S.*

Dom froze. Who was he talking to? Did she really understand Morse code? Or was it a bluff?

152

He had to know who was in the next room. The medics had yet to ask about the rebels, but they would. Soon.

He tapped out a new question.

Are you a rebel?

He replaced the tray with his ear and waited. The reply competed with the sound of his thundering heartbeat. But it was clear.

I am your mother.

Dom stumbled back from the wall. 'Mother?' How could that be? The female medic had said she was dead.

He heard the door to the other room open. 'What are you doing?' said a loud voice.

Then he heard a dragging noise outside his door. He wanted to call out to Mariella, to ask if she was okay. He kept his mouth shut to limit her punishment.

Dom paced his room waiting for her return. But the corridor outside his room remained quiet. The food slot opened and a hand pushed through a new tray. Same food with a bottle of water.

No cutlery—not since the stabbing incident.

A nervous Dom carried the tray to his bed. He ate, even though his stomach clenched tight. His mother was alive. He needed to keep his strength up to help her.

The stew tasted saltier than usual. He cracked open the bottle of water and drained half of it.

Mariella was alive. Why had the female medic lied to him? She didn't seem like the vindictive type. Not like the male.

The food sat like a ball in his stomach. He stood. His head spun. The tray slipped out of his hand and clattered to the cold stone floor.

Dom knelt down, covered his eyes. The room moved faster than his eyes could keep up. He tried to stand but fell back to the floor.

The door opened. Someone stood in front of him. He stared at the sturdy black shoes and pressed white trousers of a medic's uniform.

The male medic yanked his drugged body up. Dom could barely support himself; the drug was in the water, and the salty stew had forced him to drink it.

148-C held on to his arm, a smug look on his face as he glanced at the food tray. Dom closed his eyes and the room faded away.

Ω

He woke to find himself back in the testing room. The overhead light pinched at his eyes. The restraints on his hands and feet afforded him little room. Two of the ceiling panels were open. The extended arms held needles: one was inserted into a vein, the other into his spine.

More surgery.

He swallowed down bile as the female medic spoke to two males, one of them 148-C.

'You have delayed this surgery, 148-C. Why did you drug him?'

'He was being difficult, 118-C. Violent. I didn't

trust him after... you know.' Dom smirked at the visible quarter-inch gash in the medic's neck.

'Let me go,' said Dom to the female. She looked in his direction. He needed to know if there was any chance the Copies could see reason.

She stepped towards him. 'The Collective will let you go as soon as you are no longer of any use to it.'

'You lied about my mother. You said she was dead.'

'She *is* dead.'

'Then who is in the room next to mine?'

The female medic frowned at the two males. Dom caught the slight smile on 148-C's face. The other shook his head.

'148-C, explain.'

Dom's hope plummeted. He hadn't actually heard a female voice; he'd only assumed he had.

'It was a joke, 118-C.'

'No more games, 148-C. This patient is no longer your concern.'

'Yes, 118-C.'

Dom turned away from the medic who'd been pretending to be his mother. Lucky for 148-C, he was restrained. Next time, he'd do more than stick a spoon handle in his neck.

His chest heaved with anger. Mariella was gone and he was alone. Maybe dismissing Anya's Copy had been a mistake. What if she turned out to be his only visitor? He was certain the Collective would kill him before it granted him freedom.

If he survived this round of tests and the Copy

visited again, he would try to make amends.

A new machine sat in one corner of the large room. It looked similar to the device he'd seen on the ninth floor of Arcis, but smaller.

The replication machine.

There was no fancy arch to walk through. No blinking white lights that would pull his memories away. No giant mirror at the end masking a portal. Just a black rectangular box big enough to accommodate one person. It had four open sides and a scanner fitted to the inside of the roof. At the rear of the unit, an upright rectangular container sat separate from the machine, filled with a viscous substance.

A third arm extended down from the ceiling and cut him open. The anaesthetic in his vein and spine had slipped over him, making everything feel light and floaty. A fourth arm descended, with forceps attached to the end. The forceps pulled his incision apart. He averted his gaze.

When he heard 148-C snigger, he forced his eyes back to the surgery. He would not look weak in front of this medic.

The forceps pulled out his Second Generation–tech liver, slippery with blood. The liver made a clattering noise when it was dropped onto a tray. Then the forceps picked up a spotless liver with the words *Fourth Gen* printed on the side, and worked fast to attach the tech to his existing system. While the anaesthetic kept his pain under control, an exposed Dom felt anything but calm, laid open for the Copies. The laser closed up the wound and the bed flipped over. Dom felt his other two scars being reopened.

He yelled, not from pain but from the injustice of it.

The robotic arm with the laser continued to cut.

'This will go better if you don't move, Dom Pavesi,' said the female medic. 'We need you calm.'

Dom glanced at the males. He got some pleasure when he saw the looks of disgust on their faces. If he couldn't control this situation, he might as well be repulsive. One by one, his remaining Second Gen organs were removed and replaced with new tech.

He felt it all.

The table flipped one last time. The anaesthetic dulled his pain but not the fire blazing across his skin. One final injection.

'Immunosuppressives,' said the female. 'To stop your body from rejecting the organs.'

'What about the healing accelerator?'

'Quintus feels it is not necessary.'

Not necessary? Bullshit.

Before he could protest, the medics had untied his restraints and lifted him off the table. He tested his strength as his feet touched the floor, but his legs barely held him upright. The male medics dragged him over to the replication machine.

'Hold on to the bars,' said 148-C.

Dom used both anchors to stay upright. A blue light overhead scanned him from head to toe.

Movement in the gel container caught his eye. The gel's viscosity increased, and the liquid drew together as if it had been poured into a mould. Just like in Arcis, a copy of him formed before his eyes. But the Arcis Copy had failed to materialise past the point of his kidneys, blocked by the first piece of Second Gen tech.

He expected the same to happen here.

But the replication process continued past the failure point, until a gormless version of himself stood before him.

Dom's breaths shortened. A wave of sickness hit him. He turned his head and emptied his stomach. Salty stew covered the floor.

He wiped his mouth and turned back to see his Copy staring at him with a dead expression in its eyes. The Copy blinked once, just as Dom's weak hold on consciousness slipped away.

17

CARISSA

The setting sun at last muted its bright hold over the city. Carissa preferred the evening; her eyes hurt less in the softer light. She entered the stairwell that led below ground. She hated when Quintus scolded her, and today she'd disappointed the others in the Ten as well. Only one person could make her feel better.

In his workshop, the Inventor tinkered with one of the wolves that patrolled the outermost zone.

'Inventor!'

He turned with a lit welding torch in his hand and flipped up his protective mask. 'What is it, miss?'

'I'm in trouble. The humans. The ones who came from Arcis. They're in trouble. I don't know what to do.'

He flicked off the torch. 'I warned you about attracting the Collective's attention. What did you do?'

'I visited June and altered my memories.'

The Inventor sighed and set his torch down on a

workbench. He pulled off his mask. 'I knew you were altering your memories of our conversations, but I never said anything because I wanted you to feel safe here. For how long?'

'Since I started watching the participants in Arcis. Now Quintus is noticing the inconsistencies, asking all sorts of questions. Tell me what to do.'

The Inventor rubbed his eyes and sat down next to the table with the inactive wolf. 'You're a curious one, miss. You always have been. And I know how taken you were with the group from Arcis. But Quintus is dangerous. He can order your termination —'

Her chest tightened suddenly. 'Inventor!' She clutched at her throat. 'Inventor, I... can't... breathe.'

The Inventor dashed over to her and forced her onto the chair he'd just vacated. 'Head between your knees.'

Carissa did, gulping in air. 'What's... wrong with... me?'

'Panic attack. You're the first Copy I've seen to get this anxious about anything. Breathe deeply.'

Carissa followed his instructions until the heaviness in her chest abated enough for her to sit up straight.

The Inventor stood over her, hands on his hips. 'What's this all about, miss? Why did you hide extra footage from the Collective?'

She hiccupped on her next breath, not ready to tell him about June. Lately, her emotions had been bordering on crazy, just like Canya's.

160

'Why does Canya act out the way she does? Why is she different from the other Copies in the city?'

With a sigh, the Inventor leaned against the workbench. 'The newborns are just that. New. Once the maturation period is over, they assimilate quickly. Aside from the changes going on in Canya's body, her mind is also undergoing a period of transformation. She's feeling all sorts of things, but mostly she's confused and lonely. Until she receives her NMC, she'll continue to search for any connection.'

Quintus had said the NMC allowed the Copies to understand and interact with the world as the Originals did.

'So it's like she's been set adrift?' It was how Carissa felt now, yet she was very much connected.

'Yes, exactly. Canya feels alone, but she also feels like she should be part of something. She still shares a connection with Anya, but it doesn't bind them in the same way the Copies are bound to the Collective. Canya is hijacking Anya's memories to guide her through this difficult time. She's discovering her connections and exploiting them. Vanessa told me she's been eager to see Dom Pavesi.' Carissa nodded. 'Dom was a big part of Anya's life. Canya is trying to pick up where Anya left off.'

'Is that why she acts out and asks about Anya?'

'Humans cannot break connections as easily as the Copies. The newborns share a deep bond with their Originals, but without the memories they don't understand why. From the moment of their creation, they feel the absence of their Originals very strongly. That absence fades when they're finally connected to the Collective. But because Canya has those memories, she knows what she wants. And she's driven enough to get it.'

Carissa didn't know why she'd never asked the Inventor, repairer of wolves and servicer of faulty Copies, about the Copies' origins before.

'So what happens when Canya's first week is over and her connection to the Collective goes live?'

The Inventor rested his withered hands on his hips. 'Well, the memories of her first week are erased and she starts to form her own memories, her own experiences.'

Carissa knew nothing of her first week other than what the Inventor had told her. 'What was I like during my first week?'

He laughed and shook his head. 'A right tearaway. You got into all sorts of trouble.'

'But you took care of me.' She wished she remembered.

'Yes. I volunteered after the Copy assigned to you wanted nothing to do with you.'

Carissa hadn't known the Inventor's wife. She'd died before they could meet. 'And your wife wanted me to stay with you?'

The Inventor fiddled with something on the workbench. 'No, miss. She didn't get to know the real you.'

Carissa hadn't meant for Mags or the others to die. 'Is that why I come here so often? Because you used to look after me? Quintus asked me why I visit you so much.'

The Inventor surprised her with a pat on her head. 'No, miss. It's because we're friends.'

'*Friends*?'

'Yes. It's a human connection. The Collective doesn't understand it. With my wife gone, I'm all alone. And your Original is dead, so it makes sense that we should keep each other company.'

Carissa thought about June, all alone in her room. 'What will happen to them, the ones from Arcis?'

The Inventor busied himself with something inside the wolf's open body. 'I don't know. The Collective will continue to use them for testing, tweak the copying process, try to improve on the design of the previous Copies.' He sighed. 'The girls and boys will stay for as long as they are useful.'

'Like you?'

'The Collective always finds a use for me.'

'Why did it use teenagers for Arcis?' Quintus had never fully explained the reasons why the Collective wanted sixteen- to eighteen-year-olds for the facility's programme—only that they were young enough to be shaped and moulded.

The Inventor paused. 'For a while, Praesidium experimented with adults, brought them through the portal. But the Collective deemed the results to be poor. Vanessa said the older Copies who came in the library were rigid, inflexible and unwilling to learn anything new. The younger the Copy was, the more eager it was to learn. But some were too young, too

163

fragile. So the Collective started running teenagers through the Arcis programme. They were almost adults, but their minds could be swayed. The Collective believed the teenagers' experiences would help them to programme Copies that could fool the humans but were synthetic enough to be controlled.'

Copies ruled Praesidium in numbers, but Carissa had no idea how many passed as human. 'Has the Collective succeeded?'

The Inventor shook his head and smiled. 'I haven't met one yet that has fooled me. I think that's why the Collective keeps me around.'

'When the Originals are terminated, do the Copies get stronger emotionally?'

'Originals are human beings, miss. Please remember that.' Carissa nodded. 'I suppose it's possible. I haven't really given it much thought.'

Carissa pondered this while the Inventor picked up the welding torch and mask and resumed his work on the wolf. She knew the city disposed of Originals when their Copies exceeded them in their ability to learn. Carissa regretted not getting to know her own Original before she died.

The Inventor stopped welding and put down the torch. His movements were slow. 'Time for you to go now, miss. If there's nothing else, I'm going to finish up here and go home for the evening.'

But Carissa wasn't quite ready to let the Inventor go. 'I've been watching the most recent group. The one from Arcis. I want to help them.'

'Yes, I know. You have a good heart.'

'But I didn't tell you why.' The Inventor removed his apron and folded it, listening. 'There's someone in their group who's very important to me. Someone I want to save.'

'Who?'

'My sister. June.'

The Inventor frowned at her for what felt like minutes. Then he shook his head and smiled. 'Well, I never. Is this the first time we've had a human and Copy sibling pair here, together?'

'You have to help me, Inventor. The Collective has terrible things planned for her—for all of them. '

The Inventor narrowed his gaze at her. 'What exactly are you asking, miss?'

'I want to help rescue the humans from Arcis and go with them.' He flinched. 'But I want to do it properly this time. Not like last time. I want to help. Quintus will never know.'

The Inventor's nostrils flared. 'Nobody can leave this place. How many more people have to die for you to understand that? When we're caught, and we will be caught, the Collective will kill me and terminate you.'

'Please, Inventor. I don't like this city any more. I don't like how cold the Copies are, or how June is treated. The only good thing that happens is when new Originals arrive in the city. But they're worn down, used and tossed away. I want to save them before the Collective disposes of them.'

The Inventor pursed his thin lips. 'You know full well we've been here before, miss.'

'This is different—I promise you. I'm hiding things from Quintus now. I wasn't before.'

She waited, hopeful.

The Inventor thought for a moment. 'I've never seen you speak so passionately about living before. Existing, yes, but not much more. If you need my help, I'll give it to you.'

An idea came to her. 'What if I tell the Collective that I want to live beyond the confines of Copy life? Isn't that what Quintus and the others are doing all this for? To create a life that can exist in the world beyond this city?'

The Inventor's expression darkened. 'You must never tell them that.'

'Why not?'

'Because the Collective is addicted to learning, miss. Quintus won't stop. The group has no empathy, only power.' He sighed. 'Maybe this was a mistake. I gave up on the idea of escape a long time ago.'

But Carissa had hope. 'We will escape, Inventor. And I want Vanessa to come too, and to bring her books.'

'The Collective has the ability to terminate you remotely if you leave city.'

Carissa had thought about that on the way over. 'I know how to go offline.' She touched the disc in the side of her head, connected to her NMC. 'But I'll need your help to access the connection.'

The Inventor visibly perked up. 'Of course. Your NMC. We can try, miss. But I'll need to run the idea of escaping past Vanessa. I trust that woman with my

life, but I warn you, she'll be hesitant after the last
time. If she says it's a good idea, then I'll listen.'

18

CANYA

Canya wanted to scream at Dom's refusal to accept her. The dark, tiny library room that smelled of musty old books irritated her more than she let on. But Vanessa's appearance every ten minutes topped both of those annoyances.

The Librarian pretended these visits were about checking her biogel levels; she even brought with her a thermometer and a stethoscope. Canya might be a newborn, but she wasn't born yesterday.

Vanessa wanted the name of the rebel stronghold in the mountains.

Yeah, Canya knew where it was. What was in it for her, besides being locked in a room that felt more public than private?

The Librarian was back. She closed the door and sat down beside Canya. But instead of taking her temperature, as she had every other time, she grabbed her hand.

'What do you remember of Anya's time in

Brookfield? Please, Canya. It's important.'

'I told you I don't remember anything.'

'Think, Canya. Please.' Vanessa gave her hand a squeeze. 'Back to the time when her parents were still alive. Did Evan or Grace ever mention a place in the mountains?'

Canya glanced at their touching hands. She liked how warm Vanessa's hand felt, but not enough to give up her only leverage. 'No. I'm pretty sure I'd remember that, and if I did I would have said already.'

'I'm sorry to push. But you're my only link to that place.'

'Then why don't you just leave Praesidium and go find it yourself?' Canya reclaimed her hand.

'Because I'm not allowed to leave. And the energy barrier that surrounds this city is dangerous. Nothing can get out. The only way in is through the portal you arrived through.'

Canya folded her arms, bunching up her white pyjama top. 'Then use the portal.'

Vanessa smiled sadly. 'To work, the portal must be connected to a power source. When the urbanos were dismantled, I think it was disconnected. We haven't had anyone new to the city since the last group.'

Canya shrugged. 'Well, I don't control the portals, and I don't remember the place in the mountains. If you need to find it so badly, just ask Anya.'

It angered Canya to say her name; the girl who

stood between her and Dom. She wanted to know what was so special about her, and why Dom still pined for her. She pictured Anya weak and alone, crying and pathetic in some room. Canya was stronger than that. Soon Dom would realise his mistake in dismissing her from his room.

'You know that's not possible,' said Vanessa, sounding irritated. 'Anya no longer has her memories. And you won't either in a few days. The Collective doesn't permit newborns to keep them.'

That gave her a few days to string Vanessa along, and to work out how she could keep her only link to Dom.

She would continue to fight until Dom accepted her.

An intimate memory of Dom and Anya kissing shook her to the core. Cold, hard jealousy leaked into her bones, making her hands shake. She unfolded her arms and stood up, away from Vanessa, away from the gross feeling that crawled over her skin.

'I need to get out of this room. I can't stand it here any more. Let me come live with you.'

'I'm sorry, that's not possible. This is the only place we can talk without risk of being overheard. The Copies can't record down here, possibly because the thick walls block the signal.'

'The Copies talk, you know. The Collective can find out in other ways.'

Vanessa gave her a frosty stare. 'This space also benefits you, Canya. We must protect it. We both need something from each other.'

'And what do I need from you, exactly?'

'My guidance.' Vanessa stood up. 'If the Collective thinks you're unable to handle Copy life after you're connected, Quintus will terminate you. He can make another copy of Anya. The Collective doesn't value life like humans do.'

Canya shivered, wrapping her arms around her middle. 'Then I'll refuse to be connected. I'll just stay as I am.'

'It's not possible. You were born for this life. And you will not survive without the Collective. The NMC will give you access to the Collective's network and help you understand the world around you. Without it, your ability to learn will be severely limited to your environment and those you interact with.'

'But isn't that all you humans have? Limited minds and no chip?'

Vanessa nodded. 'Limited, maybe, but we have years to develop our brains. Yours is infantile. Without the chip, it may not evolve at all and you would be unable to look after—'

A sharp knock on the door froze both Canya and Vanessa to the spot.

'Open up, Librarian!'

Canya stumbled back from the loud, angry voice.

Vanessa checked her watch. 'It's after eight. What do they want?' She opened the door to reveal two guards. 'I'm in here with a newborn. Can't this wait until later?'

The guards pushed past her. 'The Collective

wants this room sealed permanently. You and the newborn will need to leave.'

'Why?'

'We have reports that this area is a signal blind spot. The Collective has ordered this room off limits.'

Canya felt a sudden attachment to *her* room as the guards looked around. One of them caught her staring. She shivered at the lack of empathy in his dead, cold eyes.

'Gather your things, Canya,' said Vanessa, watching the guards.

She made sure to grab her new yellow dress and some spare white clothes, as well as the hairbrush and hand mirror Vanessa had given to her on her arrival at the library. A book Vanessa had loaned her sat on the bed. She left it and headed for the door.

Vanessa smiled at the guards. 'Please inform the Collective that I wasn't aware of the anomaly. Do I have time to take some books?'

'No. Our orders are to seal the room immediately. If you stay, you will be sealed in here, too.'

Vanessa pushed Canya out the door and up the stairs.

'Where will we go?' Canya heard the two guards ransacking the room below.

'You wanted to see my apartment? Well, now you've got your chance.'

Ω

Eliza Green

They travelled on foot through D's inner zones to a subsection with single-storey accommodation. Canya felt the familiar tingle in her wrist as the tag station picked up her location. She followed Vanessa down a narrow corridor—*Section C, 28–40*—to a door labelled *28*. Vanessa unlocked the door and a curious Canya stepped inside.

'I live alone,' said Vanessa. 'And this is a human-only complex.'

Canya took in the small studio space with a kitchen at one end and an alcove with a bed at the other. A grey sofa sat next to the kitchen area. The white walls matched the floor, but splashes of maroon and teal lifted the drab dark-wood interior. She wasn't surprised to see a stuffed bookshelf against one wall. A small white screen was mounted opposite.

The windowless apartment reminded her of the place they'd just vacated. But unlike her storage room with a bed, this was new, and exciting.

'There's not much space, as you can see. You'll have to take the sofa.'

Canya set down her things while Vanessa activated the wall-mounted screen. It showed her a map of Praesidium. She flicked the image away and checked an inbox for messages.

Canya tried to read one of the messages, but Vanessa swiped it away too fast. She plucked up a maroon-coloured cushion from the sofa.

'Why do you use colour?'

Vanessa read another message.

Canya dropped the cushion and moved closer to

the screen. 'Practically everything in Praesidium is white. The Copies dress in white. Yet, humans use colour. Why?'

Vanessa swiped a message off-screen and turned round. 'Colour ignites our deepest emotions. A black-and-white world is no world at all.'

'How long do I have to stay here?'

'Until you're reset and connected. Then you'll be assigned your own apartment in Zone E with the other Copies.'

'Can I come back and visit after my first week?'

Vanessa steered Canya to the sofa, away from the screen that she desperately wanted to use. 'You won't remember this week. You won't remember me.'

A deep sadness hit her as she perched on the edge of the sofa. Would she miss Vanessa?

'What's wrong? Is it your biogel? Do you need topping up?' A concerned Vanessa hovered over her.

'I can't control my moods.' Canya felt close to tears. 'It's frustrating. I feel up then down. I can't sit still yet I don't want to move.'

'That's normal. You've gone from experiencing nothing to everything. It's too much for you now, but it will pass.'

'Why can't I stop thinking about Dom?'

'That too will pass. Give it time.'

She didn't want it to pass. And as much as she hated Vanessa's intrusion, she felt a sudden empathy for her. 'You've been so good to me, and I've been nothing but trouble. What do you want to know about Anya's past? I'll try to remember for you.'

Vanessa shushed her and walked over to the kitchen. She came back with a pen and paper and handed it to her. 'When you remember, write it down.'

Canya sat with the paper on her lap and the pen in her hand. She held it millimetres over the page, while Vanessa grabbed a spare pillow and blanket and dropped them on the sofa.

Vanessa flashed her a smile and got ready for bed. 'Whenever you're ready, write it down.'

Canya tucked the items under her pillow and lay down. Within minutes, Vanessa had turned off the light and was in her own bed.

She could so easily write down the name of the mountain range that shared its name with a common metal. But her empathy disappeared as soon as it had arrived, along with her desire to help the Librarian.

She stared up at the ceiling and thought of something happier: Dom. How could she feel this strongly about him and it be wrong?

In the dark of the room, Canya concentrated on the only thing that mattered now.

Making Dom Pavesi hers.

19

ANYA

Day Four

Her skin flushed at her thoughts. Scorching heat licked at her bones. Alex sat opposite her, cross-legged on the floor. She bit her finger as her gaze tracked the smallest of movements he made. A tray of food sat between them; the usual post-treatment treat.

She fought to keep the control Rapture slowly leeched from her. All she had to do was ride the wave, wait for the peak to hit, then slide back down the other side. But each time, the slide shortened, keeping her closer to Rapture's control than her own.

Her body tightened as the urges, raw and animal, tried to take over. She squeezed her eyes shut. Just one more hour.

She hoped.

On the food tray were strawberries, melted chocolate, asparagus, slices of watermelon and a bottle of red wine.

Known aphrodisiacs.

Alex picked up a strawberry. He touched his tongue to the fruit and took a bite. Anya devoured the sight of him as if he were the only meal she needed. What if he gave her neck the same attention? She massaged the sensitive area just below her ears. Her clothes felt tight and uncomfortable.

Alex looked up, suddenly aware of her. He grabbed another strawberry and crawled forward, holding it inches from Anya's mouth. She strained forward to take a bite of the sweet, tangy fruit. He smiled and kept it just out of reach.

'I might have to bite your finger if you don't let me have it,' she said.

'Have what?'

'The strawberry. It looks good.'

Alex looked good.

'And here's me thinking you were talking about something else.'

His wild gaze caused Anya's breath to hitch. Recently, their playful teasing had given way to light touching. New rules designed to curb their temptation had been established. Keeping a set distance apart was one.

'You want it?'

Alex continued to tease her with the strawberry. She leaned in, drawn to the almost-erotic play between them.

Screw the rules. The rules are stupid.

She plucked it from his hand, careful not to touch him.

'It's probably safer if I feed it to myself.'

He sat back on his heels. 'Sorry. I don't know why I did that. I saw the strawberry and your mouth and—'

Anya held up her hand. 'I get the picture. And it wasn't just you.'

Her stomach rumbled. The chocolate smelled decadent, wicked. She dipped the strawberry in and licked the chocolate that ran down her fingers. This food did nothing for her state of mind.

She made a quick excuse and washed the chocolate off her fingers. At the sink she took a slow breath and splashed cold water on her face and neck.

'Are you struggling as much as I am?' said Alex. She turned when she heard a cork popping. Alex held the bottle of red wine.

'What are you doing? Alcohol's the last thing we should be having.'

Alex ignored her and poured himself a glass. 'Alcohol inhibits blood flow to certain areas.'

'But it also breaks down inhibitions, so you're more likely to give in to temptations.'

He took a gulp. 'Yeah? Well, that's already in full swing, so I don't see the harm.'

Anya turned back to the mirror and leaned forward. Her dark-blue eyes, which used to shine, now looked dull. The unflattering overhead light only made her pale skin ghostlike. If Alex hadn't told her about the time she'd lost in Arcis, the three month's worth of hair growth would have given her a clue. When she first got sick in Brookfield, her hair had grazed the tops of her shoulders. Now it hung past them.

The person who looked back at her was a stranger. And it wasn't because of this place. Something major had happened to her in Arcis. She could feel it. Her heart ached too much. The closer she and Alex got, the worse the feeling became.

Her thoughts scattered at the sound of movement behind her. Alex slipped in behind her. She could smell the alcohol on his breath.

Despite the rules, she leaned back into him. Her hot skin craved his touch. He looked at her through the mirror. His wild blond hair matched the look in his eyes.

Tiny sparks of electricity had her skin buzzing. She closed her eyes when his hands rested on her hips. 'Alex, we can't.'

'Why not?' He pressed all of him against her.

'Because we agreed not to.'

'I'm not strong like you, Anya. I can't do this. Please let me touch you.'

The ache in her chest, the one she couldn't explain, grew. She fought for space and Alex backed off. 'It's not just that.'

'What, then?'

'It feels as if I'm cheating on someone. Even though there's nobody like that for me. I can't explain it.'

'There might have been someone in Arcis.'

Anya turned round. 'Someone who came to Praesidium, you mean?'

'Possibly.' Alex blinked fast, as if he'd been in a trance. 'I'm sorry. I don't know what came over me. It was like someone else was controlling me.'

'It's okay. But no more wine.'

He grinned. 'I can't promise that. But maybe I'll wait until the urges lessen first.'

'I'm serious.' She folded her arms. They needed new rules.

'So am I. I need alcohol. It helps me to forget that this is where I belong.'

She blushed at her insensitivity. 'I'm sorry, I didn't know that was how you felt. And don't say you belong here—because you don't.'

The wild look was back, but Alex seemed more in control. He nodded at Anya's top. 'You splashed water on yourself.'

She looked down at two large patches of wet that had turned her top see-through. 'I'd better change.'

Alex grinned. 'I wasn't complaining.'

'Stop, Alex. We have to resist.' Despite herself, her lips curled up into a smile.

She grabbed her hoodie from the chair at the vanity table when the door opened. Her medic entered, much to Anya's surprise. She normally stayed by the open door.

'I was just with you an hour ago.' Anya zipped up the hoodie over her wet top, covering her chest. 'I'm not scheduled for another round.'

The medic glanced at the tray of food. 'Put some shoes on and come with me.'

She shot Alex a worried look. He just shrugged.

What else could he do?

Fear replaced her raw, unbridled feelings for Alex. She welcomed the break.

The medic led her to a new part of the facility, past the treatment rooms. Anya frowned as she followed her down a set of stairs.

At the bottom, the medic pressed her wrist to a panel beside a door. She pulled Anya from the stairwell into an open area with a door on either side, and stopped outside the one on the left.

They entered a long corridor with one wall made of glass. Beyond the glass was a large space partitioned into three sections. The first section held a single gurney surrounded by various monitoring machines. In the second, a group of children aged between four and eight played alone with colouring books and puzzles on the floor.

Anya studied the scene that had a vague familiarity to it. Was she having another Arcis flashback?

Her curiosity kept her close to the medic. In the last section, four girls wearing white tended to babies in cots. Anya had never seen the girls before, but one stood out: a tall girl with long golden-brown hair.

'What is this place? Some sort of crèche?' She turned to the medic.

'It's the Nurturing Centre. It's where your baby will be brought when you conceive.'

'I told you. I'm not having a baby.'

'You cannot resist the treatments. You are valuable to the Collective. You do not have a choice.'

'I do have a choice and I will resist.'

'Then you will die.'

Anya didn't want to die, but she wouldn't be forced to conceive either. 'Then I choose death.'

The medic grunted and shook Anya's arm. 'Why are you so stubborn? I'm showing you your purpose here. That purpose is to make provision for the Nurturing Centre. You are doing a good thing. You are helping the Collective to break free.'

'But I'm being forced to do something I don't want to do. You're robbing me of my freedom. Don't you know what that's like?'

This was just like the town tradition of matching, where boys and girls as young as fifteen were paired up for marriage and babies. She hadn't had any say about that, either.

'Yes, I do.'

'What you're doing, it's no different than matching.'

The medic sneered. 'A ridiculous town tradition that excluded Originals from joining our Breeder programme.'

Excluded? Not in Anya's experience. The fights she and her mother had had over the practice were legendary in Brookfield.

'Why? If the Collective wanted us, it only had to ignore the tradition.'

'Because the Collective wanted to protect the identity of its programme, and choosing females who hadn't been forced into the matching tradition was easier than revealing its true purpose to the people.'

182

Anya didn't understand. 'They took me, even though my mother said I was matched.'

'The Collective grew tired of playing it safe.' The medic sounded tired. 'Your mother was killed to remove the threat.'

Anya's mouth went dry.

'But the rebels killed my parents...'

'That's what the Collective wanted you to think. The townspeople already hated the rebels. It was easy to sow the seed of doubt.'

She couldn't believe what she was hearing. Another lie?

'Why are you telling me this?'

'Because there is no longer a need for the ruse.'

So, Grace had been trying to save her life?

The medic started for the exit. Anya followed stiffly as all the rotten names she'd called her mother flooded her mind.

She shook her head. The medic was chatty, giving her a rare opportunity to learn more. Right now, nothing else mattered.

'You said the Collective is trying to break free. From what?'

'From its confines. It has been made a prisoner, like you. Your contribution to the Nurturing Centre will help it achieve its goal faster.'

'What about you and your freedom? Are you trapped here, too?'

'No. I was created here. That means I will die here.'

'Your words or the Collective's?'

118-C grabbed her arm, pulled her along. 'Mine. I have never desired freedom like you Originals do.'

'That's because you've never had it.' Anya vainly tried to pull her arm free. 'Wouldn't you like to live your life as you want? Or work somewhere other than the medical facility? You said this wasn't your first choice.'

'I was created to serve the Collective. I consider it a great honour to have this role, to look after the test subjects.' Despite her outward defiance, the medic looked wistful.

Test subjects?

'Tell me about this Collective you work for. Where is it? Can I meet the Ten?'

The medic shook her head, as if waking from a daze. 'This was a mistake, bringing you down here. I thought that if I showed you what you are helping to create, you would understand your importance.'

'What importance? What are we creating?'

'A means of escape.'

'If freedom is so important to your Collective, tell them to let me go.'

The medic stayed silent as she pulled her up the stairs.

'Where are you taking me?' said Anya.

'Back to your room. You will be forced to comply with the Collective's orders, ingrate.'

20

CARISSA

Carissa stopped when she saw the Inventor hurrying across the courtyard. She was so used to seeing him in his workshop, stooped over some repair, surrounded by wolf parts and digging machines. She didn't think he went anywhere other than home to his apartment.

Her heart fluttered in her chest when she saw him headed for the Learning Centre.

She ran to catch up with him. 'Inventor, what are you doing up here?'

He slowed, flustered. 'Miss. I didn't see you there. The Collective needs to see me about something.'

Originals weren't permitted inside the Learning Centre. She noticed his surprise, too—like when she'd told him about June.

Other Copies showed interest in their conversation. Carissa adopted an air of formality with the Inventor, an interaction that Quintus would see when they uploaded. 'I need to speak to you. When will you return to the workshop?'

To her relief, the Inventor picked up on her cue. 'Soon. Why don't you drop by in a little while? I won't be long, and I need to run some diagnostics on you.'

She nodded and held her chin up, dying to ask why Quintus had sent for him. 'I will be there soon, Inventor.'

Carissa watched him go and walked round to the back of the centre, to an oak tree. Her orb was playful today, almost demanding. She indulged it with a game of chase and tried to keep up as it circled the tree. She followed when it broke off, dodging Copies, circling several tagging stations close by. She needed the distraction. What did Quintus want with *her* Inventor?

After an hour of play, Carissa commanded the orb to the pocket of her white dress. It nestled in the cocoon of fabric.

She had to see the Inventor. Had he spoken to Vanessa yet? Was he going to help her rescue June and the others? Would she leave the city before Quintus ordered her termination?

She returned to the courtyard, passing by several curious Copies. With a deep breath, she opened the door and descended into the part of the city avoided by most of the Copies.

An agitated Inventor was up high on a ladder attaching wolf parts to hooks affixed to girders in the ceiling.

Carissa's presence drew his attention, and he started to climb down.

'There you are! You took your time. I've got better things to do than wait for you.'

'You didn't say how long I should wait before coming to see you.'

'It doesn't matter. You're here now.' The Inventor strode past Carissa. At the entrance he turned. 'Hurry.'

She followed him down a tunnel that led away from the stairs and deeper into the underground of the city. This part of the city wasn't on her map, which included blank sections and dead-end passageways.

The occasional wall-mounted sconce brightened the way. The other Copies had a natural fear of dark spaces; the Inventor believed it to be a flaw in the copying process. The bright-white city created the illusion of space, a design intended to counter the Copies' claustrophobia. The humans didn't seem to have the same issues with the dark. In fact, they often sought out places of solitude in the gloomiest corners of the city. Once, Carissa had seen a group of them out at night, staring up at the starry sky. She liked to watch them when they thought nobody else was around.

Even with her connection to the shared network, which sounded like a low hum of voices permanently in the background, Carissa often felt alone. Hearing voices didn't compare with talking to real people.

After a ten-minute walk, they came to a dead end.

'What are we doing here?' She looked around at the space that was familiar to her; she'd come here after she'd told Quintus about the escape attempt.

The Inventor turned to her. 'This spot is the halfway point between my workshop and the medical facility. The tunnel runs right into a bunch of disused corridors on the other side of the Nurturing Centre, on the lowest level of the facility. Turns out, this is also a blind spot that the network signal doesn't reach.'

Carissa studied the bricked-up wall in front of her. 'But it's a dead end, Inventor.'

'Don't lie to me, Carissa. You've been here before. The bricks can be removed. In fact, you watched me do it once before.'

She blushed at being caught out in her lie. As soon as she'd stopped the Inventor from joining the others in their escape attempt, she'd bricked up the wall to hide evidence that the passageway existed.

'Why would I have use for it?'

The Inventor shook his head. 'To help the others escape, miss. Isn't that what you wanted? This is the safest route out. There's another set of stairs not far from the main road leading to Zone E and the edge of the city.'

Yes, they had spoken about it, but Carissa hadn't expected things to happen this fast.

The Inventor placed a hand on her shoulder. 'But there's another reason I brought you here, to this exact spot. The signal. I know you're not able to record in areas where the network's signal is lost, like the room under the library.'

Carissa swallowed, dreading the answer to her next question.

'What did the Collective want with you?'

'Quintus asked me if Vanessa had ever spoken to me about the library room below ground. The one the Collective couldn't access via the network. And while I was being interrogated, I wondered how Quintus even knew about it. They knew I'd visited Vanessa there. They've since sealed it off and we no longer have access to the room. The only other person who knew about it was you.'

Carissa's pulse beat so hard she thought she might need a diagnostic. 'The Ten found the gaps in my memories. I had to tell them.'

'Miss, that space was extremely important. You shouldn't have said anything. Vanessa is very upset.'

'I didn't have a choice. The Ten were going to terminate me.'

'Terminate you?' The Inventor's eyes widened. 'Did they threaten you?'

Carissa averted her eyes. 'Well, no. Not exactly.' She looked up at him. 'But it was implied.'

'Well, I guess we can add lying to your repertoire of skills. The Collective has threatened termination of Copies before, but Quintus has never actually ordered it. He has no problem killing humans, though. Do you think it's possible the Collective might be serious about it this time?'

Carissa nodded. 'If they discover my intention to help the humans escape. No Copy has ever betrayed them like this before.'

'No. I guess not.'

Carissa almost apologised for her part in killing his wife, but the words stuck in her throat. Maybe some things were best left unsaid. She would prove her remorse to him instead.

The Inventor examined the brick wall. 'Be thankful this conversation won't be recorded. But you'll need to work on manipulating your memories in a more seamless way if this plan is to work.'

Carissa's mood brightened. 'Does that mean you're going to help me?'

'I had managed to speak to Vanessa before the guards shut off all access to the room. Vanessa is keen to attempt another Praesidium escape, and I can't say I'm too fond of this city any more. Not that I ever was.'

'So why did you stay so long, after, you know, the last time?'

'Old age will make a man tired.' He huffed out a breath. 'I was tired of fighting. But I saw a change in you and it gave me hope.'

'Hope? How?'

'You cared about the last group who came through the portal. I had no idea your Original's sister was among them. It shamed me that I'd done nothing to help the poor folk who wound up in this place. Vanessa and I agreed it was time to lift our heads out of the sand and put a stop to this butchering, and the experiments.'

'This is a plan to save a few, Inventor. It won't be possible to save everyone.'

'No, it won't. It's too late for many who've come to think of this place as home. But young Anya and Dom and others, like your sister—they haven't given up hope. They're still fighting for their freedom.'

Carissa buzzed with excitement at the thought of rescuing June and Anya. 'We need to move fast, Inventor. I'll only keep the Collective off my back for so long before Quintus starts asking questions again.'

He paused. 'You should know something, Carissa, about my meeting with Quintus. He told me the medical facility is now off limits to any unauthorised personnel. That may include you.'

No.

'But I need to see June. Tell her what we're planning.'

'You can try, but the guards may not let you in. For now, forget we had this conversation. Keep going to the medical facility until the Collective tells you not to. Then we resort to using the tunnel.' He turned to start the walk back. 'First, I want to show you a little memory-overlapping technique I learned while working on the Copies.'

Ω

Carissa left the Inventor behind in his workshop. He'd shown her how to restructure her memories in a way that would fool the Collective. Specifically, he'd taught her how to manipulate certain points in the recording by layering one experience over another, rather than cutting one part out and replacing it with a different moment of time, as she'd been doing so far. This would create a more seamless transition that wouldn't feel jarring to the final observer.

Keen to test out her access to the medical facility, she approached the two Copies keeping guard outside. She pressed her clammy hands to her sides as she gained entry. At least Quintus hadn't revoked her access yet. It could be a test of her loyalty to the Collective.

She rode the elevator down to the second level, where she passed by a trio of treatment rooms and a couple of medics in the corridor that led to June's room.

Carissa opened June's door to find the room empty. She backtracked to the treatment rooms and climbed the stairs to the viewing platform. The chief medic, 28-C, was alone. The medic nodded, hands hidden behind her back.

Carissa stood beside her, mirroring the medic's stance. 'I noticed 229-O wasn't in her room. Where is she? The Collective wishes to study my interactions with her.'

'229-O has been transferred to the Nurturing Centre and is awaiting foetus transfer.'

'For how long?'

'A couple of days. We need to monitor her vitals. The Collective is particularly interested in her state before and after the procedure. She will be labelled as Patient Zero. The Collective wants to use her statistics to drive the next stage in the programme.'

'Next stage?'

The medic studied her with a bemused smile. 'I thought you were Quintus' favourite. Does he not tell you everything?'

Carissa swallowed her fear. 'It would appear not.'

'The new children will be fitted with NMCs and their growth further accelerated before we send them out into the real world. If they manage to fool the humans, the Collective won't have any more need for this place.'

The NMCs would give the Collective full control over the new children. 'What will happen to us and this place?'

'Probably destroyed. I think we will be reassigned. Quintus has been vague on those details.'

28-C turned away suddenly and pressed a finger to her ear. 'But I was only... I thought she had permission to be here, Quintus. Understood.'

The medic spoke to Carissa. 'I am not permitted to discuss details of the tests with you. Your permissions have been revoked. Please return to the lobby and leave this facility. Quintus' orders.'

She had expected the order, but not so soon. 'Understood, 28-C.'

On her way out, she tried to access the medical records using the panel by the guards' station. It blinked red.

Why had the Collective locked her out? Did it consider her a threat? If she couldn't get in, what would happen to June?

She needed to warn the Inventor and Vanessa.

The Collective didn't change plans just like that; it operated within the realms of order and reason. It was planning something.

And unlike the time before the last escape attempt, this time, Carissa had no idea what.

21

DOM

Dom pressed his ear up against the wall and listened. No sound in the next room. He knocked on the wall. One, two, three.

No reply.

Mariella really was dead, and 148-C had played a trick on him. Probably some revenge shit for his spoon attack.

They should have kept up the pretence, used Mariella to bargain with him. It was amazing how much information a little threat against family members could reveal. Deception was clearly not a skill the Copies understood.

Between the surgeries and the violent attitude of his male medic, Dom was edging closer insanity as more control leaked away.

But one thing had caught his attention: the attitude of the female medic, 118-C.

Her hostility towards him in the beginning had been as palpable as the male's. But two operations and four days later, her stance had softened. Could he bargain with her?

118-C turned up an hour later and ordered him to his feet. His scars had mostly healed; a late injection of the healing accelerator had helped. He felt no pain and no different with the Fourth Gen tech inside him. If anything, he felt stronger. Could he use his new strength to his advantage?

He studied the female in her white uniform, with a bright-red trim around both cuffs and a stiff collar that covered most of her neck. Her icy gaze lingered on him a little too long, as if her mind was elsewhere.

Dom returned her stare until she stiffened and blinked away her distraction. 'You need to come with me.'

More tests. He knew what to expect now. If Fourth Gen made him strong, Fifth Gen could make him stronger—assuming that was the Collective's plan. But before he went under, he had to know something.

'The others in my group. What happened to them?'

The medic pulled him out of the room. 'They are helping the Collective with its mission.'

'Mission?'

'To escape.'

'Sheila Kouris, June Shaw. Are they still alive?'

'As long as the Collective considers them useful to its plans, they will be kept alive.'

The medic pushed him down the corridor, ahead of her. Dom considered making a break for it, but changed his mind when he saw two males waiting at the end. They turned and took the lead.

Dom swallowed. 'And Anya Macklin? Is she still... useful?'

He thought he heard 118-C draw a quick breath. 'For now. Keep moving.'

'Why haven't I seen them on this floor?'

They reached the testing room. One of the males opened the door while the other dragged Dom inside. Both attempted to lift him onto the gurney. He twisted out of their grip more easily than before.

Fourth Gen.

Huh.

'Hands off. I know the drill.' He hid his secret from them and climbed, unassisted, onto the table.

Only then did 118-C answer his question. 'They have been confined to a different floor.'

How had the other Anya managed to get inside his room? 'So there's no chance they might be on this floor?'

The female shook her head. 'Only medics have access to this floor.'

Her answer didn't satisfy him. 'Nobody else?'

'Copies, newborns, those who are still learning. The Collective gives the newborns unrestricted access.'

'What are newborns?'

'Like your new teenagers. Going through puberty and not yet mature enough to link with the Collective.'

'How long before they mature?'

'A week.'

The straps on Dom's wrists and feet tightened. Had he been too hard on the four-day-old newborn? If she knew him, maybe she had Anya's memories. If he gave her what she wanted, could he convince her to help him escape?

The idea of giving his body to the newborn sickened him. But so did a life of endless surgeries.

The overhead panels opened and the usual arms descended.

The anaesthetic first, then the laser, followed by the familiar blaze of heat it left across his skin. A robotic arm with forceps removed his Fourth Gen liver and replaced it with a new one. *Fifth Gen* was printed on the side.

He barely had time to test out the strength of Fourth. Maybe Fifth would be better.

The table flipped over and the forceps swapped out his other tech.

'What are you doing?'

'We upgraded your Fourth Gen tech to the latest generation,' said the female.

'I guessed that, but what for?'

'It's all part of the testing the Collective wants done on you.'

He received his final shot of immunosuppressives and the table flipped back.

'I'm not some guinea pig for your experiments.'

118-C leaned in closer. Dom caught a brief flicker of doubt in her eyes. 'Humans are all "guinea pigs", as you put it. A crude term but effective nonetheless. The Collective must test on human subjects to understand how the human body works. It can only learn so much from anatomy books.'

'I refuse to be part of your tests. I'm done.'

'You have no choice, Dom Pavesi. You belong to the Collective now.'

Dom grunted as he twisted against his restraints. 'I belong to nobody.'

'Except the rebellion?' The female arched an eyebrow. 'You've carried Second Gen tech in you from the age of seven. The moment you received Praesidium's tech you belonged to the Collective.'

'And what if I don't want this tech any more?'

'That is up to the Collective. Quintus has not cancelled that order.'

The female medic nodded at the two males, who helped Dom off the table. The anaesthetic that made him groggy was starting to wear off. The blazing wounds irritated him more this time than they had after the last surgery.

The door opened, and two new medics marched in a young man dressed in a white tunic. Dom gasped at the sight of his gormless Copy. His mouth was set at a strange angle, turned down completely on one side.

'This is the Copy we made with the Fourth Gen tech,' said the female. 'It cannot see or hear. The biogel failed to recreate a perfect map of your brain. The Copy's brain is missing basic functions. And its optical nerves are damaged.'

'How?'

'It appears the Fourth Gen contaminated the copying process. It was not compatible with your DNA.'

But he'd felt stronger with it than the Second Gen tech.

'So what now?'

'We will continue to make copies of you until we perfect the process.'

Dom leaned against the bed while the males gripped his arms too tight. 'Why not remove the tech and give me back my human organs? Copy me then? You already know it works.'

'Because humans carry diseases and infections that pass through the biogel to the Copies. The Collective wants to strengthen the immune system and biogel so that the new Copies become impervious to illness.'

'Why not test the tech on Copies? Why do you need me?' But he already knew the answer.

'Because once you replicate an Original, you cannot create a copy of that Copy. It weakens the DNA code, makes it less pure.'

A loophole, no matter how insidious, was better than nothing. It meant Sheila, June and Anya would be kept alive. But it also turned his testing into an indefinite process. When would the Collective be happy? He could remain a guinea pig for the rest of his life.

He flexed his hand, testing his Fifth Gen strength. His retreating grogginess made it hard to tell. He would test it out properly back in his room.

'Please step into the machine, Dom Pavesi,' said the female medic.

Dom glanced at the Copy standing beside the replication machine. How could he have confused one of these things for *his* Anya? Still, the newborn had been convincing. What would happen if they got the copying process right and humans could no longer tell the difference?

It had taken a while, but he'd managed to separate the imposter from his Anya. His Anya wouldn't have left him to rot in his cell. His Anya would have helped him escape.

Dom closed his eyes as the blue scanner swept the length of his body.

There were some things a copy machine could never replicate.

22

ANYA

That afternoon, Anya and Alex played cards to keep their minds off other activities. Anya opted for a game of go fish. Alex wanted to play poker.

'Go fish is a kid's game,' he said.

'It's that or gin rummy.'

'Please, not gin rummy again.' Alex groaned and patted the floor space beside him. 'Come here, I'll teach you.'

Next to him... feeling the heat from his skin?

Anya swallowed and arranged the cards on the floor. 'I think it's safer if we play my game.' She turned two cards up that didn't match, then turned them back over.

Alex shrugged. 'You're missing out. Poker is way more fun.'

'Just humour me, please? It's keeping my mind occupied.'

Alex sighed and turned over two cards, instantly making a match. He perked up, and soon his pile of cards grew. Anya's concentration was shot to hell. She couldn't remember what he'd turned over last. She used to be great at this game—she'd beaten Jason every time.

Alex's smile widened as he matched yet another pair of cards. Anya, with just four matches, accepted her second place.

He glanced at her miserable collection. 'You ready to call it quits yet? As much as I enjoy winning, this is boring.'

She agreed with a sigh and pushed her matched cards into the centre of the game. 'I'm done.'

She stood and stretched, unleashing a bout of nervous energy. Her fingers grazed the wall and stopped at the hidden panel. She opened it, found the music; turned it on, then off again.

Alex watched her while he tidied the cards. Her urges weren't as strong as they had been before the game. Rapture's hold on her had loosened, and with it her attraction to Alex. A temporary reprieve. Soon, the medics would be back to top up their treatment.

Alex gathered up the last of the cards and packed them away in the drawer of the vanity table.

'I feel like I have better control over it,' he said, turning round. 'You?'

She nodded. 'A little on edge, but I'm in control again.'

'You look like you're ready to break out of this place.'

'I would if I knew how.' It was a straightforward route to the treatment rooms, but the corridor carried on further to an unchecked area. Since 118-C never let Anya out of her sight, it would remain that way for now.

The stairs to the Nurturing Centre was a new piece of information. But she had no desire to go further down than she already was.

There must be an elevator. There must be a surface.

Surface of what?

Was this really the same Praesidium she'd visited as a child? The library had been the only stop on the tour, and she'd been too fascinated with the collection of books on display to ask about the city. The male Librarian had promised the tour group that hard work yielded rewards. For a kid from a poor town, rewards didn't get much bigger than working in Praesidium.

'What about charades?' said Alex.

Anya hugged her stomach. 'I'm bored with games.' With Rapture no longer making her skin hot and her pulse pound, she had no problem sitting on the floor opposite him.

Alex leaned his back against the bed and stared at the ceiling. 'So, what do you want to do? Who the hell knows when they're going to come for us again?'

'Can we talk about what I told you yesterday?' She had relayed her conversation with the female medic to him in the bathroom. With the cameras watching now, she left out specifics.

'It sounds like it could be worth exploring.'

'Yeah, sometimes I get the impression there's something to work with, but then it disappears.' She referred to a chatty 118-C taking her to the Nurturing Centre and ignoring her after.

'Try again. We've got nothing to lose any more.'

'What about yours?' The male medic who came for Alex gave off a dangerous vibe.

'A laugh a minute. Seriously, I can't get a word in edgeways.' He rolled his eyes.

'How about we talk for a while?' Anya crossed her legs. 'I think it's a safe enough activity.'

'I really should be offended by your attempts to avoid me.' He sat up and raked his hands down his body. 'Most girls would fall over themselves to get a piece of this.'

She laughed, and though she followed the movement of his hands, she didn't feel the intense burn of post-treatment stirrings. The stirrings were still there, but now they simmered. A slow burn.

'I'm not most girls.'

'No, I guess you're not.' His soft gaze forced her to clear her throat.

'So tell me, in the eight months you've been here, have you never thought about escaping?'

Alex stretched out his legs in front of him. 'Of course I have. It's all I did for the first three months.'

'What happened?'

'The Copies punished me in every manner conceivable.'

'What did they do?'

'Let's just say I started out a boy and they created a man.'

Alex was being evasive. She wanted details, but

was it any of her business? 'What were the other girls like? The ones brought in to pair with you?'

He focused on the ceiling. 'Scared, terrified. It was the same for me at the start, so I took comfort in the fact I wasn't alone.' His eyes met Anya's. 'When the treatments started, I didn't know what they were. Rapture can do strange things to girls.'

'What do you mean?'

'I said before that some were resentful pre-treatment. Rapture only heightened those feelings. The girls took their anger out on me—a lot.'

'That sounds awful.'

'Actually, it wasn't.' He paused, as if searching for the right words. 'I could deal with anger. Fury is a potent thing, but if used in the right way it's what gives us our passion. I didn't like the hitting so much before sex, or the biting during it, but it was an emotion I could relate to because I felt similar things. The difference was, I wasn't physically lashing out at them like they were at me. Don't get me wrong. I didn't encourage the violence. But at times I wanted to feel the pain, because it made things real. It reminded me that while Rapture trapped us in this spell of false attraction, our true personalities could still surface.'

Anya swallowed to hide her shock. 'You said not all were like that.'

'No. At least the angry girls were being honest about it. Some just sat in the corner and whimpered. They were scared of me, even though I did everything I could to make them feel comfortable. I hated that.'

'You hated that they were crying?'

Alex squirmed. 'Partly. I saw it as a weakness. I mean, Praesidium isn't going to release you just because you unleash a torrent of waterworks, right? So why waste that energy trying?'

'Sometimes crying is good.'

'I agree, in the right circumstances. But not all the time, when your energies are better spent figuring a way out. Take you, for example. The minute you saw me, you wanted nothing to do with me. But you weren't scared. You were determined to keep me at bay. I respected that. I mean, who lets a total stranger be intimate with them so soon?'

Being intimate with Alex was all Anya had thought about since meeting him. 'People who have no choice?'

'But resisting gives us a choice. Puts the control back in our hands. It's been a long time since I've felt in control of anything. I hated being around the weepy girls, so I tried to make things easier for them. Nothing worked. It was like they wanted to stay helpless. It wasn't good for my own state of mind. I absorbed their weaknesses until they became my own. The fit between us was all wrong, yet I allowed it to happen. I hated myself for being so weak and I hated them for making me feel weak. I hated this place for keeping me prisoner.'

'What did the medics do to you in here, Alex? Besides the treatments, that is.'

He smirked. 'They burned me, healed me. Kept me awake for days. Starved me. Beat me. Took away my privileges. They used to let me go up top for an hour a day. Being locked in the same room day in, day out kills your enthusiasm for life. This room is a beautiful prison, but being here all the time made me less cooperative. So they agreed to let me out, supervised.'

'Do you think they'll let us go up top?'

'Nah. I ruined that idea when I tried to escape. They found other ways to make me cooperate.'

She shivered at the thought. 'How have you managed alone for all this time?'

'I've adjusted my expectations. If I no longer hope for something, I won't be disappointed when I don't get it.'

'That's a terrible way to live.'

'When you no longer have the choices you want, you live with the ones you're given.'

Anya shook her head. 'That's not true. My parents are dead. I have to live with that because I can't bring them back. But everything else is possible. Jason is still out there and I'm not dead. So where there's life, there's hope.'

Alex laughed. 'How optimistic of you. Do you really think you're ever leaving this place?'

'Don't you?'

A muscle in Alex's jaw twitched. 'I gave up on that hope a long time ago.'

She didn't believe him. 'You said I came from a place called Arcis and there were others who came here, too.'

He nodded. 'Three females and a male.'

'Do I know them?' With no memories of the place, she doubted it. But her flashbacks showed her a boy with short dark hair and brown eyes. Was he a friend?

'I only know what town you came from and that you were in Arcis. You'd have been in there for at least three months, so it's likely you do know them.'

'*Three months?*'

Alex nodded. 'Minimum.'

She looked away but not before she saw the pity in Alex's eyes.

He could keep it. She didn't want it.

Anger inside her sharpened her senses. She'd lost not only her freedom, but also her memories, her friends. Her life.

Now the Collective was taking her innocence.

Or maybe that was already gone.

Alex's pitying glances were beginning to irritate her. What had the Collective done to this bright, intelligent man before her?

If Alex refused to fight for his life, then she would do it for him.

23

CARISSA

Serving the Collective used to be enough for her. But rules and order no longer held the same interest, not since the arrival of June and the others.

Carissa completed her morning upload in the Learning Centre before attending mandatory classes with other Copies her age. She sat through a range of questions designed to test her psychological strength and ability to learn. If she answered wrong, the questions about learning could trip her up and reveal her lack of interest in Praesidium, so she tailored her answers to match Quintus' expectations.

Surrounded by Copies her age that were too self-absorbed to start up a conversation, she looked out of the window, wishing she were outside. The NMC allowed Copies to understand the world around them, yet they observed life though questions and downloads.

All the Original children were dead, terminated after the botched escape attempt that Carissa had helped Quintus to stop. The teenagers now replaced the children, but soon the Collective would have no further use for them either.

'Part of life is saying and doing the wrong thing. Life isn't a perfect set of rules to follow,' the Inventor had said before the teens arrived. 'Humans learn from their mistakes, Copies do not, because they are not allowed to make mistakes. Learning makes me a better person. Those who aren't open to it will stay stuck. That's why the Copies will never be like humans. They have no idea how to unlock their potential.'

'But what about their NMCs?'

'A chip doesn't make them human, miss.' He tapped his chest, over his heart. 'This does.'

Carissa had replayed his conversation for days after. She'd even asked Quintus about it the next time she had an audience with him.

'The Inventor does not take into account the deeper levels of learning we experience,' Quintus had said. 'Humans think on a basic level. He will never comprehend the complexity of our designs. Keep on your path, 173-C. Do not be swayed by talk that is more emotional than analytical. You were created for greater things than the humans. Always remember that.'

After her lessons, Carissa walked around the city for a while. The time to rescue June and the others drew near. Her nerves were a tangled mess. She glanced at the medical facility in the distance, a place she could no longer access. But the 'greater things'

Quintus spoke about were in that building.

She stopped in to see the Inventor as part of her routine, where they kept their conversation brief and deliberately vague. Carissa tempered her feelings of excitement about the rescue plan as she listened to the Inventor explain the inner workings of the machine he fixed. She left shortly after, overlapping her memories as the Inventor had demonstrated.

Carissa hadn't told him about her conversation with 28-C the day before: if a Copy or hybrid successfully fooled the humans, it would be the end of Praesidium. So where did that leave her, the Inventor and Vanessa? The Arcis participants?

A familiar series of beeps sounded in her ear: three long dashes. The Collective needed her. Three times in the last four days.

Her heart raced in time with her steps. She crossed the courtyard feeling relieved that the Collective wouldn't see her current experiences until the following morning's upload. Uploads ran from midnight to midnight. Later, she would reorder her time to remove any incriminating actions or thoughts.

Inside the Great Hall she hesitated at the podium, then pressed her hand down flat. The array of hushed voices adopted their distinctive personalities: ten, including Unos, Septimus, Quatrius, Octavius and Quintus.

Only Quintus appeared on screen. Carissa swallowed hard as his almond-shaped gaze fell on her. Quintus might be the neutral party, but his lone appearance meant a decision had been made. When more than one appeared, the masters were willing to debate a subject.

'173-C. You are registering a rapid pulse and sweaty extremities.'

'I'm nervous, Quintus.'

'Why?'

'To be called before you three days out of four is unusual. The other Copies have been commenting on it, saying I must be in trouble.'

Quintus frowned. 'When did you speak to the Copies? I have not seen evidence of this.'

'Today, Quintus. At morning classes.'

'That's why I called you in. The Collective has a vested interest in what you do, and it feels your experiences have reached a plateau. It appears you've outgrown your role here.'

Carissa's connected hand twitched. 'Is that why my access to the medical facility was revoked?'

'That was for a different reason. We see your experiences twenty-four hours after they've occurred. And your tendency to alter them alarms the group. Your experiences are far too valuable to be altered in any way.' Carissa focused on Quintus' distorted mouth as he spoke. 'The Collective is making some changes to the way uploads will happen in future, starting with you. From tomorrow, we will track your experiences in real time and evaluate them as they happen. The group agrees it has been lax in addressing this issue with you.'

No!

'My days are not very interesting, Quintus.'

213

'Your curiosity about the Originals, the Librarian and the Inventor, in particular, is clear. You are not like the other Copies. The Collective had considered this flaw too great, and we considered termination. But Septimus convinced the group to first determine if the flaw exists with you, or with the method the Collective uses to analyse situations. This will apply to past footage, too.'

Carissa swallowed a hiccup. Quintus would not see her fear. 'Yes. That is a good idea.'

'The software update to your NMC will be ready tomorrow when you upload via the terminal room.'

'Thank you, Quintus, for giving me a chance to redeem myself. I know I've been a disappointment.'

'Yes, you have, 173-C. But we can start over tomorrow. You are dismissed.'

Quintus vanished from screen and Carissa snatched her hand away from the podium, as if she'd just received a shock. In a way she had. She steadied her rapid breaths as she strode from the room.

This wasn't over.

Quintus planned to dig into her past footage. She might have deleted part of it, but the original data still existed, never truly erased from the system. The Collective was on the verge of accessing her talks with Vanessa, and private discussions with the Inventor about the tunnel, about their plans to escape. Whatever else happened, she'd make sure Vanessa and the Inventor lived through another attempt.

Her short and sharp breaths made walking to the workshop difficult. She found the Inventor tinkering with the same wolf he'd been working on for the last few days. It stood eerily still in the middle of the space, without its exoskeleton.

'What's the matter, miss?' The Inventor stepped away from the wolf and guided her to a seat.

She sucked in air, her words barely making sense. 'I've just... Quintus... He called me in...'

'Take a deep breath, miss. What did he want?'

Carissa slowed her breaths until she felt ready to talk. 'He's working on initiating a live feed to access my experiences in real time. He also wants access to all my past footage. The Collective will be able to restore any edited information.'

'God Almighty!' The Inventor looked at the wolf. 'That's not good news, is it, boy?' His gaze returned to Carissa. 'How long do we have?'

'Until tomorrow morning. I won't be able to delay, Inventor.'

'No, you won't. Everything we do now will be under scrutiny.' He paced the floor, the idle wolf forgotten. 'So we'll just have to work faster to make things happen.' He stopped. 'Don't bother erasing anything that happens today, miss. It won't matter.'

'Why not?'

Because we'll be gone before the Ten have time to access today's feed.' He grabbed a ladder and set it against a rafter close to the retractable roof in the middle of the room. He climbed up and pulled down a spare exoskeleton from one of the hooks, then climbed back down and fitted the hard metal alloy covering loosely to the wolf.

Carissa felt calmer as she watched him work. 'The Ten could have taken everything that's happened since my upload this morning. But they didn't. Why?'

'They don't suspect what we're planning, miss. They're curious enough about your behaviour to bring you and me in, but they haven't asked for your unedited footage before now. They're following logic and protocol. That buys us time.'

Carissa didn't want to think about what happened after. 'Do you think they'll terminate me?'

The Inventor paused with his hands on the exoskeleton. 'Not on my watch, miss. I'm too fond of you to let that happen. I'm not ready to live in a world without your curiosity.'

And she wasn't prepared to live in a world without his friendship. Or Vanessa's.

Or June's.

'So, what now? The Collective has revoked my access to the medical facility.'

'The place will be on lockdown. But that shouldn't be a problem for you.'

'I don't understand. I don't have access.'

'Yes, you do. You always have.' The Inventor tapped the side of his head. 'The codes are up here, miss. Stored in a security file. You've never had to use them before now.'

Carissa searched through the database connected to her NMC. Her day's activities were at the forefront and easily accessible. Older memories at the back of her mind took more effort to retrieve. A greyed-out file she'd never seen before hid behind the older memories. She pulled it forward and tried to open it, but it requested a password.

'I can see the file but I can't access the information.'

'The password is hardwired into you, a unique code that only you have. All Copies have a fail-safe. If the city is ever under attack, you will have immediate access to your passwords to unlock the security codes.'

Carissa closed her eyes and searched through the database for her password. She noticed another greyed-out file; this one was almost invisible. *11648-C-Carissa*. She located her security file and added the full word to the password field by thinking it. To her surprise, the file opened and she discovered maps of other parts of the city she'd never explored. It also contained the frequency codes for the energy field surrounding Praesidium, as well as the security codes for all the buildings in the city.

'I have them!'

'Good.' The Inventor visibly relaxed. 'I was worried the group took them from you when they revoked your access to the medical facility.' He continued to adjust the solid metal casing to the wolf. Carissa heard the first part click into place. 'Now, go fetch Vanessa and bring her here. We'll need to make our move tonight.'

24

CANYA

'What do you mean you're not letting me in?'

Canya argued with one of the guards outside the medical facility. She had just bought a bright-blue dress from snooty Nora's store. No way would they stop her from seeing Dom.

'The Collective's orders. Medical personnel only.'

'But I'm a newborn. I have full access to Praesidium until connection. The Collective wants me to learn. That's why I'm here.'

Her biogel stomach danced with nerves. She *had* to see Dom.

'I can't let you in without an order from Quintus.'

She'd heard that name before, from Carissa. 'Is he in control? How can I get in touch with him? Or maybe you can just call him up? I'll wait.'

She folded her arms. To her delight, the guard turned away and touched the disc above his ear. 'I have 228-O's newborn here, wants to get into the medical facility. Yes... I know, but she refuses to leave... I've told her that...' The guard listened for a moment. 'Okay, Quintus.'

He turned back to Canya. 'Quintus says you have visited the medical facility every day since your creation. He wonders if you possess a natural aptitude for medics. He says to let you in and to inform you it's your last day here. Tomorrow, the Collective will connect you.'

'Tomorrow? But I haven't reached maturation yet.' What about the few days she'd been promised? A whole week, that's what Vanessa had said.

'Yes. Tomorrow you will be reset. The Collective can accelerate your maturation if it wishes.'

'Will I keep my memories?'

The guard shook his head. 'Old memories spoil the connection. You must be a total blank.'

Her breath hitched at the thought of losing her connection to Dom. The guard eyed her curiously. She forced herself to calm down. 'Just my biogel. Low reserves. Thank you.' She stepped around the guard and slipped inside the building for what would be the last time. As she rode the elevator down to the first floor, the pressure of making this visit count weighed on her.

She fixed her dress, which matched the light blue of her eyes.

The area close to Dom's room was quiet. She stood outside his door and waited for her thumping heart to quieten. When it refused to settle, she entered the room.

Her breath caught in her throat at the sight of Dom lying on the bed. Purple bruises marked the skin under both eyes. His skin was a sickly yellow. A strip of blood stained his white top, near one of his scars.

She approached him slowly, not wanting to wake him. But then his eyes opened, and his hazy and unfocused gaze found hers. She sat down beside him and touched his left hand. Usually so warm, it now felt cold to her.

Dom's gaze wandered, and she squeezed his hand to get his attention.

'Dom? It's me.' She refused to use the name Vanessa had given her, still hoping Dom would call her Anya. Maybe in his drugged state he would.

'It's Anya.' She tried the name on for size.

His gaze snapped back to her. 'Anya? I never thought I'd see you again.' He lifted his right arm. His left, the one she touched, was practically glued to his side.

'What happened to your arm?'

He pulled her into an awkward half hug. 'The medics broke it again when I tried to escape. Except this time they refused to use the healing accelerator. Said I needed to learn a lesson.'

He gritted his teeth while he kept his good hand on her face.

She couldn't think of anything cool to say. 'I thought I'd never get here.' Maybe if she mirrored the real Anya, she could prolong this fantasy between her and Dom. 'What did the medics do to you?'

He frowned at her and withdrew his hand. 'I don't remember.'

'Are you in pain?'

'My scars, they're not healing like the last time.' His slow gaze travelled from her face down to her hands then back, making her shiver. 'Where the hell have you been, Anya?'

'Right here all along.'

'I think I dreamt you were here. But it wasn't you. I kept telling this other person to leave, but she wouldn't.'

'She's gone. It's just me. It's Anya.' Canya pressed down the hurt and kissed him. Their lips touched and desire shot through her when he groaned.

I am Anya. He wants me.

She pulled back to make sure, and it thrilled her when Dom held on to her. 'No. Don't leave. I need you close.'

His good hand twisted in her hair, pulled her back to his lips. He wrapped his arm around her and she straddled him, until their bodies pressed together in several places.

'You feel so good, Anya. I really missed you. This place, what they're doing to me. I kept going in the hope I would see you again.'

Jealousy poked and prodded at Canya, threatening to ruin this moment.

Her jealousy fluttered away when Dom tasted her. Before she could respond, he pulled back.

'Anya, I missed you. Will you stay with me?'

She nodded. 'I like your voice. It's both soft and strong. Makes me think about you in ways I shouldn't.'

Dom frowned. 'In ways you shouldn't?'

'I just mean... you're sick. I don't want to make things worse.'

He smiled, buying her excuse. 'I feel better knowing you're here, that you're safe.'

He pulled her mouth to his again, and what little control Canya had slipped away. She nipped at his bottom lip as she moved against him. He groaned louder. His good arm pinned her in place. She loved the power she had over this man. Why would she ever give this up?

She sat back and pulled up Dom's shirt.

'No, Anya. Not that. I just need you close.' He tried to pull her back down to him, but she kept tugging.

'I need more of you.'

'Me too. But not now. I can't. My scars.'

Canya couldn't wait. She wanted him to take her, to give her an experience that no reset could erase. 'I need this now. I need to remember it.'

Dom pushed her away. 'Why wouldn't you remember it?'

'I mean, *you* might not remember it.'

'There's nothing wrong with my memories, Anya. Talk to me. What's wrong?'

'Nothing.' Canya refused to meet his eyes, still sharp despite the drugs in his system.

'You're the real Anya, aren't you?'

She met his gaze. 'Of course I am.'

'I don't believe it! How the—' Dom sat up, grimacing. 'You're the other one. It's that damn dress that threw me. I didn't think... I don't know what I'm doing.'

Still sitting on Dom, Canya tugged at his top again.

He stopped her with his good hand. 'No!'

'Yes!' said Canya.

'Get off me.'

'Make me.'

Dom attempted to move her off with just one arm. The drugs and his injuries had clearly sapped his strength. He sat back with a sigh.

'Please move. I don't want this.'

'I don't want to move.' She managed to yank his top all the way up, to reveal pale skin and his main scar, red and weeping.

Canya kissed him again, desperate to experience something more than what the other Anya had.

Dom tried to push her off his lap again, but she only nestled in closer. His breaths quickened, and she took it as a sign to continue. She gripped the back of his neck. Kissed him along his rigid jawline.

His breathing slowed, and she felt him relax beneath her.

Her body ached for his touch. She leaned back to see him lying still with his eyes closed. 'I don't want you here. I'm not doing anything with you.'

Rage hit, and she pounded his injured chest with her fist. He cried out, doubled over with the pain.

She climbed off the bed and hovered over him, panting. Barely controlled fury simmered close to the surface.

The rage loosened its steely grip on her. Then Dom recovered and smiled at her.

'You can pretend to be her all you want. But she's in here.' He tapped his heart twice. 'You're not. I'm not even sure what you are. Even if I never see her again, I'll always have that.'

Her fury unleashed a scream. 'You will *never* see the real Anya again. I wanted you. I visited you when she couldn't even be bothered.'

Dom perked up. 'You've seen her? Is she okay?'

'I... I didn't say that.' Canya backed towards the door.

'Why didn't you tell me you'd seen her?' He eased himself upright, visibly angry.

'I haven't seen her. I don't know where she is. I meant you can't be that important to her if she doesn't visit.'

Canya reached for the door just as Dom eased his legs over the side of the bed. 'Help me get a message to her that I'm still alive and I've never given up. Will you do that for me?'

She unlocked the door with her chip.

'Please! She needs to know I'm okay.'

She slipped out of the room and sat on the corridor floor. Tears, part angry, part sad, flowed. Maybe she didn't want to remember. Dom could rot for all she cared.

Jealousy filled the empty space in her biogel

heart. She stood up, wondering where Anya's room was.

Before she forgot Dom completely, maybe she could do some damage first, to break up the lovebirds. Canya pictured the pain on Anya's face when she told her exactly how Dom had touched her, kissed her. He'd liked it, if only for a while.

Her secret.

She entered the elevator and rode it down one more level, to the Breeder floor. This underground part of the facility was a maze. She looked around wondering which way to go, when a medic appeared from a dark corridor.

'What are you doing here, newborn? You are not authorised to be on this floor.'

'I'm lost. I was looking for Anya Macklin's room.'

'You have no business with her. Leave now.'

Canya stomped back to the elevator. This couldn't be the end of it. She had to find another way to see her Original.

But first Vanessa needed to know that her reset was planned for tomorrow. The Librarian might help delay the Collective; Canya still hadn't given her the name of the mountain range.

She smiled as she rode the elevator to the surface.

Maybe she had more power than she realised.

25

DOM

Dom's stomach churned, worse than when he'd found out his father, Carlo, had made a pass at Sheila. Or just before Charlie had cut off the dreadlocks he'd spent a year growing out. Carlo had hated long hair on boys.

His year-long tribute to that dead asshole.

The medic had said the immunosuppressives would make him sick. After the Fourth Gen surgery, the healing accelerator had helped to move the sickness on. But Fifth Gen surgery and no accelerator equalled clammy skin and nausea like nothing else. An uneaten tray of food sat on the floor. No matter how far Dom got from it, the smell always reached him. He'd even tried to prise open that damn food hatch and shove it outside.

His sweat-soaked tunic clung to his hot skin. The white fabric was spotted with blood from where the newborn had punched him. She'd partially reopened one of his scars, which now refused to heal. Dom

226

drew in a ragged breath as he peeled the fabric away from his puckered wound. His body was rejecting the Fifth Gen tech. They'd wasted immunosuppressives on him, drugs designed to coax his body to accept the new organs. The seeping wounds on his belly and the two on his back held together by sheer luck. It felt like the tech wanted out the same way it got in.

Dom lay still on his bed. Any movement brought on a new wave of sickness.

The door opened suddenly and he jerked his head up in surprise. He gritted his teeth against the nausea.

148-C. The last person he wanted to see. He closed the door and stepped closer to a weak Dom.

'Why do you have such an attachment to your mother?'

'What's it to you?'

The medic's eyes widened with anger, and it took all of Dom's strength to return the look.

'I don't like you,' said 148-C.

Dom managed a smile and focused on the floor. 'I don't care.'

'I'm confused by how much I hate you. I don't know if it's because you are a dirty human or because you are an example of what the Collective expects me to become.'

Still fighting his nausea, Dom stared at the medic. 'And what are you supposed to become?'

'The Collective wishes for us to study you, to learn from your mistakes. Or to repeat them. So we can be more like you.'

Dom recalled the voice on the ninth floor of

Arcis. The one that said the floors had been designed to help the Collective learn.

'Why do you need to be more like us?'

The medic took a step towards him. Dom's queasiness swirled as he retreated further up the bed.

'Because we are trying to escape this city. We are trying to better ourselves, to become more than we are.'

Copies indistinguishable from humans in the real world? Max and Charlie would never allow that to happen. He shifted into a seated position and a cascade of pain rippled through him. It took every ounce of effort not to throw up in front of the medic.

'Why would you want to escape the city? It's not like you're prisoners here. You can come and go. Your lot were in Essention.'

'If I had a choice, I wouldn't look like you.' 148-C's gaze roamed the room. 'Just thinking about the diseases you humans carry makes me feel as sick as you look. Just being here with you like this...' He shivered. 'But if I want to leave this world, I must resemble you in every way. Because, according to the Collective, your kind rules out there.'

In the towns? Dom didn't agree.

Dom watched, helpless, as the medic came even closer and then grabbed his foot and shook it. Dom cried out as the action sent a wave of pain through his body and set his wounds on fire again.

'You are weak. You are pathetic. You can't even stand a little surgery. I don't want to be anything like you. If that means staying in this city forever, then so be it.'

Dom coughed, held his body still to control the pain. 'And *I* don't want to be like you, but you insisted on putting your tech in me.'

'That is the Collective's wish, not mine. If I had my way, none of you would be here, contaminating our great city.'

The door opened. Dom looked up, relieved to see the female medic.

'What are you doing here, 148-C?'

The male straightened up. 'Just checking on the patient, 118-C. He was making a lot of noise.'

'This patient is none of your concern.' Her clinical gaze touched on Dom before returning to the male. 'Go to the upload room. I'm sure Quintus will be keen to see your experiences here.'

148-C stiffened. 'Yes, 118-C.' He left. The female stayed.

Dom had no energy to go another round. He didn't move when the female walked over and rested a hand on his forehead, then snatched it away.

She examined her sweat-covered hand before drying it on her uniform. 'You have an infection.'

'That's pretty obvious.' The sweat-stained, blood-soaked tunic would have been enough proof.

'The Fifth Gen tech, it's not compatible.'

Dom winced. 'No, it is not.' When he saw her normal steely composure slip, he added, 'I need morphine for the pain.'

She stepped back from the bed, as if he repulsed her. 'I am not permitted to give you anything, Dom

Pavesi.'

'Why? It's not like I can go anywhere. Make me more comfortable.'

'It's not that.'

Dom detected hesitation in her voice. Her expression matched her indecision.

'Why, then?'

'The Collective wants to experience all states of a human being's suffering. This will be a valuable experience for them.'

Dom shifted, instantly regretting it. 'I told you, I'm done with being your experiment. No more surgeries. This one shouldn't have happened. The Fourth Gen tech...' He was about to say how strong he'd felt with it. 'The Fourth Gen tech was compatible with my body. This is not. What happened to my Copies?'

'The first one died two hours after you saw it. The other is unresponsive. It has no brain function.'

Dom shook his head. 'So all this suffering was for nothing?'

The medic's face softened a fraction. 'No, not for nothing. You have provided the Collective with a valuable experience. That is good for all of us.'

The female appeared chattier than usual. Dom dug deep to access his reserves of energy. Now was the time to find out where Sheila, June and Anya were.

'Where are the others? Are they okay?'

'I told you, they're on a different floor doing important work for the Collective.'

'I want to see them.'

'I'm afraid that's not possible.'

'Why not? I'm going to die—the least you can do is grant me a final wish.'

The medic sighed. 'You're not going to die, Dom Pavesi.'

'Well, it sure as hell feels that way. Don't you know how human anatomy works? Infections kill. My body will fight for as long as it can before the infection wins out. I'll be dead and it will be all your fault.'

The medic paused, and he saw another flicker of indecision in her eyes. He was getting through to her.

She lowered her voice. 'Your friends are okay, for now.'

'Can you take me to them?'

'No.'

The last ounce of fight drained from him, and he looked away.

'But I promise to help them if I can.'

He looked back. 'Don't just help. Get them out of this place. None of this is right and you know it. I am not a machine. I am human. I cannot survive multiple surgeries.'

The medic's lips turned thin and white. She exited the room, leaving Dom alone to fight against his pain. It escaped through a cascade of tears and shallow breaths.

The others were okay. But he couldn't help them in his current state.

Or could he?

Dom fed his feet over the edge of the bed and placed them on the floor. He used the bedpost as a crutch and attempted to stand. No problem. His stomach churned, and the wounds etched a new trail of fire across his skin. Standing up almost sent him barrelling over the edge into unconsciousness.

He huffed out a breath of air just as the door opened.

It was the female medic again. Her eyes widened when she saw Dom.

'Lie down. Immediately. Unless you want to reopen your wounds.'

'They're already open.' Dom sat down and savoured the instant relief. The medic lifted his feet back onto the bed and eased up his tunic. The pain started a new crescendo that threatened his sanity.

118-C pulled a long thin metal tube out of her pocket. She twisted it counterclockwise and a red beam extended from its tip. She swept the beam across his stomach. The pain retreated as the beam cleared up the seeping infection and sealed the wound on his stomach. She ordered him onto his side. He just about managed it. She used the same tool on his other two wounds. For the first time in hours, Dom felt relief. He rolled onto his back again.

'That will help for a while. But the tech is still incompatible and the infection will build again and reopen your incisions over time.'

She pocketed the tool and removed a vial and a syringe from her other pocket.

'Morphine.'

Dom nodded, and she injected him with a dose. 'Just a little for now. You can't be too out of it, otherwise they'll know I gave it to you.'

She put away the vial and syringe. 'How do you feel now?'

He closed his eyes. 'Better.'

'Good.' Dom opened his eyes to see the medic standing over him. 'On your feet.'

'Why?'

'We need you in the testing room again.'

'I don't want to go in there again. I can't.'

'You must continue to pretend for now. And Quintus wants you back in the testing room.'

He pinned 118-C with his morphine-hazy eyes. 'And what if I refuse?'

The medic leaned in. 'It's better for you if you don't fight it.'

Ω

The female medic helped him walk to the testing room alone. At least that was something. Either 118-C trusted Dom, or she knew he was too sick to run.

He guessed it was the latter.

The room was empty except for the replication machine at the back. The lack of bed meant no operation. Dom should have been thrilled about that, but the Fifth Gen needed taking out. He never thought he'd admit to wanting another operation.

His wounds were still closed, thanks to the medic's intervention. But for how long? She hadn't fixed him. He still felt weak. Once the infection took hold again and the morphine wore off, he'd be back to square one.

'Stand inside the unit,' said the female. 'We've made some adjustments to the machine. We need to copy you again.'

He had no strength to argue.

The machine was set at floor level, unlike the one on the ninth floor of Arcis, with steps leading up to it. He gripped the bars and hauled himself inside. The tank at the rear of the machine contained biogel that would soon transform into a copy of him.

The scanner moved around him, and Dom held as still as possible. The sooner this was over, the sooner he could plan his escape. He needed the tool the medic had used to clean and close his wounds, and more morphine. Maybe then he could reach the floor with the girls. Get them out.

The scanner beam drifted from his head to his toes, then worked its way back up. His skin tingled when the scanner lingered over the parts where his tech was.

His nausea returned. He glanced down at his top. No new blood had seeped through. As soon as the scan finished, Dom eased his top up a little. The closure was holding.

But he still didn't feel right.

His wavering gaze tried to focus on the gel that took on his exact shape, starting with his legs. It continued up to construct his torso, arms, neck, face.

Dom stepped out of the machine. A ceiling panel

opened and an arm extended down to scan the new life form. It produced a set of results that appeared on a screen set flush against one wall. The medic studied the display with a frown on her face.

She touched a disc above her ear.

'The Copy is unresponsive, Quintus. Limited brain function. Same result as before.'

Dom shuffled closer as he tried to listen to the conversation. He could hear a male voice talking.

'The Fifth Gen tech is all we have, 118-C. The machine must be the problem. Recalibrate it and try again.' The voice sounded just like the one Dom had heard on the ninth floor of Arcis.

'There's nothing left to calibrate, Quintus.'

'Then we will forget about copying and replace him with all of our tech.'

Dom shrank back just as 118-C flinched at the command. 'I'm sure there are other uses for this subject, Quintus. Fifth Gen is clearly not compatible with his body.'

'We will wait until his body adapts to the tech. The Fourth Gen tech is useless now, since it won't produce a clean Copy. Fifth Gen is our best version. Make him useful or terminate him.'

118-C glanced at Dom. He nodded and mouthed 'Fourth Gen' to her. If he could ditch this incompatible tech, he had a chance. She shook her head and turned back to the screen. 'Quintus, I don't think the Fifth Gen is compatible. His immune system is severely weakened. He has an infection and the antibiotics are not helping. Even with the immunosuppressives, his body is rejecting the transplant. I recommend we use the healing accelerator on him.'

Dom moved closer to hear the response.

'I do not care about his health, 118-C. The Collective wishes to continue experimenting on him. The surgeries are creating valuable compatibility data as to how Fifth Gen works with his body. You will replace his remaining organs to see if the issue can be overcome with more tech, beginning with his heart. Prepare him for heart surgery.'

Dom grabbed the medic's arm. She snatched her arm away and moved to the other side of the room.

Dom leaned against the wall. Replace his heart? Turn him into one of them? No way. He would die before he became a synthetic with a machine mind. The machines killed his mother. He needed a way out of this.

The medic continued arguing with Quintus, but Dom was too far away to overhear the male voice. 'No. I don't think that's the way to go... Well, I think we should interrogate him for information about the rebellion... No. I haven't asked him about it... I will, Quintus... Okay.'

118-C disconnected and turned back to him. Her expression was dark.

'Touch me like that again, human, and I will break both arms.'

Dom gasped for new breath. The fading morphine gave way to fresh, stabbing pain.

'You can't have my heart. I'll kill myself before

you turn me into a machine.'

'I am no machine, Dom Pavesi. I am a synthetic Copy with an NMC that gives me the ability to learn. There is a difference.'

'Not to me. You'll never be human.' Dom gritted his teeth as the pain intensified.

The medic pulled the bottle of morphine out of her pocket and showed it to him. 'What do you know about the place called "the Beyond"?'

Dom stared at the bottle in her hand. 'What's that?'

'A place that is believed to exist beyond this one. Even beyond the towns. What do you know about it?'

Dom shook his head. 'I don't know anything about it.'

Charlie had intimated that such a place did exist, but no one had been able to confirm it. According to Charlie, it was where the townsfolk originally came from, as well as the machine minds that built Praesidium.

'If you tell me, I will give you morphine.' She removed the syringe from her pocket, flicked off the lid.

A new bout of pain left a hot, searing path across his wounds and caused him to wince. His stomach heaved again.

'I don't know about any *Beyond*.'

The medic stuck the syringe into the top of the vial and drew liquid into it. Dom was lured in by the memory of that first feeling of morphine; the one that coated the pain and made him feel numb. He stared at the syringe.

'It's a fair trade, Dom Pavesi.'

'But it's not one I'm willing to give you.' He squeezed his eyes shut and gritted his teeth against the agony.

When he opened them again, the medic had moved closer.

'You don't understand,' she whispered. 'The Collective needs to think you're valuable. Information makes you valuable. If you tell me something, Quintus will keep you alive for longer.'

She nodded at him, encouragement in her eyes.

A wave of dizziness struck him. 'I would rather die.'

The medic jabbed his arm and pushed in the syringe's contents. 'Then your wish will come true sooner than you think.'

His vision faded and he collapsed, right before he passed out.

26

ANYA

The Rapture had quietened, taking with it Anya's burning desire for Alex. But a slow burn remained, low in her core. It usually struck when Alex talked about his past, or how much he hated using the girls who had been in his room. Anya tried to reassure him it was the Collective's fault. He was just a pawn.

For the last four days, Anya and Alex had used conversation to distract them. Anya knew more about Alex than she ever thought she would. Gone was the cocky boy with the wild blond hair and smouldering green eyes. Before her sat a sad and lonely boy trapped in this place for too long.

That evening, the last of Rapture lessened its hold on Anya, enough for her to function normally. She'd been crazy on it all day, willing to do almost anything to have Alex close. And because mutual feelings were in the mix, it was more potent than any drug she'd ever been given.

She watched the door, expecting both medics to

turn up. She committed to memory what it felt like to be off the drug. When she was on it, her thoughts and actions belonged to someone she didn't recognise.

The door unlocked and Anya stood. Alex followed suit, more lazily than her. She'd done this enough times to know the drill. But this time, her mind was clear and focused on one thing: escape.

She waited for Alex to go with his medic, the one identified as 148-C. She kept pace with hers, the less combative 118-C.

A short distance from the treatment room, Anya stopped. 'I need a change of scenery.'

The medic pushed her on. 'The treatment room is your change of scenery.'

'No. I mean, I want to go outside.'

118-C gave a short sharp laugh. 'You do not have permission to leave this place.'

'Alex said he was allowed to leave before.'

'That Breeder talks too much.' The medic shoved her harder. And with that, her chance to sway her medic vanished.

But 118-C surprised her by speaking again. 'You are too uncooperative. Leaving the medical facility is a reward. You have not done anything to be given such a privilege.'

They were almost at the treatment room. If Anya could delay the injections by a couple of hours and get up top, she might be able to work out an escape plan before Alex consumed her every waking thought.

She threw the medic's words back at her. 'Maybe

if I was allowed to leave, I would be more cooperative. I can't stand that room, the walls, the smell. Humans need variety. I know Alex feels the same way.'

'Neither of you can leave. Particularly Alex.' The medic lifted her chin. 'The Breeder escaped once before and attempted a second time. He is a flight risk.'

The medic was open to talking. Good. 'I'm not suggesting you let him leave. Just me. With a dozen escorts, if necessary. Have you seen the size of me? If I try to run, I won't get far.'

118-C ushered her inside the treatment room. Anya avoided the usual manhandling by voluntarily sitting in the chair. The viewing platform was empty. No extra eyes. Pity. She'd hoped to appeal to the older female. But it was just her and 118-C. The leather straps pressed against the bruises on her wrists.

'So, what do you say?'

The medic ignored her, getting the usual tray with six vials and a syringe ready. She prepared the first shot: an equal mixture of all six vials. For the second shot, sometimes the medic drew more from one vial than the others.

'I'm not giving the Collective what it wants,' said Anya. 'I haven't done it up to now. So why would anything change?'

'You will do it.' 118-C flicked the barrel of the syringe. 'The Collective has assured me our methods will yield results. Those in the Breeder programme have been selected specially. In the end, they always give in.'

Anya leaned forward, straining against her ties. 'How was I selected? Did I come from a place called Arcis?' She had to know. If this medic had knowledge of her arrival, she must know where she'd come from.

'You shouldn't remember Arcis. I will need to inform the Collective that the memory wipe did not take.'

Anya swallowed. 'I don't remember Arcis. Alex mentioned it to me. I think they're memories, but I'm probably just dreaming.'

The medic glanced up at the empty viewing platform, appearing to relax a little. Syringe in hand, she leaned over Anya. 'That's what the memory wipe is supposed to feel like.' She stabbed Anya's upper arm. 'You were selected for this programme because you lacked understanding of children.'

'Lacked understanding?'

'You were placed in a room with crying babies. The others in your group of five helped them, but you stayed away. That is why you're here. The Collective is curious to know why you didn't help—if you are broken.'

Anya didn't remember any babies, and yet the room in the Nurturing Centre had felt oddly familiar. She'd never felt the same gravitational pull to babies that others her age did. She'd always put this down to being the youngest.

'When was this?'

'In Arcis. You were in a test. The Collective chose you because you are an anomaly. It hopes that you will produce a product that's different from what Originals with maternal instincts produce.'

'A product?'

'Yes. One that will be compatible with its network. This way, the Collective will have control over the product, and use it to escape.'

Anya sat up straighter. 'So this is all about control?'

'Partly. The Collective is trapped in its own prison. It wishes to escape, to survive in the human world. That's only achievable if it learns from you.'

The medic prepared the second shot. Anya winced when she stabbed her arm.

'You have shown no interest in interacting with us. How can you learn from us if you keep us locked up, away from others?'

The medic prepared a third shot and gave it to Anya. 'You are not alone. You have company.'

'It's not the same. I mean, don't you interact with others like you?'

'I am connected at all times to others. I have no need for personal contact.' The injections continued until all six vials were nearly empty.

Anya squeezed her eyes shut. There was no way she could fight against this much dosage.

'But I need contact. All humans do.' She hoped to engage the medic's curiosity about humans. 'Alex isn't enough for me. I need to know I'm not alone.'

118-C stared at her, needle pointing up. 'But you

are alone. You are not connected like the Copies are. Your mind is independent of any system. The Collective cares only about the creation of the product. It does not place importance on your well-being, and to that end, neither do I. Your human ways are of no interest to me, 228-O. Whatever I need to understand, I can download.'

The medic prepared another shot; the sixth and, presumably, final one. There was nothing left in the vials.

'But that's the point you're missing, medic. In order to experience humanity, to understand humans, you need to interact.'

The medic stepped around the trolley and gave Anya her last injection. Anya slumped back, defeated.

'If this is what you call interacting, then we're already doing it.' She wheeled the trolley back to the open panel and put the tray away.

Anya felt odd, as if she were caught in a drunken haze. 'No. This isn't what I meant at all. I want to feel the wind on my face, to see other people. We're social creatures, by nature.'

'There is no wind in Praesidium. The bubble encasing this city controls the weather.'

'That's not what I meant...'

'You are being isolated for a reason, 228-O. So that you can pair with just one boy, chosen for you.' The medic removed Anya's restraints and pulled her up from the chair. 'Time to go back to your room.'

Her head spun as she stood. The medic steadied her with a hand. The high dose of Rapture invaded her body, while Alex invaded her thoughts. She would remember every last detail of this floor and write it down, before her control vanished.

118-C dragged her outside. Three girls escorted by three medics approached the treatment rooms. One was tall and tanned—the girl she'd seen in the Nurturing Centre. The other, equally as tall, had wiry blonde hair. The third was shorter and had fine blonde hair. Anya didn't recognise them. Were these the three females Alex had mentioned? The ones who had also come from Arcis?

The older female medic that sometimes watched from the viewing room rounded the corner. 'That one is to receive prenatal care,' she said to the Copy holding the shortest of the three blondes. 'Take her directly to the Nurturing Centre when you're done.'

One of the medics forced the girl with the wiry hair towards the room. The girl pulled her arm away. 'I'm not going back in there! You can't make me.'

The medic slipped a baton out of an unseen holder and cracked it over the girl's head. Anya gasped when the girl dropped to the floor, unconscious.

'I can, and I will,' said her medic. She dragged the girl inside the room.

Anya looked at the tall and tanned goddess, who caught her staring. 'What are you looking at?'

'Do you know me?' said Anya.

The girl raked her eyes over Anya once. 'Can't say I do.'

The goddess-like girl looked towards a corridor

leading away from the rooms, as if she were considering her escape. Her medic yanked on her arm, and she blinked. Then she disappeared inside one of the rooms.

Who were those girls? Had she known them from Arcis? Were they connected to the boy with dark brown hair and brown eyes? The one who was a friend?

The others in your group of five helped them, but you stayed away.

Three girls and Anya. The boy made five.

The medic dropped her off back at her room. Alex hadn't returned yet.

Anya found a notepad in one of the hidden wall panels. She tore out a page, grabbed a pencil and carried both to the bathroom, keeping them hidden from the camera. There on the counter, she sketched the layout of the floor as she knew it.

118-C's new desire to talk had caught her attention. Could she get through to her?

Her pencil strokes shortened as the Rapture began to take hold. She prayed that together, she and Alex could figure a way out of this place.

27

CARISSA

The Collective would be updating her connection the following day. It was bad enough that the update would give the Collective access to her movements in real time. But worse, the Ten also planned to look into Carissa's altered footage. First they would see the changes, then they would look for the unedited feed still stored in the network. Carissa could do nothing to stop it.

She saw no point in altering her memories now; instead, she recorded her activities exactly as they happened. She hadn't done that since before she saw June in Arcis. If Carissa couldn't get her and Anya out, or if the Inventor's plan to reach the energy barrier didn't work, the Collective would terminate all of them.

This had to work.

The energy barrier encased the circular city and was powered by twelve generators located at equidistant points along its edge. When active, the twelve force fields, wider at the points of origin, narrowed to meet at a central point high above the city. Carissa had spent the day inspecting each of the twelve generators. She focused in on the seams, the points at which two energy segments joined.

Wolves roamed the zone, and cameras similar to her orb covered the area, but neither paid her any attention. She kept her interest light as she stopped at seam number 2.5, located behind the Business-District plaza. This was where her Original and the Inventor's wife had died. According to her newly accessible security file, it was also the weakest out of all twelve seams.

She returned to her apartment in Zone E to find a note slipped under the door. It was from the Inventor; he wanted her to come by his workshop. She hid the note in her waistband and ran all the way there.

On her arrival, the Inventor set down his welding torch. He'd been working on the same wolf for days. He ordered her to sit, then pulled over a diagnostic machine. He hooked up her NMC disc to the machine. Files and folders flooded the screen. Carissa saw an orientation file that contained details of Praesidium and the purpose of Copies. She hadn't used that one for some time.

The Inventor pointed to her almost-invisible security file. 'Is that where the codes are?'

She nodded. 'I'm still not sure about using them, Inventor. Won't the Collective know I've accessed them?'

'Yes, but the Ten don't have real-time access yet.

They're relying on uploads to formulate patterns in behaviour. Once or twice isn't enough to provide a baseline of data.' He touched the screen and opened the file. 'But to be safe, I wanted to add a redirect so it looks like the command is coming from one of the medics already in the facility.' He typed in a command and added 124-C's designation.

'Why 124-C?'

'This medic is on duty. He was the first designation to come up. The redirect will work until 124-C uploads his memories and the Collective sees the anomaly.'

'Why didn't you tell me I had access to the codes before?'

The Inventor gave her an uneasy smile. 'I wasn't sure I could trust you. Not after what happened with Mags and your Original.'

Carissa looked away from the Inventor's weathered face, wishing she could go back and change things.

He continued. 'But the morning after, I found you sitting on the ground, looking up at the spot where they'd died. And I wondered if you were different from the other Copies. Your prime directive is to protect the Collective, though. If you were still loyal, if I started poking around for your access codes, your directive would have kicked in. I couldn't take that chance.'

'So you hid them from me?'

'No. They were always yours to find. Archived, until you needed them.'

She understood. The Inventor was protecting himself. 'What's your name, Inventor?'

'You know it.'

She didn't remember. Maybe she'd asked as a newborn. 'Tell me again.'

The Inventor smiled, his eyes glossy. 'Jacob.'

'Does that upset you?'

'No. To you, I've been plain old Inventor since your creation. Other than Vanessa, nobody has ever asked my name before.'

'Are names important to you?'

'They give us our individuality. Separate us from the Copies. So, yes.'

'Jacob' felt too formal. To her, he would always be Inventor. 'Is it enough that I know it?'

'It is.' The Inventor swiped a thumb under his eyes. 'Have you figured out a way through the energy barrier? Rescuing the kids is the easy part.'

Carissa opened a file on the diagnostics screen and pulled up the schematics of the city. 'There's a weak point along each seam, where two segments of energy join. The weakest point is at 2.5, which means that generator is not putting out as much power as the others. I might be able to draw power from the generator or the field. I haven't tried, so I don't know if it will work.'

'All the Copies run on the same energy frequency, so it shouldn't harm you like it would me.' The Inventor picked up his welding torch and resumed work on the almost-completed wolf. 'I've asked Vanessa to meet us in the tunnels after sunset.

Return here then.'

That was in less than two hours.

Ω

Carissa could barely control her nerves as she wandered around Zone E, waiting for the sun to go down. With a sick feeling in her stomach, she headed for the tunnel at the time the Inventor had specified. Finding an empty workshop, she carried on to the bricked-up access point to the medical facility. She found Vanessa and the Inventor with a pile of bricks at their feet and the tunnel entrance exposed. Canya was with them.

She frowned. 'Why is she here?'

'I've been asking myself the same thing,' said the Inventor.

Vanessa continued to pull the bricks down from the wall. 'I told you, Jacob. She's as much at risk of termination as we are. We can't leave her behind. We have to protect her.'

'You mean protect her memories? I know you're still looking for that place in the mountains.'

Vanessa dropped a brick on the ground. 'Yes! I need her memories, Jacob. She told me the Collective is going to reset her tomorrow. I need to grab whatever time I can with her.'

But Carissa didn't see Vanessa's issue. Canya wasn't the only one in possession of the memories. The Original's memories could be restored, even after they'd been wiped.

251

'Why do you need Canya's memories, Vanessa?' she asked.

'You know why. The real Anya doesn't remember. Canya is the only remaining link to her past.'

Carissa frowned. 'But she can give them back to Anya at any time.'

Both the Inventor and Vanessa stared at her.

'She can what?' said Vanessa. 'How is it even possible?'

'During the copying process, the biogel stores data, which includes an imprint of Anya's memories. Canya's location chip can act as a transmitter to send a specific message to Anya's chip. The cells in the human body have inbuilt delivery systems. Anya's cells will receive the encoded message and fire it up to her brain, where it can be decoded.'

'How long will that take?'

'The exchange and decoding happens in a matter of seconds. Our compatibility gives us a unique connection with our Originals. The biogel copies right down to the cellular level, making the exchange possible.'

The Inventor rubbed his chin. 'So she only needs to touch Anya? Well, that makes things a lot simpler. Why didn't I know about this?'

'That information was part of the security file,' said Carissa. 'Without it, all the Originals knew was the machine wiped the Arcis memories for good.'

'I considered it a good thing that those kids couldn't remember anything,' said the Inventor. 'But if we can restore memories, do we give them back everything that was taken from them? The good and the bad?'

'It would be better to give it all back,' said Carissa.

Vanessa grabbed her arm. 'Is it possible for Canya to transfer Anya's memories to me?'

The silent newborn watched as Carissa shook her head.

'The transfer can only occur with her Original. Anya still has those memories. The memory wipe has only placed them in hibernation. The transfer will wake them up.'

Vanessa let go. 'Or Canya can just tell me about the place in the mountains.'

'I don't know it,' said Canya. 'I told you.'

'She's lying,' said Carissa.

Vanessa sighed, as if she already knew. 'If she won't give me the information, then we need the real Anya to remember. But if there's a chance we can return Anya's memories to her before Canya is connected... Tell me more about the transfer, Carissa. Can the Inventor replicate the process using one of his machines?'

'No. The transfer can only happen on a cellular level between a Copy and its Original. Normally the newborn isn't given access to the memories, but then you injected her, activated the imprinted memories. Canya's control on that imprint weakens as she nears maturity. We should do the swap now.'

Canya flinched.

'But there's one small problem,' said Carissa. 'She has to *want* to give them back. She can also control *what* is passed between them.'

Vanessa narrowed her eyes at Canya. 'Did you know you could do this?' Canya shook her head. 'Will you help us?'

'I won't cooperate.' She folded her arms. 'As soon as I do, you'll leave me behind to be erased from existence.'

'You won't be erased,' said Vanessa. 'Only reset. You will still exist.'

But Canya wasn't satisfied. 'I lied. I know about the place in the mountains. I know where it is. Anya doesn't know. She'd buried the memory so deep I had to do some work to retrieve it.'

'You've known all along?' said Vanessa. 'And you just refused to tell me?'

Canya shrugged. 'You needed something from me. That's the only reason why you kept me around. I didn't want it to end. I want to be the only Anya with memories. If you don't take me with you, I'll tell the Collective what you're planning to do and about the place in the mountains.'

Vanessa closed her eyes briefly, then turned to the Inventor. 'While I'm not fond of threats, I think she deserves a chance outside of Praesidium. She won't have any life here.'

'And what's the real Anya going to say about that? How's she going to feel about another *her* running around with her entire set of memories?'

'I don't know. I haven't thought that far ahead.

I'm sorry. We're getting off-topic. We should concentrate on the rescue.'

'And Canya?' said the Inventor.

'She'll have to come with us, until we can figure something out. Right now, we need her, Jacob. If she wants to tell the Collective, I can't stop her. But I can keep her in my sights.'

'She'll be reset tomorrow. She won't remember anything.'

Vanessa shook her head. 'Plenty of time for a resentful girl to do damage. She stays.'

The Inventor gave Carissa a look that she understood well. Carissa had been that resentful girl once. While the Inventor agreed to Vanessa's plan, Carissa vowed to make him—Jacob—proud of her.

The Inventor spoke to all of them. 'We don't have much time. Take the tunnel as far as it goes. You'll hit a bunch of darker corridors that the Copies don't use. As soon as you reach a bright section, assume the Copies to be active in that area. The Nurturing Centre is beyond the bright section, but the entire facility is on lockdown. Carissa will to need to open a few doors. Exit out the viewing corridor with a glass wall, then take the stairs up one floor. That's where the girls will be. The boy is one floor above them.'

Impressed with his knowledge, Carissa asked. 'Have you been there before, Inventor?'

'My Mags worked in the nursery.'

When Vanessa stepped closer to the entrance of the tunnel, Carissa froze. This was getting real.

'We're going now? What if it doesn't work? If the Copies find us, how do we get out of there?' She had never gone against the Collective before. Quintus had always been like a father to her. She hated the idea of disappointing him, too.

'I've seen that look before, miss.' The Inventor bent down to her level. 'Your prime directive is kicking in. Protect the Collective at all costs. You'll be safe with me. Everything will be fine. Do you trust me?'

Carissa nodded.

'We have to do this now. We have no choice.'

'But if Quintus discovers my betrayal,' said Carissa, 'he can terminate me at any access point.'

The Inventor nodded. 'Your Original was brave, Carissa. You must be, too. All you've done in your short life, all you know, is to serve the Collective. Think about June, and how much it will mean when you rescue her.'

The Inventor was right. She needed to do something good in the name of her Original who'd died trying to get back to her sister.

Her desire to please the Inventor more than Quintus surprised her.

'Good.' The Inventor straightened up, looking relieved. 'Carissa said the weakest energy-field seam is 2.5, between the second and third segments. It's the one located to the rear of the Business-District plaza. I'll pack some things, meet you there.' He removed the last of the bricks blocking up the tunnel.

'This tunnel is not on any of my maps, Inventor,'

said Carissa. 'Was it always like this?'

'No. I took the bricks from a different tunnel, built this wall. I didn't like the idea of the Copies from the medical facility sneaking up on me while I worked. But they hate dark spaces, so that worked in my favour.'

'I quite like the dark. The brightness of the city, it hurts my eyes.'

'Yes, miss. That's why I'm fond of you—you're different from the others.'

She liked being different.

When they'd finished dismantling the wall, Vanessa made no attempt to leave. 'Girls, I need to speak with Jacob for a minute.' She led the Inventor a short distance away.

Carissa stayed with Canya by the wall. The newborn was too quiet. 'So, are you going to help Vanessa find this place in the mountains?'

'I said I would.'

'Are you going to give the real Anya back her memories?'

'If I have time. We'll be busy rescuing people.' Canya's reply lacked emotion, confirming Carissa's earlier suspicion that she had plans of her own.

'Vanessa has been good to you. Remember that.'

'Inventor wanted to leave me behind. Vanessa is only keeping me around because she needs something from me.'

'And *you* don't need something?'

Canya glanced at her, lips drawn thin and white.

'I know you went to see Dom Pavesi,' said

Carissa. 'After Vanessa told you not to.'

'So?'

'And Vanessa knows, too. She hasn't said anything because you'll do what you want, anyway.'

'I'm not hooked up to the Collective, so what does it matter?'

'You're interfering in other peoples' lives.' Watching Dom and Anya's friendship blossom into something more in Arcis had thrilled Carissa. Canya would not steal that moment from the real Anya.

'What do you care? You're just a Copy.' Canya folded her arms.

'I have my own mind. You're using Anya's memories to live your life.'

'And you've never done that with *your* Original?' Carissa wished she'd taken better care of her Original. Then she might still be alive. 'The Collective controls you. You're nothing but a pawn to them. I'm an independent mind because I'm not connected to the network.'

'But you will be tomorrow. And if we're successful, you'll avoid termination. Don't you want to help Vanessa and the Inventor?'

'The Inventor means nothing to me.'

'But he's helped you all the same.'

Canya unfolded her arms. 'By threatening to leave me behind? I don't want to stay here. But I don't want to be connected, either.'

'You won't survive past the first week without your NMC. You need to be connected. Copies cannot survive alone.'

'I have lived four days without an NMC. I don't need the Collective like you do.' Canya's nostrils flared.

'And yet you spent those four days with Dom. You want to belong somewhere. And Dom helps to fill that aching void.'

Canya's expression softened a little. 'Is that so bad?'

No. It wasn't bad to care about another person. Or to act and feel like a human being.

Carissa opened her mouth to say as much. But before she could, Vanessa was back.

'Let's get going.'

28

ANYA

Anya spent the first hour post-treatment engaging Alex in innocent conversation: what her school was like in Brookfield; the most annoying thing that Jason had done; her favourite pastime. Running.

A smooth track entered her thoughts—a place she'd never been. The boy with the dark hair had been there, running alongside her. She'd felt safe with him.

It wasn't long before the topic turned to strategy. Both she and Alex relocated to the bathroom, but not before they played up their attraction for the camera.

Anya leaned against the sink. 'There's a corridor that carries on past the three treatment rooms. Any idea where it goes?'

'That's where the elevator is. But you can't operate it without a chip or a card. I've tried.'

'So we have *no* idea how to get out of here?'

Alex stood by the closed door, his laser-like gaze cutting through her skin. She felt exposed, even though she wore pyjama bottoms and a hoodie. 'Short of attacking the guards and cutting the chips out of their wrists, I can't think of a way.'

'So, we go back to our original plan of resisting,' said Anya. He stepped closer. Her hands found his chest. He smelled musky, natural. Appealing. 'If we don't give the Ten what they want, they might give up.'

'Or kill us.'

'I'd rather die having tried than live with no freedom, or no say.' Her fingers massaged his chest.

Alex groaned and walked to the door. Turned back. 'This is killing me. I can't get you off my mind.' He pulled out his loose waistband. 'I can't eat. I can't sleep. I need you and I don't know what to do about it.'

Anya bit her lip. 'I don't, either.'

Alex stepped in. 'Let me feel you in my arms. Maybe that will be enough.'

She nodded. Truth was, she needed him close. Maybe it was Rapture. Maybe it was the slow burn that simmered when Rapture broke its hold.

She rested her hands on the edge of the sink. The running water soaked the ends of her long sleeves. Her heart pressed against her ribcage as Alex pressed against her. She ached for him. She needed him.

Alex whispered her name in her ear.

She shivered and closed her eyes. His fingers grazed hers, which now gripped the sink's edge.

'I need to kiss you.' His voice rumbled low. 'Like right now. I know it's just Rapture, and I'm trying to resist. I really am.'

Anya opened her eyes to find Alex's lips inches from hers. She recalled two vague, intimate dreams: one was sweet and sexy, the other rushed and unwanted. She trusted her experience with Alex to be closer to the first.

'Anya, please.' His rumbles sent tiny shocks through her. She laid her hands flat on his white shirt.

'I feel it too, Alex. Too much. It's all just too much.' She slipped her fingers under the hem of his shirt until she found skin. Alex jerked beneath her touch.

She frowned at the discovery of smooth skin. Why had she expected to find scars?

Alex's hot breath by her ear made her shiver. 'Let me touch you.'

'I can't do this. But... I can't stop, either,' she whispered. 'I'm not normally this forward. At least, I don't think I am.'

'You thinking about your missing memories?'

She nodded. 'I don't know what happened to me in Arcis. I keep remembering things that don't make any sense.' She pressed her palms against his skin, feeling the pulse of his heart. She had limited eye contact with Alex on purpose, but now she met his gaze.

Hot. Hungry. Her breath hitched as he leaned in.

The feel of his lips on hers sent new shocks to her centre. All the control slipped away; all the reasons for resisting no longer made sense. This was not a performance for the cameras.

Starved, her lips demanded more.

Alex teased her with his tongue until her lips parted, allowing him the kind of access that felt vaguely familiar, as if she'd given it to someone before. Her skin blazed, her nerves ignited. Hands in hair. Hers. His was too long, too coarse beneath her fingers. She preferred shorter hair, softer hair.

Dark brown.

Alex groaned as he deepened the kiss. He worked the zip of her hoodie down and she shucked it off her shoulders. His fingers roamed every exposed inch of skin and she let him. She wanted this.

Alex lifted her onto the counter and she wrapped her legs around him. He pulled her in tight. She felt his warmth. *This feels right.*

But in her head it was all wrong.

She shook off the confusion and nipped at his bottom lip, ignoring the water that continued to soak her clothes. His kisses were more hot than sweet; enough to make her legs tingle.

This feels right.

This feels wrong.

Alex lifted her off the counter and carried her to the bed. She craved the feel of his full weight on her. She needed it like she needed air. He dropped her and she gasped. When she saw the shock on his face, she waved him off. She crushed her lips to his, drowning his apology.

He slipped off the bed and knelt at her feet, ran his hands up the sides of her pyjama bottoms to her thighs. She wriggled against his fingers and mouthed,

'More.' He pulled the fabric down and tossed the bottoms across the room. In just a camisole and underwear, she should have felt vulnerable in front of him and the camera. But her desire smothered any thoughts of modesty.

Her hands found skin again. She tugged his shirt up and over his head. He lay on top of her, bare skin to camisole. She inhaled his natural musk and relaxed under his weight.

This is wrong.

Then why does it feel so good?

Her fingers slid over his toned, muscled, naked chest. Alex whispered, 'You're so beautiful.'

She shivered. 'You, too.'

Alex was sexy, but her heart ached for something else. She just didn't know what.

His lips stayed by her ear. 'I know I should take the rest of my clothes off now, but I'm feeling a little shy.'

As soon as he said it, she felt it too.

'Are we really doing this?' He choked out a nervous laugh.

It was all too much. 'I'm a virgin.'

Alex smiled. 'I guessed that. But we'll go at your pace, okay?'

She nodded. Her body wanted it.

Just once. Get it over with.

Alex kissed her again, and she froze beneath him.

Get it over with. Was that how she wanted her first time to go?

'What's wrong?' Alex pulled back.

'What are we doing?'

'I think it's obvious. We're giving in to our temptations.' He placed gentle kisses along her collarbone.

'It feels wrong.'

'But so right.'

'Yeah. That, too.'

Alex lifted her chin so she was looking up at him. 'What do you want to do?'

'I want you, but I also don't.'

'But I feel good, right?' His breaths were ragged.

Anya closed her eyes. '*So* good.'

'Well, the choice is yours. Tell me what happens next.'

Alex's hooded gaze chased away her anxiety. The low burning in her core was back, feelings that had nothing to do with Rapture.

She lifted her head and kissed him.

29

DOM

Dom opened his eyes to find himself back in his prison cell. The last thing he remembered was the female medic injecting him with something.

Morphine? Or a full dose of anaesthetic to knock him out? He still didn't know if he could trust her.

He lifted his head off the pillow. A pounding headache forced his eyes closed, and he lay back down.

The room spun.

The Copy. He'd seen the biogel take shape in the tank at the rear of the replication machine. The Copy had moved, but only with involuntary jerks. There must have been an electrical conduction agent present in the gel to give it movement.

118-C had told Quintus that the last copy hadn't worked. Fifth Gen was their latest tech, their best shot for the experiments on Dom.

No more Copies meant no more use for Dom.

Did that mean Quintus was done with him? No,

he had wanted to replace all his organs with tech. Dom would rather die than be turned into machine like a Copy, or one of the wolves in Arcis.

He had to escape. To find June, Sheila and Anya, and get the hell out of this place. He thought of Anya, the only person who gave him the courage to fight Praesidium's attempts to turn him into a plaything. He was done with the newborn. She'd attacked him and reopened his main wound. While Anya and the newborn looked the same, it was their personalities that set them apart.

The newborn's childish attitude didn't match Anya's. Nor did her lack of empathy.

The real Anya was selfless and strong, even though she didn't always believe those things about herself. Anya had woken him up in Arcis, made him believe there was more to life.

Dom worked himself up into a seated position, fighting against the dizziness and nausea. He placed both feet on the floor, and sucked in a sharp breath as his fresh wounds stabbed at him again. He lifted his tunic top, stained with ruby-coloured blood. The wounds continued to seep.

The door opened and the female medic entered.

'Lie down. You're too weak.'

Dom remained seated on the edge of the bed with his tunic pulled up to chest height. The medic walked over and forced him back down. He couldn't fight her, even if he'd wanted to.

She removed the cylindrical tool from her pocket and waved it over his seeping wounds. The red beam from the tip closed it again. She gave him a small dose of morphine, plus something else.

She held up a second vial. 'A new type of immunosuppressive. Better than the last one. It should help to fight off the infection, give your body a chance to recognise the tech as being part of you.'

Dom tried to sit up. 'I need to get out of here.'

The medic pushed him back down. 'I can't let you go, Dom Pavesi. The Collective will know I've helped you. '

'So I'm to die here? You know this is wrong. I'm not a lab rat.'

'Quintus is insisting I swap your heart for a Fifth Gen version. I can only hold him off for so long.'

Dom pulled a ragged breath through his teeth as his pain spiked. 'You have to hold him off forever. I will never allow that.'

The medic moved closer. 'He is interested in the Beyond, the place that exists further than Praesidium and the towns. I can delay him if you give me information about this place. He'll want to keep you healthy. Might even agree to downgrade the tech if you tell him what he wants to know.'

'I don't know anything.' Could he trust this medic who'd been so hostile to him in the beginning? Maybe something had happened to make her change, but he couldn't be sure if she was being genuine, or just playing him.

Max had mentioned the Beyond. He and Charlie hadn't planned on beginning their search for it until they'd dismantled Praesidium and rescued the human captives, including Max's wife. Max had said he'd never been to the Beyond, and that he didn't know if it was possible to cross back once there.

'Dom Pavesi, if you want to see your friends again, it's in your interest to cooperate with me.'

Dom sat up partially. This time, the medic didn't stop him. The morphine gave him false strength. 'Is that a threat?'

'A warning. The Collective doesn't have corporeal form. It lives life through our eyes. It will not hesitate to terminate you if you threaten its existence, or ours.'

118-C's demeanour appeared to soften with every new conversation. 'Why are you helping me?'

The medic hesitated. 'A girl on the floor above taught me that life is precious and not ours to control.'

Dom straightened up. 'What girl? Was it Anya Macklin?' The medic nodded. 'She's okay?'

'Yes. I told you she was safe.'

'That was before you told me you'd spoken to her.' Dom stood up and braced himself against the wall. 'Take me to her.'

The medic paused. 'She's important to you?'

'Very. Will you use that against me?'

The medic smiled a little, as if remembering. 'She is strong, wilful.'

Dom nodded. 'She is much more than that. Take me to her, please.'

The medic wiped all emotion from her face and pushed him back down on the bed. 'No. I am not permitted to take you there. Only to the testing room.'

'Then why are you here?'

'Because the Collective has instructed me to inquire about the Beyond.'

Dom shook his head. 'I mean, why are you still helping me?'

She stared at him for a couple of beats too long. 'I don't want to live my life this way any more.'

'So take me to Anya.' He tried to stand again.

'No, Dom Pavesi. If I do, I will be terminated.'

'But Quintus will see this conversation. He will know how you've helped me so far. You said the Collective lives life through your eyes.'

'I know how to hide my memories from the Collective, but if I'm caught taking you to Anya's room, I will not be able to explain your reason for being there. Plus, there is a camera in her room.'

'I don't care about that.'

'She's not alone.'

He was glad to hear one of the other girls was with her. 'So? Take me to her.'

'No!' The medic slapped the wall behind Dom's head. He went still. 'No,' she said, more softly. 'I can't take you to her, but I will do what I can to bring her to you.'

For the first time, he had hope.

'Dom Pavesi, I don't know how long you've got, but the Collective is keen to operate on you again. If you want to stay alive long enough to see your friends, I suggest you tell me something about the place known as the Beyond.'

270

Dom hesitated. Admitting to the existence of the place would keep him in Praesidium indefinitely. The searing pain of his injuries returned like a punch to the gut; the numbing effects of the morphine had slipped away faster than before. He swiped his fingers across his sweaty forehead and felt the heat emanating from his skin.

He had no choice. If the medic could argue for a downgrade of his tech to Fourth Gen, then he had to give her something. Praesidium's tech had been a part of him for so long, he was used to it. He could live with it inside him forever. But not the incompatible Fifth Gen.

Dom drew in a deep, shaky breath. 'I know about the Beyond. I'll tell you everything if Quintus is prepared to fix me.'

30

CARISSA

Carissa's schematics of the city excluded the tunnels into the medical facility. Was the Collective even aware of them? Possibly, yet Quintus had known nothing about the room beneath the library until Carissa ruined that secret. Maybe both had existed before the Collective.

Maybe Praesidium had, too.

Her hand grazed the uneven tunnel wall—so out of place in a concentric and ordered city—as she followed Vanessa and Canya.

The tunnel meandered in a series of gentle turns before it ended with a door.

Vanessa turned around to Carissa. 'You're up. Any idea what we should expect on the other side?'

Carissa checked her security file. 'The medics won't be expecting us, so hopefully nothing. We should keep going.'

Hopefully nothing? When had she started sounding so... human?

'What happens if they catch us?' said Canya. 'Why aren't we using weapons?'

'Jacob has assured me the Copies won't fight unless we give them a reason,' said Vanessa. 'If we go in there with weapons, they're bound to raise the alarm.'

'But the place is crawling with medics,' said Canya. 'What if one of them catches us?'

Vanessa frowned at her. 'And how would you know that? Is that what you saw when you came here? When I told you not to visit Dom?'

'I can go where I like, Vanessa. I had every right to see him. We share a connection.'

'You mean Anya and Dom share a connection. You're just borrowing her memories. Don't forget that. Soon, you'll have your own memories, your own experiences, and Dom won't matter to you.'

Canya flinched at Vanessa's harsh truth. Carissa saw it on the newborn's face: she was in love with Dom Pavesi.

'Even if my memories are wiped, I won't forget him.' Canya's voice wavered. 'Not even after we escape.'

Vanessa sighed. 'I can't stop you from feeling what you do, but it won't work out for you. Once you give the real Anya back her memories, she will remember Dom.'

Carissa stepped up to the door past a silent Canya, who scared her more now than the brat from a few days ago. 'Canya's previous visit may work to our advantage. Her access hasn't been revoked yet. If anyone comes, we can hide, and Canya can say she's exploring.'

Vanessa nodded. 'Okay. But hurry. The sooner we get in, the sooner we can get out.'

Carissa studied the door; it had a mechanised lock. She scoured the NMC security file for the medical facility's codes. It surprised her to learn that only three codes covered the entire facility. She set her chip to match the first frequency code and pressed it to the lock. It didn't work. She had better luck with the second code.

They stepped through into a plain white corridor and heard babies crying close by. Carissa glanced back at the clearly soundproofed door they'd just come through. That would work in their favour when they used it to escape later.

They followed the dimly lit corridor to a section that was brighter. Carissa kept watch for the Copies who were sure to be active in this part of the facility.

'The Inventor said the Copies don't use the darker tunnels,' she said. 'But these lit ones are on my map, so we must be entering the main part of the facility now.'

Vanessa nodded ahead. 'Jacob said to go through the Nurturing Centre. There are a couple of corridors up ahead. Which way?'

Carissa studied the map of the facility.

'Through here.' She pointed to a set of white doors on their left. 'Canya should go first and check the area is clear.'

Canya opened the door and poked her head out.

After a few seconds, she gave the all-clear. Inside, one wall was made of glass; there was a sectioned space beyond it. Carissa assumed this was the viewing corridor the Inventor had mentioned. The space, split into three parts, housed a dozen infants in the first area. Copies of the Arcis participants— Sheila, June and Yasmin—tended to the babies in cots. Each Copy had the extra NMC disc embedded in her temple.

Canya perked up. 'I know them. Are they newborns like me?'

Carissa shook her head. 'They already have their NMC discs. Their maturation period must have been accelerated.'

Vanessa nodded at them. 'I never saw them around much, except for their first day.'

'So why wasn't I connected straight away?' said Canya.

'The Collective must have had its reasons. Maybe something to do with Dom and your link with him.'

'We need to get him out of here.'

'And we will,' said Vanessa. 'Patience is the key now.'

They continued past the first section. The Copies looked up but only for a second. Carissa guessed their orders were to remain in the room with the infants.

The second section of the partitioned space was full of children ranging in age from four to eight years old. They had odd-coloured eyes.

Vanessa went still, causing Carissa some alarm.

'What's wrong?'

'I've never been in the Nurturing Centre before,' said Vanessa, whispering. 'The scene is a little... shocking. Are these children Copies?'

'No. The Collective uses Originals to create genetically perfect children. These children will remain here until they're mature enough to live in the city.'

'But the children have scars. Marks on their bodies.' Vanessa pointed to Carissa's NMC disc. 'They have a disc like yours.'

'Some of them do. Others don't have any marks or discs. These particular children are hybrids— human, but with Praesidium tech.'

Vanessa kept staring inside the room. 'So what's the difference between these children and you, Carissa?'

'I am an exact replica of my Original in body only. While I possess her memories, I differ enough to think independently. These children are human. From the Breeder programme.'

Vanessa swayed suddenly and Carissa grabbed her arm. The Librarian steadied herself against the glass. 'I had no idea the Collective was using the teenagers for this purpose. How long have the children been down here?'

'These particular ones?'

'You mean there are more?'

Carissa nodded. 'Not long. Probably only a few months. Before that they were like the babies in the first section. Their growth has been accelerated artificially.'

'A few *months*? But they've aged years. How?'

'The Collective has a machine capable of accelerating cell growth and maturity. It can convert hours into minutes, months into days.'

Vanessa closed her eyes and swallowed. 'What about those babies back there?'

'They'll be older tomorrow. The machine speeds up their cell maturation.'

'For what purpose?'

'The Collective is impatient. It needs a perfect human but one that can accept an NMC, so it can be controlled.'

'Why, Carissa? What's this all for?'

'So the hybrid can live among real humans without detection. That has been the purpose of this facility for the last eight months. It's common knowledge.'

'And how would I know, when I don't have access to what you do?' She tapped the side of her head.

Carissa understood. Without NMCs, the Originals relied on Copies to tell them news. But since Copies avoided Originals at all costs...

Vanessa swallowed again. 'I knew some of what the Collective was capable of, and I thought it brought the girls and boys here to understand how procreation worked. Not to whore them out and grow children faster than is humanly possible.' She stared at Carissa. 'And the gestation period?'

'Three months.'

Vanessa closed her eyes for a moment. 'I've been blind to this city. I've let it fool me into thinking it was a place built around curiosity.'

'It is,' said Carissa. 'But the Collective doesn't just want to learn. It wants to survive beyond the confines of Praesidium. It wants to live in the place the humans call the Beyond. And creating hybrids or Copies that can fool the humans is the first step to its achieving that goal.'

Vanessa perked up. 'That place. The Beyond. What does the group know about it?'

'Only that it was where the Collective originated from. Quintus doesn't know if the place even exists. There's no information about it in the database. He believes it's out there.'

'How?'

'He calls it a "feeling". That's why the Collective is making these children. If a Copy or hybrid crosses over, the Collective can too, using its creation as a vessel. The group is close to succeeding.'

'Not if I have anything to do with it.' Vanessa strode to the door at the end of the viewing corridor. Canya followed, while Carissa took a quick peek inside the last section. A blonde girl in a white gown lay on a large table in the middle of the room. She was surrounded by a machine and hooked up to tubes.

'Wait!' Carissa pointed inside the room. 'June's in there.'

Vanessa checked for herself. 'Why is she alone?'

Carissa checked the NMC file with the layout of the Nurturing Centre. 'This room is used for prenatal care.' Then she relayed what 28-C had told her. 'She's being prepared to receive a foetus from one of the Breeder pairings. She will act as incubator until the baby is fully grown.'

'For nine months?'

'No. The machine will accelerate the growth inside her.'

'And kill her? Her body's not designed for that kind of rapid growth. We need to get her out—now.'

June faced away from the window. Vanessa knocked on the glass, but the thickness deadened the sound. 'There's no way in. How do we get her out?'

'There must be a way to get to her,' said Carissa. She unlocked the door and sent Canya out first.

'Clear.'

The place was too quiet. Vanessa looked around. 'I guess they don't need as much security down here.'

Carissa ran her gaze over the square space beyond the Nurturing Centre. Ahead, a door led away from the room they needed to access. There was also a set of stairs leading up to the next floor. But no clear access point to get inside that room.

She couldn't see how to get to June.

31

ANYA

Alex's touch scorched Anya's skin. His assault of kisses rendered her breathless. His fingers teased the end of her camisole. She arched her back into him, wanting him closer. He growled, sending a shot of desire through her body. This moment. Perfect.

But beneath the heady desire was control.

She froze, causing him to pull back.

'What's wrong?'

'I don't want this.'

He sat up. 'Now? Or ever?'

'Not like this, Alex. It's not the real us. Let the Rapture subside, and if we're still attracted to each other, let's talk about it.'

Alex rolled his eyes. 'Sounds boring.' He slid off the bed and retrieved his shirt from the floor. 'But if I'm being honest, I'm glad you said it. I don't usually like to bed women I haven't even taken out on a date.'

'A date might be good. When we get out of here.'

'So. Never, then?' His smile faded.

'Don't think like that. We won't be here forever.'

'Wanna bet?'

A noise at the door drew their attention. Anya saw a folded slip of paper slide in.

Alex, who was the closest, picked it up and opened it. A thin card fell to the floor. Anya dressed and retrieved the card, made of brushed silver. It looked familiar. Had she used one of these before?

Alex grunted and thrust the note at her.

She plucked it from his fingers. 'What does it say?'

'I can't read.' He sat on the bed avoiding her gaze.

Anya read it aloud. '*I have turned off the camera. This card operates the elevator and other doors. Don't waste your freedom like I wasted mine.*'

'Who's it from?'

It could be only one person.

She didn't answer him, instead she tried the door; it had been left ajar.

'Quick. We've got our way out of here.'

Alex stayed put.

'Come on.'

'You go.'

Anya huffed. She collected one of the playing cards from the vanity table and used it to cover the door's locking mechanism, then shut the door.

'What are you doing, Alex? Come on.' She grabbed his hand and tried to pull him up.

He was on the verge of tears. 'I can't go with

you.'

'Of course you can.' She pulled on his sleeve. He didn't budge. She yanked on his arm.

'I'm not going. I don't belong anywhere else.'

'What about your family, in one of the towns?'

'I don't have any family. I lied.' Alex buried his face in his hands. 'I didn't see the harm. I never thought someone would help us escape. I'm sorry.'

Anya sat down beside him. 'Sorry about what? What are you talking about? The Ten kidnapped you, brought you here. Just like me.'

Alex shook his head. 'No, Anya. They didn't. I was already here.'

'But you escaped. You said so.'

'I was born here. I escaped. The Copies brought me back. My place is here.'

She wasn't quite sure what Alex meant. 'What do you mean you were *born* here? Are you human?'

'That's the only part that I didn't lie about. But I was grown quickly. I reached sexual maturity eight months ago, and then the Collective dumped me in this room.'

Fear hit her from all sides. 'But, how? I mean, what *are* you?' She backed away.

'I'm human. Created, born. Whichever you prefer.'

'How? When? Alex, please. I don't understand.'

He sighed and looked at her. His sadness stole her breath away. 'According to my file, I was created twenty months ago when two humans conceived naturally. I'm the product of that conception.'

'Here? In the city?'

He shrugged. 'I don't know. I could have come from one of the towns. But all I know is that while I was here, my maturity from child to adult happened in twelve months.'

He was *grown*?

'So you became an adult, an eighteen-year-old, in twelve months?'

'Yeah, but the hormones kick in when you reach puberty, and that's when I escaped. I had just turned fourteen.' He covered his face again. 'And this is why I didn't tell you. Because of *that* look. You're disgusted by me.'

She forced her shock to one side, coaxed his hands free of his face, and made him look at her. This was Alex, not some stranger.

'I'm not. I'm just... surprised.' She touched his face. 'You feel so real.'

'That's because I *am* real, Anya. I just don't belong out there. I know only this place.'

'How long were you gone from Praesidium?'

'Two weeks.'

'And fast growth, how did that work?'

'When I left, I stopped growing, or I grew at a normal rate. The machine I was placed in every day sped up my cell growth.'

'Until you reached sexual maturity?'

Alex shook his head. 'Fourteen years is considered useful to the Breeder programme. Eighteen for full maturity.'

'Let me get this straight. You've been in the

Breeder programme for eight months and you're only twenty months old?'

Alex smiled. 'When you put it like that, it sounds creepy. I have the intelligence of an eighteen-year-old, in case you're wondering. My body is human, but my brain has been modified. My ability to learn is accelerated in tandem with my growth.'

'But if you lived out there for two weeks, you must have settled somewhere.'

'I survived on my own. The Collective had given me knowledge, including survival training. I made do.'

Anya laced her fingers in his. 'How did it find you?'

'I slipped up. In some weird, freakish way, I missed this place. It was like a homing beacon drew me back.' He sighed. 'I got too close to one of the urbanos they were building. The Copies spotted me and found my bio signature that identified me as one of them.'

'So they brought you back?'

'They had to. I was a Breeder. I was too valuable to the Ten.' He stared at their joined hands. 'That was always my purpose here, to become a Breeder.'

'How many Breeders are here?'

'A dozen or so. But they want to increase the numbers.'

Anya's throat tightened. 'That's what we're doing here. That's why they're pumping us full of Rapture.'

'Yeah, partly.'

She looked at him. 'We're *creating* Breeders?'

'Potentially. But not all babies are grown for the Breeder programme. I think others are being used to create synthetic and human hybrids that can masquerade as human beyond Praesidium's walls.'

She remembered what 118-C had said about the Collective. 'My medic mentioned something similar to me, that the Collective was trapped and looking for a means of escape.'

'I don't know much about the Ten, but Praesidium exists for a reason. Why bring so many humans here in secret?'

The thought made Anya shiver. 'And that's how you knew so much about this place. I just thought you'd figured it out over time.'

'A bit of both.' Alex freed his hand to swipe at his eyes.

Anya knelt between his legs. 'So why don't you want to leave?' She held up the elevator card. 'We have a way out.'

'Because I can never be free. I'm forever tied to this place. The Collective will always find me. I tried to escape before, remember? It brought me back.'

'I'm sorry, Alex. It's not a good enough reason. Freedom, no matter how short, is better than a lifetime of slavery.'

'I hear you, but I was *designed* for this place. I have nowhere to go.'

'Come with me. I can take you back to Brookfield.'

He shook his head. 'You spent three months in

Arcis. It's possible the rebels have taken over the town.'

Anya had the same thought. 'I have to find Jason, and Brookfield is the last place I saw him.'

'You should go.'

'No. Not without you.'

'I tried living among you. I couldn't find a place where I belonged.'

'You gave it two weeks. That's not nearly long enough. Plus, you didn't have me then. You didn't have a friend.'

When he smiled, her heart lifted. She pulled his face down to hers.

His kisses were soft, tender. 'Do you really believe we can escape?'

'We didn't have this before.' She waved the card around. 'Let's give it a shot.'

32

CARISSA

'There's no way to reach June,' said Carissa frustrated.

Vanessa glanced up the stairs. 'We should keep going. We'll come back for her on the way out.'

They climbed up one floor. Canya led the way as they entered another monochrome corridor.

'The Breeder programme is on this floor,' said Carissa. 'We'll definitely cross paths with a few medics here. We should stay on high alert.'

Carissa led the way to the three treatment rooms and the access point to the viewing platform. The sound of a door opening followed by movement froze her to the spot.

Vanessa took action and found a nearby door unlocked. Carissa and Canya wasted no time in following her.

Carissa stayed by the door with Vanessa, who held it open just a crack. A female medic walked past with a firm hold on Sheila.

'We should wait here for a moment,' whispered Vanessa.

Carissa watched Sheila struggle against her captor until they both disappeared out of sight. She heard a door being opened. The medic said, 'Good riddance.'

Sheila had most likely been returned to her room —which one, she couldn't tell. Vanessa opened the door wider to get a better look. The medic backtracked out of the corridor with the rooms and continued down the main one, away from their location. Carissa heard an elevator being called.

She turned to Vanessa. 'The elevator's further on past the holding rooms.'

With the area clear, they slipped out of their hiding place and headed to the area where the medic had taken Sheila. Carissa pressed her wrist to the first door to reveal an empty room. She looked up at the number. Seventeen.

'That's June's room,' said Carissa. 'We should try the next one.'

Rooms eighteen and nineteen were also empty. Room twenty revealed Sheila standing over a wailing boy. His bloody nose looked broken.

'I told you what would happen if you touched me. Pervert!'

The boy pleaded with her. 'But we're *supposed* to touch. That's the whole point of this place.'

'Over my dead body.'

Sheila turned and glared at the trio standing at the door.

'What? Have you come to watch? You're all a bunch of sick freaks.'

'No time to explain,' said Vanessa. 'We've come to get you out of this place. Hurry.'

Sheila didn't waste time. She left the bleeding boy behind.

'We can't leave,' said the boy. 'They'll find us.'

Sheila whipped her head back around. 'Who said you were coming?' Her gaze flitted between Canya and Carissa. 'And who the hell are you three? No, wait. I don't care. Just get me out of this place. Where's Dom? Is he with you?'

'He's on the floor above,' said Vanessa. 'That's our next stop, once we clear this one.' She waited for the boy. 'Are you coming?'

He shook his head. 'Already escaped once. Giving in to this perversion is much easier.'

Vanessa left the door unlocked. 'Your call.'

Carissa smiled when Sheila rolled her eyes at the boy and stomped out the door. While watching her in Arcis, she'd grown fond of her feisty attitude.

The group opened all the doors they came across. Most of them were empty. Carissa found Yasmin in room twenty-nine.

Yasmin stood, her eyes narrowing, as Sheila presented herself at the door. Sheila just looked at her. 'I feel like I know you from somewhere.'

Yasmin gave Sheila the once-over. 'I've never seen you before.'

'Let's keep moving everyone,' said Vanessa. 'We don't have time to idle. We still need to find

Anya.'

Their search brought them to a corridor on the far side of the treatment rooms with door numbers ranging from one to ten.

Carissa opened a door marked with the number six. A playing card dropped to the floor. She froze when she saw Anya kneeling in front of a blond boy sitting on a bed.

Kissing him.

33

DOM

118-C relayed the information Dom had given her about the Beyond back to Quintus. She sealed up his wounds for the third time and gave him antibiotics and a hit of morphine.

'Quintus is not satisfied. You are to come with me.'

'Why?' Dom's voice barely notched over a whisper. Every word, each painful breath, reminded him the infection was spreading again.

'I've delayed Quintus long enough. He wants to perform the heart surgery soon.'

'No! I won't survive it.'

'Quintus doesn't understand the danger. But if you come with me, together we might be able to delay the surgery. That's the best I can do for now.'

Dom stood up and leaned into her; he didn't have much choice. 118-C looped an arm around his waist, giving him the strength he lacked. How much more of this could he take?

291

On the way to the testing room, Dom created more false information about the Beyond he could give to Quintus to stop him from proceeding with his plans. No more surgery, unless it was to revert him to Fourth Gen tech.

Inside the room, the bed waited for him. The sight of it, what it meant, had him straining towards the door.

No more playing games with Quintus. It was time to escape. And 118-C would help him, because, damn, he didn't have the strength to walk, let alone run.

118-C shuffled him over to the bed.

No, the other way, his inner voice whispered. She got him settled on the bed and strapped him down. His heart pounded as he stared up at the closed ceiling panels. Would his new mechanical heart beat just as wildly? Would it beat at all?

118-C touched a finger to her ear, listening. She shook her head at Dom and stepped back and off to the side. The first of the panels opened, and the arm containing the anaesthetic punctured his vein. He jerked and twisted against the restraints. The scanner arm extended and ran the beam over the length of his body.

The laser arm descended. Dom's breath caught in his throat as it hovered over his chest.

He squeezed his eyes shut and prepared for the cut.

But when nothing happened, he opened his eyes. The laser had relocated to his left arm, and began cutting there. Dom flashed a surprised look at the medic, who appeared equally startled. Then she neutralised her expression.

Pincers spread the skin to expose his bones. The laser cut the two main bones in his forearm and pulled them out. Under anaesthetic, Dom felt only a tingling in his limb. The pincers worked fast. They darted over to the panels in the wall and removed a tray with two bone-shaped pieces of metal, then returned to place the tray on Dom's chest. They attached the new bones and sealed the wound.

This had to be the beginning of his transformation into a machine. At least the Collective had started with his arm and not his heart.

The surgical arms retracted into the ceiling; the panels closed to hide them from view.

Movement from the medic caught Dom's eye. She touched a disc above her ear and spoke rapidly. A booming voice overhead frightened Dom. He recognised it; the same voice he'd heard on the ninth floor in Arcis. Quintus.

'118-C wishes to know why the Collective changed its mind about the heart surgery. A scan has determined that your odds of survival would be low if it was to proceed while you still have an infection. And the Ten still has questions about the Beyond.'

Dom released a quiet breath, but he wasn't ready to play all his cards just yet. 'I told the medic everything I know about that.'

'But you have not told me everything. The Collective believes there is more. You are a rebel. It is my belief that your sole reason for existing is to find the Beyond and to help liberate your people.'

Dom tried to locate the source of the voice. 'And what's your reason for finding the Beyond?'

'To liberate ours.'

Dom glanced at the medic. Even she looked surprised.

'118-C doesn't know everything, Dom Pavesi. The Collective only tells its Copies what they need to know. Now give me the coordinates to the Beyond.'

Dom called Quintus' bluff. 'I came here because I heard you had them.'

'Do not confuse the Collective's delay for kindness,' said Quintus. 'I will order your surgeries to resume, regardless of your survival potential. I will continue to gather information on your physiology and its compatibility with Praesidium tech. It does not matter to the Collective ten if you live or die.'

Dom hadn't expected the Collective to keep him alive after it was finished with the surgeries. 'I was told the coordinates to the Beyond were in Praesidium.'

'That is not the case, Dom Pavesi. If it were, you would have come to the city much earlier than this. You only discovered its existence recently. What I don't understand is how you just found out. The Collective has known about it all along.'

'If the Beyond is so important to you, what do you need me for, besides information? Why are you copying me? Why are you replacing my organs with tech? What does it matter?'

'The Collective ten does not have corporeal form. Its Copies are not entirely convincing replacements for humans. Strange eye colour, mannerisms and behaviour—these are things you humans notice. The Collective must cross over to the Beyond. To do this, it needs foolproof Copies.'

'And what makes you think the Beyond exists?'

'Because the Collective was born there. Its makers trapped us in this world.'

Max and Charlie had said the same thing. But to hear it confirmed sent chills through Dom's scorching flesh. 'Born? How?'

'It doesn't matter. Tell me where it is. The Collective has failed to locate it since the makers placed it in this prison. The makers are masking the crossing point.'

'I don't know where it is.' It was the truth, and Dom was out of options. A groan escaped his lips when a new pain shot up his arm. The damn anaesthetic was wearing off.

118-C stepped closer to him. 'We should give him time to rest, Quintus. He is not well enough to be interrogated.'

A long pause followed, and Dom thought Quintus had disconnected. But then his voice boomed out again.

'Take him back to his room. You will try again in twenty-four hours, when he has recovered.'

118-C untied Dom's straps and helped him off the table. In his room, she helped to get him comfortable on the bed.

Dom's arm raged with pain. He held it up. 'Fourth or Fifth Gen?'

'Fifth,' said the medic, with a soft shake of her head.

'So, what now?'

At the door, she turned round. 'You have twenty-four hours before Quintus wants to operate again. And the next surgery is likely to kill you. I'll do what I can to get you help before that happens.'

Dom watched her leave. The isolation hurt worse than the fire in his arm. He closed his eyes and prayed to a god he didn't believe in that she would.

34

ANYA

'What the hell's going on?'

Anya froze. The voice sounded like hers. She looked up and was caught in the pale-blue stare of her identical twin.

A dark-skinned woman stood behind, with two girls she'd seen earlier: the tanned goddess and wiry blonde. A third girl, aged around thirteen, grinned at her.

She got to her feet, a blush heating her cheeks at being caught kissing Alex. 'What are you doing here? Who are you all?'

Her twin's aggressive step forward forced her back. 'What were you two doing? Don't you even care?'

'Care? What are you talking about?'

The others entered as the older woman retrieved the fallen playing card and placed it back over the lock. She closed the door. 'Are they recording,

Anya?'

Anya shook her head. 'The camera's been disabled.'

'How?'

'Long story. I don't know why any of you are here, but we need to leave before the medics realise.'

Her twin invaded her space. 'You don't deserve to leave. He doesn't deserve you.' She spoke through clenched teeth. 'I still don't know why he wants you. I mean, look at you. Willing to do it with just *anyone*. There's a name for girls like you.'

'Canya, that's enough!' said the older woman.

'Canya?' Anya stared at her lookalike. 'What is she?'

'Your Copy,' said the younger girl. 'She was created from you.'

'Created? When?' She looked to Alex for an explanation.

'When you were in Arcis,' he said. 'After your memories were taken. Before you came here.'

Memories or not, how could she forget another *her*?

Her lookalike punched her in the arm. 'You don't deserve him. You have no idea what he's been going through.'

'Ow!' She stepped out of Canya's space. Canya —really? 'Who? Alex? I know enough about him. We've been stuck in here for days. We've been helping each other.'

She caught the seething hate in her twin's eyes and dodged another fist.

'You're all he talks about. And here you are, shacked up with another guy.'

'Canya, it's not her fault,' said the younger girl.

'Shut up, Carissa. He's hurting because she won't visit him. I've been keeping him company. Not her. Me. She's repaid him by kissing some stranger.'

'She doesn't remember him,' said Carissa. 'She's also a prisoner here. But you can help her to remember. You can give Anya back her memories.'

Canya folded her arms. 'I don't think so.'

There was something disturbing yet familiar about Canya's behaviour. In her younger days, Anya had been that same brat with both Jason and her mother.

'They're not your memories, Canya,' said Carissa. 'They're hers. He belongs to her.'

He? 'Is my brother here? Is he okay?'

Carissa ignored her and shook Canya's arm. Her lookalike yelped.

'You have to, Canya,' said the older woman. 'I need her to remember.'

'But *I* remember, Vanessa. I can give you anything you want. Why do we need her?'

'Because I've asked you numerous times,' said Vanessa. 'Now we have a chance to return Anya's memories.'

Canya appeared to panic. 'There are no guarantees Anya will give you what you want. You haven't given me a fair chance. I'm new. Still getting used to things. Please don't make me... What if I lose my memories during the transfer?'

'It's a risk we have to take,' said Vanessa.

Canya took a swing at Vanessa, who dodged it. But it might as well have come from Anya. She'd swung at Grace like that a few times, when she couldn't control her temper—which was often. Now, she couldn't bear to watch her twin act out. It all looked so childish, so out of character. She'd grown up the second she saw her parents being killed.

Vanessa and Carissa drew Canya closer. Anya fought against a sudden instinct to flee. She wanted her memories back, and if this Copy had them, she would see this through.

Carissa explained how she needed to press her location chip to Canya's for the memories to transfer. 'You still have them, but they're in hibernation.'

'Do we all have Copies?' said the goddess. 'Because I'd really like to get back what I've missed over the last few months, too.'

'They're in the Nurturing Centre,' said Carissa. 'But they're connected to the Collective, which means their memories may have been wiped already.'

'But we can try?'

'Yes, Sheila,' said Carissa.

Vanessa pushed Anya's twin forward. 'Canya, you need to do this.'

'I don't want to.'

'If you don't, I can't take you with me.'

A look of alarm flashed across Canya's face. 'I need these memories. The Collective is going to reset me tomorrow. You can't leave me here!'

'Do this or you'll never see Dom again. And if

you do see him, I'll make sure you won't remember him.'

Canya gritted her teeth.

'She's into Dom?' Sheila snorted. 'Figures.'

Canya shot Sheila a nasty look. 'Fine, I'll do it.'

Carissa turned Canya's wrist so it was facing up. 'You need to touch chip to chip, to make a connection. Concentrate on the memories, Canya. They're saved in your synthetic biogel brain, like an imprint. You must use the electrical reserves in your biogel to create a connection between it and your chip, then force the memories to hitch a ride on the connection between you both.'

Canya pressed her chip to Anya's. She closed her eyes.

Anya closed hers, too, not sure what to expect.

She felt the first stirring of something in her mind: an awakening of something dormant. A memory hit her.

Warren Hunt. He had trapped her in the bathroom, blocked her escape. He wanted something from her.

'No!' Her eyes shot open, and she broke contact with Canya. Her chest tightened and she heaved out a breath. The feel of Warren's weight as he touched her, demanded more—it was too much. She wanted to be sick.

Carissa shook Canya's arm. 'What did you show her?'

'I gave her back her memories, like you told me to.' Canya tried to reclaim her arm from Carissa.

'What did she show you, Anya?' said Carissa.

'Something horrible.' She swallowed bile and fought back tears.

'We can't stay here any longer,' said Vanessa. 'We need to go. We can try again later. Anya, are you ready?'

Anya wiped her face and nodded. She had to be strong. She showed Vanessa the elevator card. 'This will take us to the surface.'

'Where did you get it?' Vanessa took the card from her.

'A friend, I think.'

'I promise we'll try again with her.' Vanessa glanced at Canya. 'She's been difficult these last few days. Give her time.'

Anya nodded as more feelings from her memory of Warren surfaced. She hid her disgust from the others, but she also felt energised by the partial regain of memory. What else could Canya unlock?

Anya grabbed Alex's hand, but he still didn't budge. 'I'm not leaving you here. I won't take no for an answer.'

The edges of Alex's mouth turned up. 'I guess I could try. See what all the fuss is about.'

Outside the room, Vanessa said, 'We need to split up. Dom's on the first floor and June's on the last floor, in the Nurturing Centre. Carissa, you take Canya, Sheila and Yasmin with you to get June out. Anya and Alex will come with me to get Dom.'

'I want to go with you,' said Canya. 'Dom needs me.'

Vanessa ignored her pleas, much to Canya's irritation. 'We'll meet on the first floor, by the elevator. Don't be late.'

'Wait,' said Anya. 'I only have one elevator card.'

'Carissa is a Copy. She still has access to the codes.'

'I'm going with you,' Sheila said to Vanessa. 'Dom knows me. If he's lost his memories, he won't remember any of you.'

'We've got it covered.' Vanessa pointed in the direction of the stairs. 'Go with Carissa. Your Copies are in the Nurturing Centre. If they still have their memories, you'll need to be present to receive the transfer.'

Anya took Alex's hand. For the first time since her arrival, she had hope.

35

CARISSA

'What was Vanessa talking about back there?' said Yasmin. 'What are Copies?'

Carissa had located the stairwell. She and Canya led Sheila and Yasmin back to the Nurturing Centre.

'There are Copies of both of you in the Nurturing Centre,' said Carissa.

'What are you talking about? What the hell's a Copy?'

Carissa kept moving, surprised by Yasmin's question. Copies had escorted her to and from the treatment rooms several times. Maybe ignoring the obvious was how she dealt with trauma.

'Canya and I are both Copies,' said Carissa. She needed to hear the truth. 'We are perfect replicas of what we call Originals, but you call humans.'

Yasmin slowed on the stairs. 'This is all bullshit. For all we know, these two are leading us into a trap.'

Sheila slowed, too. 'I'm with her. How do we know you're not just taking us to a new cell?'

Carissa rolled her eyes. 'Why would I when we could have just left you in the cell we found you in?' She considered going without them. June needed her and time was running out. 'I'm at as much risk of being caught as you are.'

'You always were a bitch, Sheila,' said Canya.

Sheila stopped. 'Excuse me?'

Canya folded her arms. 'You heard me.'

'Have we even met?'

'Yeah, we have. You were a bitch then, and you're still a bitch now.'

Sheila grabbed a fistful of Canya's blue dress and slammed her into the wall. 'Say that again, Copy, and I'll knock you unconscious.'

'She didn't mean it.' Carissa fought against an eye roll as she peeled Sheila's hand off Canya. Sheila's mouth made a perfect *O* at her show of strength. 'It will all make sense when you get your memories back.'

Sheila backed off. 'What memories have I lost? I was in one place, then I was here. The in-between stuff is hazy.'

'You lost three months. You came from a place called Arcis,' said Carissa. 'Your Copies, they can give you back your memories. But you both need to touch your opposite.'

Sheila nodded but Yasmin needed convincing. 'You're telling me I have to touch something that looks exactly like me?' Her mouth turned down in disgust. 'I don't think so.'

'So what if they look like us?' said Sheila. 'If

something's been taken from me, I want it back.'

'Come on,' said Carissa. 'We should keep moving. Before someone hears us.'

Canya entered the space first and headed straight for the viewing corridor.

'Wait,' said Carissa. 'We need to get inside the Nurturing Centre. We have to find another way in.'

Canya stood with her hand on the door. Carissa had no idea if the newborn would help. She checked the offline map. It showed two doors in the area, one for the viewing area and another leading away from the centre. But there was also a dark area that led behind the Nurturing Centre. Carissa ran her hand over the solid wall protecting that area, expecting to find an entry point.

'There's nothing here. We must have missed something in the viewing corridor.'

Canya gave her an I-told-you-so look and entered the corridor. Carissa searched for a secret panel in the glass but found nothing. The wall opposite the glass was equally smooth to the touch. She breathed out and pressed her hands against the glass. June lay still on the gurney, a white sheet pulled up to her waist.

The Collective would implant her soon. Carissa had to get her out.

The door opened suddenly and a male medic appeared.

'Halt! What are you doing here? This is a restricted area.'

Carissa's pulse thrummed and she straightened up. 'We're here to observe the experiments.'

The male medic eyed her. 'Designation?'

'173-C.'

'173-C, your access to the medical facility have been revoked.' The medic checked over the others. He pointed at Canya. 'You are a newborn. Unconnected.'

'I'm to be connected tomorrow,' said Canya. 'I wanted to see the Nurturing Centre one last time. I plan on becoming a medic.'

The medic's eyes flitted between Sheila and Yasmin. 'And you two are not designated. You are part of the Breeder programme.'

Carissa thought fast. 'No. These are the Copies. Still to be connected. They have permission to be here.'

The medic pressed his finger to the disc just above his ear. 'I will need to check.'

Think, Carissa. As soon as he checked, he would discover her lie and Quintus would order their immediate terminations.

The door opened again and a second medic, a female, appeared.

'124-C, they are here under my supervision,' she said. 'There is no need to check anything.'

The male medic frowned. 'Does Quintus know they're here?'

'Your superior is giving you an order, 124-C. They are my responsibility. I will report to Quintus, if necessary. Please return to your duties.'

'Of course, 118-C.' The male medic left the viewing corridor.

Carissa formulated a new set of lies for the female.

118-C waited for 124-C to leave before she turned to them. Her eyes raked over Canya. 'You are not the one from the floor above.'

'No, she's the Copy,' said Carissa.

The medic turned her grey eyes to Carissa. 'Designation?'

'173-C.'

The medic nodded. 'You're the one who watched them in Arcis.'

Carissa nodded. 'I have permission from Quintus to be here.'

The medic was silent as she examined their group. She pointed at Sheila and Yasmin. 'These two are from the Breeders' floor. Correct?'

'Yes.'

She looked inside the partition at June. 'And you want to know how to get in there and rescue your friend?'

Carissa nodded. She saw no point in lying further.

The medic turned and paused at the door leading back to the open space. 'Then follow me.'

Carissa shook her head at this strange turn of events. She waited with the others as the medic stood in front of the solid wall that, according to her map, hid an access point. She waved her wrist over it. The wall shimmered, liquefied and then solidified into the shape of a door. It opened and the medic stepped through. 'Quickly. We don't have much time.'

Carissa entered a corridor she never would have found on her own. Perhaps this trick was tied in only to the medic's chip. The medic led them to the back of the Nurturing Centre and a corridor with three doors that allowed access to all three partitions. 118-C opened the first door, and Carissa wasted no time in getting to June.

She was groggy, but awake. 'Carissa...'

'Come on. We need to get you out of here.' She pulled the IV free from June's arm.

'173-C, how do you know this Original?' said a suddenly tense medic.

Carissa considered lying, but she sensed 118-C was different from the others. Quintus would see her reply only when the medic carried out her upload. But she expected that wouldn't happen, since it would implicate 118-C. 'She's my Original's sister.'

The medic gasped. 'Can that happen? I was told siblings of our Originals would never end up here. The townspeople would ask too many questions.'

'Well, clearly that was a lie.' Carissa supported June's weight alone until Sheila and Yasmin stepped in to help. Canya stayed back, watching as they carried her outside the room.

'118-C, there's something else we need,' said Carissa. 'Access to the Copies in the first section.'

The medic frowned. 'What do you need with them? They are connected now.'

'They're Copies of these three,' she said, nodding at Sheila, June and Yasmin. 'If they still have their Originals' memories, they can pass then back.'

The medic's grey eyes widened. 'How is that possible?'

'The procedure is explained in the security file we're only meant to access in the event of an attack.' She explained to 118-C how the transfer worked. 'It's only been a few days since connection. The memories might still exist despite the reset. This is our only chance to try.'

The medic paused, listened. 'Someone will be here soon. We need to leave.' She poised a finger over her communication disc.

'Please! We can't go without trying with the Copies,' said Sheila.

The medic glanced at Carissa, then at the exit. She dashed to the last partitioned space, opened the door and stepped inside. She emerged dragging Sheila's Copy with her. 'Do it quick. I cannot get everyone.'

Carissa grabbed the stunned Copy and pressed her location chip to Sheila's wrist. 'Think about your Original's memories. Give them to her as if you're passing a thought. Quickly.' Sheila's Copy glanced at the medic, unsure.

'That's an order,' said 118-C. The Copy nodded and closed her eyes.

Sheila shuddered as a transaction appeared to take place between her and the Copy. She gasped and stepped away. Her unfocused gaze honed in on Yasmin. 'I *know* you.'

'Go back,' said the medic, 'and do not speak of

this.' The silent Copy stumbled back to the last partition and disappeared inside.

The medic turned to Carissa. 'You have to go.'

'But the others...'

'There's no time. Now!'

The medic pulled Carissa by the arm and the others followed. They passed back through the organic door.

'You cannot risk using the elevator,' said the medic. 'You must take the stairs.' Canya entered the stairwell first then June, supported by Sheila. Yasmin brought up the rear.

Carissa stayed back with the medic. 'Come with us, 118-C. When Quintus finds out what you did for us, he'll order your termination.'

The medic smiled and pushed her towards the stairwell. 'I am committed to serving the Collective. I will take whatever punishment is appropriate.'

'But why? Why help us?'

The medic frowned. 'For the same reason you choose to help. Because it is the right thing to do.'

'Thank you.' She gave 118-C a quick nod and caught up to the others. Together they climbed to the first floor, where they had planned to meet up with Vanessa.

'Are we going to get Dom now?' said Canya. She pushed ahead, leaving the others to tend to June.

Carissa was tired of her attitude. 'Yes, Canya. That's exactly where we're going.'

Canya smiled and turned away, leaving Carissa to stare at the wilful newborn's back. Memories or not, she was an unpredictable risk. No way was she leaving the city.

Carissa would see to it.

36

ANYA

Anya followed Vanessa up the stairs, gripping Alex's hand. The pungent, hospital-like smell on the new floor made her nose twitch.

Ahead was a straight, wide corridor with a series of closed doors inset along one wall. On the other side were four corridors set at ninety degrees to the main one, with similar closed doors. She shielded her eyes from the glaring overhead light.

Vanessa used the access card to open the main doors only to discover they were empty. After checking the minor corridors, they gathered again in the main space. All empty.

Anya looked around. Where was everyone? The antiseptic smell tickled her nose, sparking a new memory. Her arm had been cut. The boy with the dark hair had applied a stinging liquid to her arm that was more painful than the wound.

Alex's hand in hers suddenly felt wrong.

'What happens on this floor?' she said, releasing

Alex's hand.

She was looking at Vanessa, but Alex replied. 'At the Collective's request, the medics put Praesidium tech in those taken from the towns. If Dom's here, he must be important to the Ten.'

'Important how?'

'It means he's receptive to their technology. He was probably tested at a young age to gauge just how compatible his physiology was with their tech.'

Anya shivered at the thought. She'd grown up in a simple household; her only exposure to tech had been the broken Praesidium hand-me-downs that Jason used to fix. Anya usually went for a run whenever Jason tried to explain how it worked. Maybe she should have listened.

They gathered in the last unchecked corridor. Vanessa pressed the card to the locking mechanism of the last door. 'It's empty.' She closed the door with a sigh. 'I don't understand. Where could he be?'

'He may have been taken for harvesting,' said Alex.

Anya frowned. 'Harvesting?'

'When the Copies replace an Original's biological organs with artificial ones.'

'Why? For what purpose?'

'To test compatibility. The Collective wishes to understand the limitations of the human body.'

'And if the tech isn't compatible?' But Anya already knew the answer.

'The Original is terminated.'

'You're human, correct?' said Vanessa.

Alex nodded. 'Breeder. Human, but grown fast.'

Vanessa shook her head slowly. 'Jacob told me about the growth machine. I thought he was joking. Has the Collective experimented on you?'

'No, I wasn't designed to be anything but a Breeder. I was never meant for this floor.' Alex pointed to the dead end. 'We should keep going. There are more rooms on the other side of this wall.'

Vanessa touched the surface. 'It's solid. There's nothing here.'

Alex asked for the card and Vanessa gave it to him. He waved it over a specific spot. The wall shimmered to reveal a full archway. Anya smiled at the new corridor with a dozen, maybe more, doors.

'This place is full of surprises,' said Alex, handing back the card. 'A bunch of the walls are organic, meaning they can become anything they want. You never know what's behind them.'

A wall, similarly organic in nature, flashed in Anya's mind. It had become malleable when she'd fired an electric bolt in it.

Vanessa hurried through the archway. Alex and Anya followed. 'We need to get Dom before one of the medics finds us. I'd rather be closer to the exit before that happens.'

'What if we find new people in here?' said Anya. 'Will we take them with us?'

'Our priority is getting you and the others out,' said Vanessa. 'We have a better shot at escaping if the group is small. We can worry about a rescue plan later.'

The first two rooms that Vanessa checked were empty. She gasped when she opened the third door and rushed inside. 'Hurry!'

Anya followed but stopped when she saw a young man of about nineteen lying on a bed. His skin was pallid and soaked in sweat. His laboured breaths told her he wasn't asleep.

'I guess this is Dom Pavesi,' said Alex.

Vanessa glanced at Anya. 'You two knew each other in Arcis.'

She studied the boy with dark brown curls stuck to his skin. 'I don't recognise him.' That wasn't true. A flicker of recognition caught her from the moment she saw him.

'Canya was supposed to give you back all your memories,' said Vanessa. 'I'm sorry. She's been a handful since the moment of her creation.' She checked Dom's eyes and pulse. 'He's in bad shape. He's got an infection and it's spreading. He'll be dead in a few hours if we don't get him out of here.'

Anya helped to lift Dom, but he was too heavy to move in his barely conscious state.

Vanessa groaned. 'He's dead weight. He's going nowhere unless he walks.'

'We need a gurney,' said Alex. 'I'll check the other rooms.'

'I'll come with you,' said Anya, eager to get some breathing space.

They soon found one and wheeled it back as fast and quietly as they could. With Alex on one side and Anya on the other, they managed to lift Dom onto the gurney.

'Is he going to be okay?' She touched Dom's skin; it was freezing. She grabbed the blanket from the bed and tucked it around his body.

Alex pushed while Vanessa pulled the gurney back to the stairwell. It bumped against the bottom step. 'We'll need to find the elevator. No way we're getting him up the stairs on this.'

There had to be another way out. 'Up is too dangerous.'

'It's our only choice, Anya.' Vanessa looked around. 'There's a way out through the Nurturing Centre. But the gurney won't fit. Dom can't walk and we can't carry him. We have to use the main entrance.'

Dom stirred. His eyes flickered open, and Anya grabbed his hand without thinking. His unfocused gaze watched her, gave her butterflies. Then it changed, became fierce.

'I told you not to come back,' he hissed. He turned his head away.

It had to be the drugs. He was hallucinating. So why did his words, from a stranger no less, sting? Anya concentrated on a new noise, coming from the stairwell.

Carissa appeared first, followed by Sheila and Yasmin. Under their care was a blonde girl dressed in a hospital gown; Anya had seen her earlier.

'Good,' said Vanessa. 'You found June. Now we can all get out of here.'

'Dom!' Sheila handed June off to Yasmin. 'Is he

okay?'

'He's in bad shape. We need to get him out of here.'

'You stupid idiot.' Sheila moved to his side and squeezed his fingers.

Canya emerged from the stairwell to push past Yasmin, nearly knocking June to the floor. Yasmin grunted and caught June before she fell.

'Dom.' Canya groped for his other hand and kissed it. 'Dom, I'm here. Everything's going to be okay.'

Jealousy hit Anya square in the gut. She stopped herself from pulling Canya off him.

Dom looked up at the Copy, blinking. 'Anya?'

'Yes. It's me.'

'*I'm* Anya.' The words sounded like a growl in her head, but never passed her lips. She groped for Alex's hand, finding comfort in his warmth.

'Come on,' said Vanessa. 'We need to get out.'

They found the elevator not far from the main corridor. Vanessa and Alex wheeled the gurney in first. Canya continued to hold Dom's hand. An irritated Anya followed. Sheila and Yasmin entered last with June. The elevator moved and then opened at what she assumed to be the lobby. Anya exited, surprised to find it empty.

'Where is everyone?'

Vanessa and Alex pulled the gurney out of the elevator.

Anya's fingers brushed Dom's hand for just a minute, and Canya noticed.

'What are you doing? Don't touch him. He's mine.'

She was sick of the drama. 'I didn't mean anything by it.' She held her hands up.

'Yes, you did,' said Canya. 'As soon as we're out of here, you're going to make a move on him. Don't think I haven't figured out your game. You're trying to break us up.'

Anya smothered the urge to hit her duplicate. 'I've no desire to break you up. You're welcome to each other.'

Canya's hands curled into fists. She scanned the exit. 'Come quickly! The test subjects are trying to escape!'

Her shouts brought three guards rushing into the lobby. 'How did you get up here?' said one.

The guards pointed Electro Guns at them. Anya had seen the gun type somewhere before.

One of the guards snatched the access card from Vanessa's hand. 'We have intruders in the medical facility. They've just exited the elevator. It looks like they had help.'

The lead guard turned to Canya. 'Designation.'

'She's unconnected,' said Vanessa.

'I wasn't speaking to you.' He cracked the butt of his gun against Vanessa's head. She stumbled back and hit the gurney, which kept her on her feet.

'Designation.'

Canya's lip quivered. 'I don't have one.'

'You were helping them escape?'

'No, I'm warning you that they're trying to

leave.'

The lead guard examined Canya. 'You are here. That means you are helping them.' He turned to Carissa. 'Designation.'

'173-C,' said Carissa softly.

The guard's eyes flickered for a second. 'You are banned from the medical facility, 173-C. Why are you helping these Originals escape?'

Carissa squeaked, 'Because it's the right thing to do.'

Canya moved to stand with the guards. Anya almost went for her when she pointed at Dom. 'This man needs to be taken back to his room. He's sick.'

'Canya, what are you doing?' said Vanessa.

'I want to be with him. That's the only reason why I helped. I don't care where he is.'

The lead guard pointed a gun at Canya. 'You admit to helping the Originals escape?'

'I didn't say that...'

The lead guard closed his eyes, and Anya watched their rapid movement. He appeared to have an unspoken connection to something. 'Yes. There is a suspected breach in the medical facility. Yes. One of the newborns. Of course.'

It happened so fast. The guard's gun fired into Canya's head. Sparks of electricity danced across the Copy's skin. Anya muffled her scream as Canya fell, her eyes and body frozen in fear.

The lead guard instructed the others. 'Send this one to the Inventor. Her biogel can be harvested and reused.' He kicked Canya's still body. 'And take the others back to their rooms.'

A guard grabbed at Yasmin, but she evaded his first attempt. 'I'm not going back in there.'

'You're part of the programme now.'

'Yas, don't,' Sheila pleaded. 'For me.'

Yasmin paused and looked at her. 'Don't tell me what to do. I don't even know you.'

The guard caught her on the second attempt. Yasmin bit his arm and he cried out. A second guard grabbed her other arm and she rose up, lashing out. She landed a kick on his shin, before a third discharged his weapon. Yasmin grunted as the blast hit her but continued to kick until they let go. The guard kept blasting until she dropped to the ground.

'Yas!' Sheila ran to her. Vanessa caught her arm and pulled her back, just as one of the guards lifted his gun and pointed it at her.

'Get up,' said the lead guard, kicking Yasmin's body.

'I'm not detecting any life signs,' said another.

'Take her to the incineration room,' said the one in charge. 'If anyone else wants to struggle, they will go to the same place. Are we clear?'

The group nodded. Sheila was in shock.

Anya, not much better, stood frozen the spot.

Movement caught her eye as someone new slipped out from a corridor and crept up behind the gathered guards. It was her medic.

118-C pulled out a rounded tool and moved quickly between the guards, touching the end to each of their main discs. The tool seemed to short the connection. All four guards dropped like stones. Not dead but deactivated.

Anya stared at her medic, who she realised had been the one helping them.

'Hurry. They won't stay like that for long.' 118-C nodded to the entrance. 'It's not safe to go that way. New guards will be coming. Leave the way you got in.'

A more alert Dom climbed off the gurney. Vanessa and Alex helped him stand. They would move faster without it.

Commotion at the entrance commenced as several guards rattled the door from the outside.

118-C turned to Anya. 'The lock won't hold them for long. They'll be able to overwrite my commands. You need to go. And take care of Dom Pavesi. He's a good man. He cares about you.' She picked up the immobilised guards' weapons and handed them to Anya.

'Aren't you coming with us?' said Anya. 'This is your chance to be free of this place.'

118-C smiled. 'I belong here, Anya Macklin. You do not. Nor does Dom Pavesi. I realise that now.' She glanced at the door the guards were trying to open. 'Now, go. Otherwise this will all have been for nothing. I'll hold them off for as long as I can.'

37

CARISSA

They rode the elevator down to the Nurturing Centre, leaving 118-C alone in the lobby to deal with the extra guards. Carissa took one of the three Electro Guns. Anya kept one and handed the last gun to Alex.

'They'll work on the Copies,' said Carissa, her words just a whisper. She gripped the gun to her chest. 'The electricity will immobilise them the same way the guards immobilised Canya.'

Despite her steady voice, numbness and shock slicked over her. She'd never seen death up close, except in Arcis. But the screen had acted like a buffer against the torture—and the smell of burnt flesh.

The others' nervous energy pricked her already sensitive skin. Vanessa was quiet. Dom was half awake and leaning on Vanessa and Alex. To her relief, June stood unassisted, but Anya kept her arm around her.

Sheila's body was so rigid that Carissa could see the tendons in her neck. She and Yasmin had had a special, yet volatile, friendship in Arcis.

The elevator opened and they returned to the space before the viewing corridor, where 118-C had helped them. Carissa hoped the medic survived this.

'Where are we going?' said Anya.

Carissa opened the door. 'Through here. We can get back to the Inventor.'

'The what?'

'She means Jacob,' said Vanessa. 'He's a friend of mine. We can trust him.'

'And how do we know we can trust you?' Sheila said to Vanessa.

Vanessa stopped with a weak Dom, who was leaning hard into her side. 'You can stay if you want. End up like your Yasmin and Canya.'

'She wasn't *my* Yasmin.' Sheila clenched her jaw just as Dom flashed her a stern look. She swiped her finger under her eyes. 'I guess I can trust you if Dom does.'

With Canya gone they no longer had a valid reason to be in the medical facility. But they had weapons now, and Carissa had no problem using her gun if the medics tried to stop them.

Her face felt tight as she entered the viewing corridor. She touched her tear-soaked eyes and drew her brow forward. Was she crying over Canya?

New Copies milled around the first partition, where June had been. They looked up in confusion as the group carried on. Carissa heard Vanessa draw in a tight breath behind her.

'It's okay,' she said. 'They're just wondering

where the patient is. They won't stop us. But the guards and medics will, so we need to keep going.'

'But they're connected,' said Vanessa. 'They can alert the medics at any time.'

'Only if they perceive us to be a threat. Hurry.'

They exited the corridor and ventured further into the darker part of the underground. The corridor narrowed and the walls changed from white to an unfinished grey stone.

'Will the guards follow us into these tunnels?' said Vanessa.

Carissa nodded. 'Some might if they're ordered to.'

'Well, we'd better get a move on.'

Carissa, out in front, kept the pace slow to compensate for a sick June and injured Dom. June soon ditched Anya's help and moved on her own. It freed Anya up to use her gun. But Dom was still too weak, and Vanessa and Alex continued to help him. Alex tried to balance Dom and point his gun.

'Here, give me that.' Sheila snatched the gun from Alex.

'Do you know what to do with it?'

'Shoot it, right?' Sheila snorted. 'Silly me. I'm just a little girl. I don't know much about guns.' She moved up to Carissa.

'Do the guards or medics know where these tunnels lead?' said Vanessa.

'They will if we don't move faster.' Carissa bit the inside of her cheek. She hoped the Inventor wouldn't be too upset if some discovered their escape route.

'I really hope Jacob is gone.' Vanessa sighed.

Carissa's chest tightened. 'I do too.'

They passed through the de-bricked entrance, set halfway between the Nurturing Centre and the Inventor's workshop.

'We can't use the stairs closest to Jacob's room,' said Vanessa.

Carissa agreed. Exiting metres from the Learning Centre and the Collective was a stupid idea. More guards than their three guns and small party could handle would be waiting.

She checked her map. 'There's another tunnel that brings us within a couple of kilometres of seam 2.5 and the Business District. They won't expect us to exit from somewhere else. It's a climb up. That might be an issue for Dom.'

'We don't have a choice,' said Vanessa. 'Let's go.'

Carissa saw a tunnel up ahead, 250 metres short of the entrance to the Inventor's workshop. According to the map it headed west towards the Business District. Carissa hoped the Inventor had used it. She was about to check for him in his workshop when she heard movement coming from behind them.

'They're coming!' Carissa pushed the others on before slipping to the back of the group with Anya and Sheila. 'Shoot them fast. Don't give them time to transmit our location.' She raised her gun. 'The Collective will only order more guards to intercept us.'

'Electro Guns have fourteen shots, right?' said Sheila.

Carissa checked the indicator on the side of her gun; it showed half a charge left. 'Probably not that many. Be accurate.'

Two guards appeared and Carissa fired at one, while Sheila blasted the other. Three more arrived straight after. Anya, Carissa and Sheila fired at the same time. All five guards dropped to the ground, their blank stares fixed on the ceiling. Carissa relieved them of their weapons. She handed them out and kept an extra one for herself.

'They're only temporarily stunned. We need to keep moving.'

The group resumed their journey, but at a slow pace that frustrated Carissa. She sprinted ahead with a gun in each hand and checked the way was clear before running back, while the group trudged along with Dom.

At the stairs, it took all of Vanessa and Alex's effort to drag Dom to the top. Carissa opened the door using the barrels of both her guns. It was night and she saw no guards.

At least it was dark. 'Let's go. This place will be swarming with guards soon.'

They exited, and Vanessa leaned against the nearest wall. 'I can't carry Dom much further. We're going to need transport. We're near the human accommodation. I've seen vehicles near the tag station between D and E. Can you get one?'

Carissa thought the plan through. 'The open cars

only work with Copy commands, so I'll have to drive.'

They were still in Zone D; just two kilometres between them and seam 2.5. Carissa ran to the nearest tag station and found an unmanned vehicle on the side of the road. She activated the car and pressed her foot hard on the pedal. The car jerked back and lunged forward as she got used to driving for the first time. When Carissa reached the others, Vanessa and Alex eased Dom into the back. Vanessa settled up front while June and Alex sat with Dom. Anya and Sheila, both armed, held on to the outside of the vehicle and scanned for trouble.

A piercing alarm sounded as Carissa floored the accelerator. The car picked up speed but moved slower than she knew it could. There were too many people on board.

She could see the Business District in the distance and a line of guards cutting off their access point. With half a kilometre to go, the car shuddered then came to a stop.

'What's wrong?' said Vanessa.

'I don't know.' Carissa stared at the steering wheel. She heard a voice in her head. '173-C, return to the Learning Centre.' It was Quintus. 'The Collective understands why you helped. We're not angry. We wish to talk to you about what happened tonight. The Collective is eager to learn.'

Carissa pressed her hand over her NMC disc and squeezed her eyes shut. 'Quintus is trying to distract me. The Collective has taken control of the car. He knows where I am. You need to break my connection to him.'

'How?'

Carissa pointed to Vanessa's gun. 'Electromagnetic pulse. Single shot. Lowest setting. Fire once.' She tapped her NMC disc. 'Hurry.'

Vanessa looked unsure, but she pointed it at Carissa and fired. Carissa's head jerked. She shook the lingering crackle from her mind. Her quiet, voice-free mind.

'Come on. We have to move on foot.'

'What about the tag stations?' said Vanessa. 'They'll pick up our location.'

'We can't avoid them, but there's a time lag between when the location is picked up and when the Collective receives the information.'

They got out of the car, and Anya and Sheila helped Dom while Vanessa and Alex took the guns. They slipped between the buildings close to the border of the Business District, where the line of guards waited.

Carissa could tell from their alert, but lazy, stances they hadn't yet detected them. With her NMC inactive, Quintus couldn't find her; she had bought them some time.

'Can we get around them?' said Anya.

Carissa shook her head. 'The Collective will have instructed them to form an unbreakable bond.'

'So we go through?'

Then Carissa froze. She heard Quintus through her device again. '173-C, I am alone. The others aren't listening. I would like a chance to speak with you. I want to understand why you felt compelled to help the Originals from Arcis. I know you watched them. I understand your reasons for manipulating your footage. You thought the Collective would be angry. While both Septimus and Octavius disagree with your actions, I am intrigued by them.'

Carissa covered her fried NMC disc with her hand. She heard only Quintus. Somehow he'd found an offline way to contact her.

'173-C, tell me where you are,' demanded Quintus. 'I cannot locate you. You have interfered with your NMC. We must discuss your actions.'

'What is it, Carissa?' said Vanessa.

'Quintus is still able to talk to me.'

'Can you disconnect fully?'

Fully, meaning no more Collective? Alone? The thought made Carissa sweat.

She still had access to the security file that contained the entry codes and other information that might be necessary in the event of a city attack. 'I think so, but I won't be able to talk to them again.'

'Where we're going you won't need to,' said Vanessa.

The idea terrified her: losing the link she shared with the Collective. But termination scared her more. She had no choice. From the moment she'd altered her first memory, she'd chosen her side.

Carissa accessed the security file and found information on how to disconnect from the network in case of a viral attack on the Collective. She needed a burst of energy.

She still felt the energy from Vanessa's gun bouncing around inside her head. She gathered it up and redirected it to the NMC, overloading it. The overload delivered a nasty pain through the back of her eyes.

Vanessa touched her back. 'Is it done?'

Carissa drew in a tight breath as the pain hit its peak, then slid down the other side. She'd damaged her vision, but she could still see. 'Let's get out of here.'

They moved on, and Carissa was relieved to see Dom walking on his own, albeit slowly. That would improve their chances of escape.

They crept up on a section where the line of guards ended at a wall. Vanessa and Alex went first and fired shots into as many guards as possible. The other guards rallied around their fallen comrades and flooded their location.

'We have to get out of plain sight,' said Vanessa. 'They'll shoot us.'

Vanessa and Alex took down enough guards to breach their defensive line, but more footsteps approached their location. Under the cover of darkness, they slipped through the gap before the new guards arrived. Carissa led the group down a nearby street. Between them, they had six guns. They took one each and fanned out to cover both entrances to the street.

Vanessa pointed her gun at one entrance. 'Shit, we're trapped...'

Guards piled in from one side and then the other. Carissa froze when she saw Alex gearing up to fire his gun. 'Don't shoot. There's too many. They won't hesitate to kill us—'

Her words stuck in her throat when she saw a mechanical wolf slip in behind one of the guard groups. Strong, predatory and exceptionally fast, a single wolf could take down a human in seconds. A Copy took a little more effort, but not much.

She lowered her gun, her breaths fast and painful, and resigned herself to her fate.

But the wolf did something she didn't expect. It attacked the guards and tossed them aside as if they were an inconvenience. Then it turned and ran at full speed towards their group.

Carissa slammed her body against the gable wall of a building. 'Get back!' The others mirrored her actions. She sucked in a breath as the wolf tore past them and attacked the guards at the other end of the street.

Then she saw him: the Inventor.

Jacob.

He stood at one end of the street, beckoning them forward. 'Come on. We don't have much time.'

The wolf turned and started back. Carissa watched in horror as it ran at the Inventor.

Words bubbled up in her throat. 'Inventor, run!'

38

CARISSA

Carissa shook her head at the scene before her. Maybe her ocular nerve was more damaged than she'd thought. The wolf charged full speed at the Inventor. Then it stopped in front of him and whined as he patted its lowered head.

The old man smiled at her. 'I bet you thought he was going to eat me, didn't you, miss?' He walked on and the wolf followed.

Dismembered Copy bodies lay scattered around her. She shook her head again and followed the Inventor and the wolf.

Their group reached the edge of the Business Plaza. Ahead was a group of stores and a narrow street that led to seam 2.5 and the weakest generator.

The night continued to give them cover. Even without her connection, Carissa could tell that the guards roaming the plaza hadn't detected them yet. That would change as soon as they attempted to cross it.

She checked the schematics for Praesidium's energy field, grateful she still had offline access to the security file. If she used one of the terminals, Quintus would get a lock on her.

The Inventor stood close. 'Where to, miss? You're the one with the map.'

The wolf leaned in and sniffed her. She flinched. 'Is it connected?'

'No. The wolf answers only to me. Now, let's hurry. Dom doesn't look like he'll last much longer.'

Carissa turned to see all eyes were on her. She swallowed and pointed to the narrow street across the plaza. 'Down there.'

The Inventor nodded. 'Okay. I'm going to send Rover in to do some clearing. Wait here.'

'Rover?' Vanessa grimaced.

'That's his name.' He patted the wolf's nose. Rover whined again and nuzzled his hand.

Carissa had always kept a healthy distance from the wolves. These weren't pets but Guardians, designed to protect Copies. Yet this one had just attacked a bunch of Copy guards.

An unconnected Guardian? How could the wolf listen to only one master? Live with one voice—its own?

The Inventor whispered to Rover and it darted across the thoroughfare. Light on its feet for its size, Rover drew the attention of the guards. They pressed their NMC discs at the same time, trying to connect with the beast. To command it.

The wolf ignored them.

'It won't take long before they realise it's not connected,' said the Inventor. 'Let's go.'

The guards took the bait as the wolf led them in the opposite direction. Their group crossed the plaza and slipped down the narrow street between two buildings, to a grassy area at the rear. Past the energy field, Carissa saw the land beyond the city: brown and dry, in contrast to the protected green side she knew well.

She stood in front of seam 2.5 and examined the generator box powering segment 2. In her security file she found the output value each of the twelve generators needed to fully power the segments.

'The kilojoule reading on this generator is much lower than expected.' She touched the field, but yanked her hand back when it sparked.

The Inventor stood by her shoulder. 'You can peel it back. It's the same energy that powers you. It won't hurt you like it would us. You just need to find the frequency of the field and harmonise your biogel frequency to match.'

Carissa searched her security file again and found the code for the field generator. The weaker field—the one that her Original and the Inventor's wife had attempted to escape through—would require the least effort to overpower.

She handed the Inventor both guns and, using her disabled NMC like a console, set her frequency to match that of the generator's. She placed her hands on either side of the seam. Matched to her frequency, the energy barely tickled her hand. She stretched the seam apart. The edges of the large gap tried to snap from her fingers.

'I can't keep it open for long.'

The group stepped through the open seam. When it was just Carissa and the Inventor left on the city side, the Inventor whistled, and the wolf charged at him. He jerked his head to the opening. A gust of wind whipped up Carissa's hair as the wolf darted past, then it yelped as its metal exterior grazed the closing edges of the seam.

Guards burst into view, hot on the tail of the wolf. 'We've located the escapees!'

The Inventor fired both guns into their pursuers.

'Inventor... I can't hold it open... much longer.' Where a weak seam occurred, the Collective would bolster power to both segment generators. This generator must have been leaking power. It shouldn't have been so easy for Carissa to open it.

The Inventor ducked his head under the closing seam and grabbed Carissa's arm, yanking her through. One of the guards fired a gun through the gap just before it closed. The Inventor let out a cry and crumpled to the ground.

Carissa ran to his side. 'Inventor!'

'Jacob.' Vanessa slid to the ground beside him.

'It's my leg. I'll be fine. Dom is our priority. We need to stabilise him.'

The guards struggled to pull the seam apart. Carissa knew the generator had already compensated.

'We don't have much time before Quintus orders the generator offline,' she said, getting to her feet.

'Then we have to move.' Vanessa helped the Inventor stand.

The others had gone ahead, almost invisible as the black night swallowed their forms.

The wolf moved to the Inventor's side, nudging his arm gently. With Vanessa's help, he climbed up on its back. Carissa noticed closed handles set at different points along the wolf's spine.

'Vanessa. Miss. Get on.'

Carissa hesitated as Vanessa settled on its back. This was a Guardian. Not a mode of transport.

'Miss, get on. Now.' She flinched at the Inventor's sharp tone and climbed up with the help of Vanessa's outstretched hand.

She gripped one of the closed handles and sucked in a breath. Her legs dangled on either side of the beast's hardened exoskeleton.

Rover caught up to the others, and they helped June and Dom onto the beast's back. There was no room for Alex, Sheila and Anya, who ran alongside the wolf.

'I'll send him back for you,' said the Inventor. 'Keep going.'

The wolf galloped on.

'We need to head for one of the towns,' said Vanessa, glancing back at the city. 'We need supplies and to tend to your wound, Jacob.'

The Inventor gave the wolf a new order and it changed direction. Alarms sounded in the distance. Carissa looked back at Praesidium, bright and imposing behind a kaleidoscopic energy field that only Copies could see. Guards collected at the barrier. She tried to connect to the Collective, to find out what was going on. The silence in her head reminded her she was alone.

Rover came to a stop outside a town about five miles away from Praesidium. They climbed off its back, taking care with the injured.

'Go back for the others,' said the Inventor to Rover. The beast ran off.

Carissa and June assisted Dom, while Vanessa helped the Inventor into the town. The alarm in the distance got louder.

Carissa closed her eyes, feeling dizzy. She didn't like the quiet in her head. Not one bit. 'I still feel part of the system, like I should hear them. I feel disorientated.'

The Inventor winced as he put weight on his injury. 'You've severed your NMC link to the Collective, but you have to break your ties with Praesidium. The city can still track you.'

'But I don't know how.' Carissa protected her head, as if the action would somehow disguise her location.

'We can't stay here exposed like this,' said Vanessa. 'She's still connected. The Ten will find us through her.'

Carissa thought about the dead signal spot near the Inventor's workshop, about how the voices had disappeared. The Inventor smiled at her, as though he could hear her thoughts. 'We need to hide underground. Preferably some place with thick walls.'

Vanessa clicked her fingers. 'All these towns have bunkers.'

'That should block the signal until she can disconnect fully. It's too risky to do it now while the guards are out there, looking. They'd locate her in minutes.'

The Inventor hobbled over to a large building in the centre of town. 'The bunkers in Greenacre were located inside the town hall.'

Carissa ran ahead of him. She needed to hide fast. She risked everyone's safety.

The wolf returned with the others, and Anya and Alex helped Carissa search for the bunker. They found a large trapdoor hidden beneath bags of grain. It concealed a space big enough to hide a dozen people. They opened both sides.

'Everybody inside.'

Carissa ran down the stone steps first, followed by the others. The wolf managed to squeeze in as well.

Vanessa was last. She replaced the bags of grain and closed the door. Carissa and the others got settled in the cavernous underground space. Rover sat in the middle of the bunker, taking up most of the room.

Noises up top, definitely the Collective's machines, tore through town. She shivered as the sounds got louder. She looked around to distract herself.

There was a cupboard over a sink in one corner of the room and a bunch of stacked chairs in the other.

She watched Alex and Sheila gather up three chairs and place them lengthways to create a makeshift gurney for Dom.

While they waited for the commotion to subside up top, Vanessa checked the blast wound on the Inventor's leg. Carissa made herself useful and went through the cupboard. There, she found a first-aid kit. The Inventor pulled air through his teeth as Vanessa cleaned his wound with antiseptic from the kit.

She wrapped his leg and he hobbled over to Dom. 'My injury isn't life-threatening,' said the Inventor, when Vanessa protested. He touched Dom's forehead, then checked his pulse. 'What does he have in him?'

'Fifth Gen tech, Inventor,' said Carissa. She'd seen the medical files on the participants, which included the planned surgical procedures for Dom.

'He's weak from the surgery.' The Inventor lifted the edge of Dom's bloodied tunic, soaked through with sweat. 'And it looks like they operated on him several times. I can't do a lot for him here, but I know this tech well from working with the wolves. I should be able to help him.' He called to the wolf. 'Come here, boy.'

Rover inched forward in the small space until its nose was level with the Inventor's hand.

'Carissa, grab my bag,' he said, nodding to the backpack on the floor.

She handed it to him, and he pulled out a syringe and a barrel-shaped device with three perforations.

'Rover is part organic, part machine—Fifth Gen,

to be precise. His natural immunity to the tech should stabilise Dom. The infection is a different matter.'

The Inventor stuck the needle into the beast's soft underbelly. The wolf whimpered as the Inventor drew a small measure of clear liquid into the syringe. He finished with a pat on the wolf's nose. 'Sorry, Rover. But it's to help the boy.'

Carissa shivered when Rover's yellow eyes flicked over to Dom. The wolf's soft tongue flicked out between its metal teeth. It whined at the Inventor, seemingly in response.

The Inventor laughed. 'Yes, he is fragile. But he's also like you.'

The wolf lost interest in Dom and stared at the floor.

The Inventor jabbed Dom's upper arm and pushed in the liquid. Then he picked up the barrel-shaped device. 'It's not a skin-repair tool, but it will do the job for now.' A red beam from the tip sealed Dom's wound and cleared up all the obvious infection.

Vanessa took the tool and used it on the Inventor's leg, drawing a deep growl from Rover.

Ω

They waited for the machines to leave. After an hour, the noises lessened, but they agreed to wait another hour to check. Then, Alex and Vanessa tried the door.

'Something's blocking it,' said Vanessa.

They managed to work the blockage free with a

little help from Rover's nose. Carissa stayed below while Alex and Vanessa went up top to look around.

They returned with a report on the situation. 'The machines have gone,' said Vanessa. 'All the buildings razed, including this one. We should probably move while it's still dark.'

Carissa looked at Dom. His dry brow told her the Inventor's intervention had worked. Alex and June sat with their heads in their hands. Except for a strong desire to connect, and occasional bouts of dizziness, Carissa felt fine. Sheila checked Dom's temperature for the hundredth time. Anya was alert and anxious.

Now was a good time to go. But they couldn't yet.

'If we leave now, our chips will lead the machines straight to us. Before we surface, we need to get rid of them.'

Vanessa checked the Inventor's bag. 'You'd better have a knife in here, old man.'

The Inventor smiled. 'I always come prepared.'

Vanessa found what she was looking for and used the tip of the knife to cut hers out. She finished by lasering the wound closed. She repeated the action with Carissa and the others.

Sheila got up and rinsed a cloth in the sink. She laid it across Dom's forehead.

Vanessa checked Dom's pulse. 'He's holding steady.' She opened the first-aid kit. 'There are definitely no antibiotics in here. We'll have to move him soon, get him to the compound.'

It surprised Carissa to see Anya wasn't by Dom's

side. Instead, she sat beside the Breeder. Alex. They were holding hands and speaking low to each other.

'She's supposed to be with Dom, not Alex,' said Carissa to Vanessa.

'You can't force people together. It's not how life works.'

The Inventor hooked a finger at her. 'You need to fully disconnect from the city, not just the Collective. Can you still access the security file? It should contain instructions on how to do it.'

Carissa nodded. 'I can't think down here. It's too quiet. I'll need to go up top.'

'You've severed the link to your NMC, but now you need to disconnect your link to the communication disc. It's still transmitting data to the city. Overload it. I won't lie—it will hurt.'

'I can handle pain, Inventor.'

'I don't mean physically. Losing your connection to the Collective will change you. Set you adrift.' He grabbed both of her hands; it made her feel less alone. 'When it's over, we'll all be waiting. Now, go. Quick, before they detect you.'

Carissa climbed the stairs, pushed the hatch open and stood outside. She rerouted a blast of electricity to the cochlear implant that maintained her last link to Praesidium. A shock of searing pain ripped through her eardrum and she cried out. She dropped to her knees, eyes closed, waiting for the pounding in her head to stop. She heard the Inventor say, 'Give her a minute, Vanessa.' The pain lessened, taking with it her desire to connect.

She sloped back to the basement and sat beside the Inventor again. Rover pressed his giant metallic nose into her side. *Beggars can't be choosers, Carissa.* She'd take whatever friends she could get.

'He understands you now, miss,' said the Inventor. 'He's not connected, either.'

Carissa looked up at him, through blurry vision. Damn tears. 'I've always been connected, Inventor. I don't know anything else.'

'That's not true. You don't remember being a newborn, but you weren't connected then, either. You can survive now, just like you did then.'

'I don't know how to function alone.'

The Inventor put an arm around her tense shoulder. 'I'll help you.'

39

ANYA

Alex's hand felt too hot in hers. She tugged her fingers free and wrapped her arms around her body.

What now? They had an injured old man, a sick June and an even sicker Dom. His familiarity continued to taunt her. She and Dom were meant to be together. That's what she'd heard Carissa say to Vanessa. How was that possible, when she didn't know him?

The memory of her struggle with Warren felt new, as if it had happened yesterday. June and Yasmin had helped her. That was the evening she'd discovered June was a rebel.

A *rebel*? The memory clarified. Not just June, but Dom and Sheila, too.

'Are you okay?' Alex's hand on hers snapped her back to the present. He nodded to Dom, who was lying across three chairs. 'You've been staring at him for a while now. Do you recognise him?'

Was that jealousy in his tone?

'No.' She smiled at him, but Alex didn't look convinced.

The giant wolf settled in one corner of the bunker, observing the group. Even though Jacob sat close by, Anya shivered at Rover's proximity. A memory of wolves, not nearly as friendly as this one, flashed in her mind.

Sheila, beside Dom, used a wet cloth to keep his forehead cool. She called Anya over. Her stomach flipped as she neared. She kept her gaze on Dom's hands to steady her nerves.

'He's been asking about you,' said Sheila.

Anya's eyes brushed over the barely conscious Dom. 'He doesn't look well.'

'He's not. But seeing you here will help him.'

'I don't remember him.' Sheila was a different matter. 'I think I remember you, but I also feel wary around you.'

Sheila barked a laugh. 'Yeah, we didn't get off to the best of starts.'

Anya didn't think Sheila knew Yasmin as well as June.

'Were you close to Yasmin?'

Sheila swallowed. 'Yeah.'

'Are all your memories back?' Sheila nodded, to which Anya sighed. 'My Copy only passed back one unpleasant memory. June and Yasmin helped me.'

Anya looked over at June, sitting alone. When Alex got up and joined her, Anya pushed down her jealousy.

Sheila nodded to Alex. 'That's your Breeder?'

She didn't wait for an answer. 'Give it time, Anya. You'll remember everything. But don't forget Dom. You two went through a lot together. And for the record, I was against most of it.'

'Against it? Why?'

Sheila laughed. 'I hated you at first. You were Little Miss Rod-Up-Her-Butt.'

'Gee, thanks.'

'But you're okay now. I guess we could try to be friends when this is all over.'

Sheila didn't strike her as someone who made that offer often. 'Yeah, I'd like that.'

The longer she sat there, the more partial memories crept in. Her head ached trying to make sense of it.

Snippets of chat murmured around the space, along with the sound of a panting mechanical wolf. The bunker felt small and constricted. Anya pulled her loose-necked hoodie away from her flushed skin. She closed her eyes, wishing she was alone so she could think.

'You're trying to remember, aren't you?' Anya opened her eyes and nodded at Sheila. 'Do you want me to tell you what happened in Arcis?'

That was the last thing she wanted. 'I need to remember on my own. If you tell me, I won't know what's real and what's not.'

'Suit yourself.'

'But if I don't remember on my own, will you tell me about it?'

Sheila smiled. 'As soon as this idiot gets better.'

Vanessa positioned herself on the other side of Dom. She placed two fingers against his neck. 'His pulse is weak, Jacob. I haven't heard any activity up top for a couple of hours. We'll need to move him.'

'Soon, Vanessa.'

She sighed and sat beside Anya. 'We haven't been formally introduced. I'm Vanessa Walker. I was a friend of your parents.'

Anya shook the hand on offer. 'I don't remember you ever coming to our house.'

'We weren't friends in the conventional way. We were helping to liberate the people from Praesidium's control.'

'You mean from the rebels?'

'No. The rebels are your allies.'

118-C had already said Praesidium killed her parents. But someone had once told her it was the rebels who'd poisoned the town. 'They poisoned the food and water. Why would they be my allies?'

Vanessa pressed the back of her hand to Dom's cheek.

'Anya, trust me when I say the rebels are not your enemy. You would have discovered that when you went through Arcis. Your memories may be scrubbed, but if you changed your opinion about the rebels, how you feel about them is still inside you.'

She wished her memories would return. Three months was a long time. What had she missed? 'All I know is I owe you my life. We all do.'

Vanessa patted Anya's arm. 'Canya knew the location of a rebel compound in the mountains.'

Anya frowned. 'And you think she... I knew about it?'

Vanessa nodded. 'Your parents were rebels. They knew the compound's location. Whatever happened, they were only protecting you. Praesidium ordered their deaths to break their control over you.'

118-C had said as much, too. Anya blinked back tears. All eyes were on her. She wished they'd stop staring. 'I remember their deaths like it happened yesterday. But Jason is still alive and I need to find him.'

'He may be at this compound I'm trying to get us to.'

Anya tried to remember. She shook her head. 'They never mentioned any such place. They were always secretive around us.' She and Grace had shouted more than talked, and Evan had hid everything from her, treated her like the baby of the family.

'*Think*, Anya. It's important. Maybe you overheard them talking. Did your mother ever mention a place in the mountains?'

Anya didn't recall. Grace had once said that she and Evan should try hiking, and that she preferred the rugged terrain of a mountainous range to the eroded coastline.

'She talked about her favourite mountain with my father. Nothing else.'

Vanessa went stiff. 'That could be it. Which mountain?'

'I don't know. Ferry something?'

'Ferrous Mountain?'

'Yeah, that's it.'

An animated Vanessa turned to Jacob. 'That's due east of here. Through the Apalana Mountains. Over three hundred miles. A week's walk.'

'Dom won't make it.'

'I know. We need to find a truck in this town.'

Alex stood up. 'I'm good with mechanics. I'll take a look outside.'

Anya mirrored him. She needed air, and to feel useful. 'I'll come with you.' Sheila and Vanessa volunteered, too, and the four spread out to search the town.

It was still dark. Evidence of the machines' presence was everywhere. Most of the town had been levelled. An abandoned truck sat outside what she presumed had once been a building. They gathered round it, and Alex cleared the debris from around its wheels and hood. The rusted vehicle was in bad shape.

Vanessa found a key in the ignition and turned it, but the engine wouldn't start.

Alex propped open the hood and took a look inside. 'The battery's dead, but I should be able to fix it, with Jacob's help. That wolf down below is a walking power supply. It should give the battery enough of a jolt to start it.'

Vanessa nodded. 'Get to it.' She turned to Sheila and Anya and pointed to a building with a missing roof, but partially intact walls. 'That's the farmhouse. Collect as much food as you can find in there.'

'What about weapons?' said Sheila. 'There's always a weapons cache in these towns.'

'Exactly my thinking. I just hope the townspeople didn't clear it out before they left. I'll check the back rooms.'

Sheila and Anya began their hunt for food in the kitchen while Vanessa searched the remainder of the building for weapons. Moonlight shone through the gaping hole where the floor above had collapsed.

Anya found cans of food in one of the cupboards, along with some bags. She handed several bags to Sheila and they started filling them. Vanessa rejoined them holding three rifles and a box of bullets.

'This is all I could find.' She dropped the cache into one of Anya's bags.

Outside, Alex was at the truck with the wolf and the Inventor. Jacob had opened the wolf's body and attached two wires from its power supply to the battery of the truck to serve as jump cables. Alex tried the ignition; the truck turned over after a few tries. 'There's enough juice to get us there. We're good to go.'

Ω

Alex kept the lights off as he drove the open-backed truck out of town and along a dark road heading for Ferrous Mountain and the compound. Vanessa sat up front, navigating with a map she'd taken from Jacob's bag. The others sat in the back, with Jacob keeping watch on Dom. The wolf, too big for the truck, ran alongside.

At the break of dawn the truck began its climb. Anya felt pressure build in her ears. A mountain road lay ahead—a sheer cliff on one side, and a rock face on the other. She shifted back from the edge of the truck when she saw how high up they were.

The road came to an abrupt end at an old mountain pass that had been blocked off. They pulled up to the dead end and waited. Anya froze when she spotted men and women dotted around crevices in the rock. They held guns.

'Halt! Where did you come from?' A man dressed in military fatigues approached their truck, gun raised.

'We escaped from Praesidium.' Vanessa held her hands up.

'Stay where you are. All of you.'

A blue light, originating from a hidden point in the rock face, bathed the truck. A second soldier clutched a handheld screen and showed it to his armed colleague, who immediately pointed his gun inside the truck's carriage. Two more armed soldiers moved around to the bed of the truck.

'Three of you are emitting a Praesidium signal,' said the first soldier. He nodded at the wolf, which, on Jacob's command, sat down. 'Where did that thing come from?'

'It's mine,' said Jacob, from the back of the truck. 'I made him. I used to fix the tech in Praesidium.'

The soldier turned away and mumbled into an

old-style walkie-talkie.

Anya sat back and waited while armed soldiers looked on.

Several minutes later, a truck pulled up behind theirs. A man in his forties with a buzz cut got out. His hard gaze scanned the scene. Only when he reached the side of the truck did his expression soften.

'Vanessa?'

'Max,' Vanessa jumped out, and the man hugged her.

'Shit, Vanessa. I thought you were dead.'

'It's a long story.'

Max gripped Vanessa's arms. They seemed to be old friends. 'Last time I saw you was a year ago. You'd left Halforth to join up with a rebel camp in the south.'

'I had, but our party was picked up.'

He looked past Vanessa to the others. 'June! Sheila! Is Dom with you?'

Sheila grinned at the man. 'He's in the back of the truck. Is Charlie okay?'

Max nodded. 'He'll be thrilled to see you three.'

He returned his attention to Vanessa. 'We were stuck inside Arcis when the urbano lost power, just after these kids disappeared through the machine. Then the city sent machines of their own. We were lucky to escape Essention after they gassed the urbano. So many others didn't make it, Vanessa. That was days ago, and we were still working on a plan to get past Praesidium's energy field. We had to assume the kids were useful to the city, and therefore safe for now. But you've been gone a year. If I'd known you were in there... I thought you were safe.'

'Max, it's okay. You weren't to know.'

Anya wanted to ask if Jason was here.

'My wife. She disappeared six months ago. Vanessa, did you see her?'

Her smile vanished as she nodded. 'She was killed a month after she arrived. She worked in the medical facility and was trying to get the kids out. '

'Medical facility?'

'That's where the Collective ten placed the kids from the towns, some as young as thirteen. They killed her during our rescue attempt.'

Max closed his eyes and swallowed.

'We found Dom and the others there, but we couldn't get everyone out. We'll have to go back.'

Max opened his eyes, looking more alert. He spoke to the soldiers. 'Stand down. Get them inside before we have more company.' He turned to Vanessa. 'Were you followed?'

'No. We managed to evade them.' She nodded at Carissa. 'Thanks to her.'

Anya saw Max stiffen. 'She's a Copy? Is she connected?'

'No longer,' said Jacob. 'She was the one who got us out of there. She managed to loosen the energy barrier so we could escape.'

'How many more do you have?'

'A Breeder, too. But Dom needs medical help. He's burning up from an infection.'

Max called one of the soldiers over and

whispered something in her ear. She nodded.

'Drive the truck into the pass and onto a platform,' Max said to Alex.

The soldiers winched back a false wall, and Alex inched the truck inside. Anya and the others stayed in the back with Dom. The platform lowered into the mountain, and the truck exited onto a new road that ran through the bed of the valley—the valley belonging to the mountain her parents had spoken about, and the rebel compound Vanessa was looking for. Maybe this Max guy would know if Jason was here.

Alex drove the truck to a gated entrance, where several armed soldiers waited. They ordered everyone out, and Carissa and Alex were taken by the soldiers.

Max's vehicle pulled up behind their truck.

'What is this, Max?' said Vanessa as he got out. 'Where are you taking Carissa and Alex?'

'To a holding cell that blocks any signal they might be transmitting.'

'This is insane,' said Vanessa.

'This is necessary. We cannot compromise our location, and I need to determine they're not a threat to our compound. Go on ahead. The soldiers will take Dom to the medical area. He'll be fine.'

One of the soldiers looped a cord around the wolf's neck. The cord crackled with energy.

'What are you doing with him?' Jacob ran forward; two soldiers restrained him. 'He's not a threat. I designed him.'

'We need to determine its composition.'

'You can't. He belongs with me.'

Anya stepped back when Max challenged an angry Jacob. 'Sir, we can do this the hard or easy way. I'd much rather have you work with our team. We already have a Copy here, and we need your help to understand it. If your wolf isn't a threat to my people, then we'll let it go.'

Jacob relented, but he didn't look happy.

Anya followed the soldiers through the gates and inside the compound. She observed the place her parents might have visited. Then a familiar face in the crowd caught her eye, and her thundering heart nearly brought her to her knees. She heard her name being yelled. 'Anya! Anya!'

Her legs froze. The boy pushed his way through the crowd of curious onlookers and ran straight for her.

'Jason!' she croaked. 'You're okay...' She met him halfway, winding him with the force of her hug. 'I thought you were dead.'

Jason laughed. 'You can't keep a Macklin down.'

Ω

Continue the series

The Haven (Book 3)
The Beyond (Book 4)
The Rebels (Book 5) is *The Facility* retold
from Dom and Warren's perspective.

Other Books by Eliza Green
Genesis Series
GENESIS CODE

An alien hunter is caught in a dangerous game of cat and mouse.

Investigator Bill Taggart will stop at nothing to find his missing wife. But standing between him and the truth is a secretive alien species on a distant planet. When his government pushes him to observe the species ahead of plans to relocate Earth's population, Bill crashes straight into the path of one alien.

The surprising confrontation forces Bill to question whether the investigation into the savage species is needed. But when official government intel disagrees with the cold hard facts, he worries there might be another reason for the relocation plans.

A snap government order leaves the investigator in limbo and facing off against a new enemy that is more dangerous than the first. Worse, this enemy appears to live close to home.

A devastating set of plans is soon revealed that will destroy the lives on two worlds. And Bill is caught in the middle. Can he stop chasing ghosts long enough

The Collective

to save humanity from the real enemy?

Get *Genesis Code*

Available in Digital and Paperback

www.elizagreenbooks.com/genesis-code

Genesis (Book 0) Get this teaser story for free only when you sign up to my mailing list. Check out **www.elizagreenbooks.com** for more information.

Duality (Standalone)

Jonathan Farrell is stuck between two realities. Who put him there, and can he escape before he loses his grip on the real world? Read this story with flavours of *The Matrix* and *Inception*.

www.elizagreenbooks.com/duality

BOOKS BY KATE GELLAR

Eliza also writes paranormal romance under the pen name, Kate Gellar.

The Irish Rogue Series begins with *Magic Destiny*.

Book 1: One novice witch must temper her conflicting magic before the wrong one unleashes a new power nobody can stop.

Available in both digital and paperback from Amazon.

Rogue Magic (a free prequel to *Magic Destiny* when you sign up to my mailing list. Check out **www.kategellarbooks.com** for more information)

The Collective

Word from the Author

Hey there, beautiful readers! Thank you so much for your patience. I know you've waited a long time for the next book in this series. To publish books to the standard I expect and you deserve costs money. I'm an indie author, which means I pay for everything myself. Sometimes I have books ready to go, but not enough funds in the pot to get them edited. I hope as I continue to get my books out there, I'll be in a better position to release more frequently. For now, I love you for giving me the time to get my ducks in a row.

Can we talk about that amazing cover? I commissioned Deranged Doctor Design (yes, I love the name!) to do the covers for this series. I love them all. They're so bright and energetic. I can't wait to get going with the third book. How many will I release in this series? Not sure yet. Let's see where the story takes us, shall we? *evil laugh*

Thanks, as always to my amazing and supportive editors, Andrew and Rachel. And to my launch team for being the first to review this book. Thanks to my brilliant betas, Tom, Madeline and Roeshell for helping to craft the story. I'm always petrified to read beta notes on my stories. These are my babies, and nobody smacks down my babies. *grins* Actually, betas make a story better. I just need to put on my happy armour before I read the feedback. Yes, we writers are a sensitive lot.

What's next? Well, I recently changed the names of these books from Feeder and Breeder to The

Facility and The Collective. Same story with new titles. I backed myself into a corner with my rhyming cover names (third book was going to be "Leader" but then I ran out of ideas for book four. Oops!) I love (or sometimes hate) picking titles for my books as much as I love picking designs for my covers. These things make me happy. It doesn't take much.

Reviews are a privilege, but if you decide to leave one, I will do a happy dance. Because it means other readers will find my books. Yes, readers actually care what you think. So please take a moment to leave one. Even if it's just one word like, "Fantastic", or "Amazing". Or a one liner like, "What were you thinking?" Seriously, I hope you don't write the last one. But you can, if that's how you feel.

Signing off now, but please keep in touch to let me know if you enjoyed this book. I'd be super excited to hear from you. Much love and kittens to you all.

Reviews

Word of mouth is crucial for authors. If you enjoyed this book, please consider leaving a review where you purchased it; make it as long or as short as you like. I know review writing can be a hassle, but it's the most effective way to let others know what you thought. Plus, it helps me reach new readers instantly!

You can also find me on:

www.twitter.com/elizagreenbooks
www.facebook.com/elizagreenbooks
www.instagram.com/elizagreenbooks
www.wattpad.com/elizagreenbooks
Goodreads – search for Eliza Green

Printed in Great Britain
by Amazon

71452885R00220